Smelted

Wings

TRICAH

BLURB

She fell to the floor. Dead. Princess Phaedra is banished after she watches her mother annihilate her best friend. Forced to leave everything behind, Phaedra pursues the only goal of interest to her: revenge.

When Phaedra learns Queen Mara plans to conquer the land and Sphere of the Fire Fairies, she departs to kill her in combat. However, she is forced to flee with Fira, the Fairy Princess of Fire, by order of the Fire King before the Sphere falls. In search of other ways to stop her conqueror mother, Phaedra sets out on a cross-continental journey and gathers the elemental Fairy Princesses to fight with her. An egg from the Campaign of the Dragons, the forgotten race of water fairies, and glass fruit trail our flock towards their final objective.

When Queen Mara takes one step too far and assassinates the Matriarch of the water fairies, the Domain of Life, backed by Phaedra and companions, declares the greatest war of their time.

As she travels, Phaedra must come to terms with who she wishes to be and what her future looks like in exile. As Phaedra wrestles with the assumption that Keres, her sister, wants to take the crown and continue the bloody tirade of their mother, Phaedra has to decide if she even wants to take up the mantle of Queen of Death.

Contents

The Frozen Sea
Dragon's Den
Castle of Life
Lake Lakira
Passage of the Dead
Teacup Hills
Swampy Marsh
Castle Fort
Bay of Stars
Heartpeak Fjord
Wind Mountain
Fire Wing Bay
Telling Woods
The Nothing Woods
The March
Fire Castle
Wreden's Opening
Key Stone Valley
Tooth Pikes
Aged Tree
Noxious Waters
Arch Islands
Witch's Pass
Flat Claws
Silver Top Bay
Turbulent Sea
Sunset Valley
Castle of Death
White Forest
Field of Lightning
Dead Forest
Wistful Reach
The Tears
Mermaid's Bite
N
The Sea
W
E
S
Ouránios
and the Land of

CHAPTER ONE

SHE FELL TO THE floor. Dead. Flecks of blood hit my face. Warm. The Queen of the Death Angels stood in her chambers, scythe in her hand. She looks up at me. Eyes widened. Queen Mara had summoned me to her chambers after dinner to begin my education on receiving foreign persons of interest to our castle. *And yet she's surprised to see me?* My stomach twisted against the heavy meat I had devoured despite my best efforts to fight her orders. *She didn't think the weaker of the Princesses of Death would devour another angel, feathers and all.*

I stared down at Liraz's corpse. It felt as though the bricks that made up the castle floor crawled up and into my feet and held me still. The Queen, my mother, extended her hand toward me, and her lips moved without sound.

My gut wrenched in fear, and I dove down the dark hallway. My black feathered wings carried me quickly through the twists and turns of my home. Something pounded in my ears, a voice just out of reach, calling me toward the bottom-most labyrinth of this fortress built upon long dead bones. I took the tight, spiraling staircase with a wing beat and glided down. My feet landed loud on the stone, and I made to rush past the guards that always protected the armory before I saw they weren't there.

My feet tripped on the uneven foundation as I hurried along toward my prize. Past the swords, shields, spears, lances, and bows, she rested. My scythe, my Weapon, Cynthia, slept upon the ceremonial altar. My hand squeezed her tight, the White Wood of her staff shifting under me at the sensation. I brought her blade up to look her over, and she glistened in the torchlight as if preening. She was undamaged, unmarred.

I slid the scabbard nearby onto my back and slipped her into it. My wings, unburdened by her weightlessness, flapped to clear the dust when I pushed open the secret stone door behind her plush bed. I held my breath against the odd, forgotten scent, and walked into the passage blind, my brain able to piece together one thought: *She's finally going to kill you too. Escape.*

The passageway led me up a steep staircase, and my hands found the steps in front of me while the dark squeezed in and listened intently to my exhausted pants. My body wasn't strong enough for this. *But I'm not ready to die.* A small light came into view. I scrambled forward, my hands pressed against the cobwebs and grime to push open the door for the first time in centuries.

I blinked in the torchlight of the throne room of the Queendom of Death. I had emerged from a nondescript sidewall. My breath stuttered as I realized what was before me. The Queen was upon her throne. Her bloody footsteps trailed away out of sight to her rooms, to Liraz's corpse. At her side stood my sister, Princess Keres. On her other side, her advisors. She was surrounded by her advisors, my sister, and her warriors. No one attacked.

My yellow eyes grew large as I stumbled back in shock. "M-mother?" I asked, my quiet voice amplified by the silence pounding in around us all unrelentingly. The crowds of dark stones that raised this castle from the cliff spied down.

"The time has come, Phaedra," as she spoke to me, her tone was even. As if I wasn't her daughter. As if I wasn't her firstborn. As if I wasn't her greatest disappointment. "Kill me and take the throne. Or be banished forevermore."

My face crumpled. I struggled to wield the Weapon she had graciously bestowed upon me. I could not keep up with even the lowest ranked soldier in a contest of flight when I had been given the chance to prove myself. I had never bested anyone at the war games we played so regularly within our ranks.

Liraz's hand, falling on the cold floor, the blood dripping down her face from her stricken skull — *is it worth it, without a single friend?* I could feel my hands shaking as I closed my mouth, forcing my expression to fall away as the Queen herself had taught me in court.

There is no way I will walk away from this alive. I glanced over my shoulder as a cool breeze stroked my feathers. The Queendom of Death spanned outside the open doors, the city below dwarfed by the old trees in the distance.

Freedom. The thought had me shift toward the only route in which I might live. I took one more look back at the Queen, my sister, and the people who I had known life with. Without Liraz, I had no one to keep me here, to invoke my will to fight and take the throne.

Without a word, I ran towards the great doors and leaped. My wings beat powerfully from the sharp takeoff and carried me close to the roofs of the buildings below. I looked down and saw the commoners still ignorant of what transpired. Some drank, some sang, and others gathered around the gallows to watch the execution of a life angel who had been unlucky enough to stray too close to our borders.

He was strung up by his hands. His head hanging as the crowd jeered at him, his wings at odd angles alongside him. His eyes connected with mine as he raised his head and as I fled for my life, his white wings stained far dirtier with blood than my black pair.

The pine nettles scratched my face as I unwillingly drifted towards the forest floor some ways outside the town and castle. My wings ached, my muscles exhausted from the sudden spurt of use after they had been categorized as ornamental. I jerked to the right to avoid a branch and tried to give a few strong flaps to dream of being able to raise myself above the treeline.

My wings gave way, and I found myself staring, dull-minded and broken, as the ground hurtled towards me stupefyingly fast.

Chapter Two

Soft material wrapped around me and squeezed me gently. A gentle light rapped on my eyelids, and I made to rub at my eyes as I wondered who had drawn the draperies so late in the morning. I yawned and flexed my body. A sudden jolt of pain shot through me, and I recoiled and curled into myself instinctively. My memories washed over me, cold water that had me drawing the blanket tighter around me.

Blanket? My thoughts belatedly filtered through as my eyes cracked open. I swept my white hair to the side from where it had tumbled onto the blanket and off the bedside. I examined the blanket and looked around. This was definitely not the forest floor that had been so gracious as to break my fall.

I shivered and drew my legs closer in as my heart sped up. This new, unfamiliar space left me feeling like a rabbit in confinement as it waited for the butcher to round the corner. My eyes swept around the room in search of danger.

The room was small albeit cultured. The walls were not those commonly found in the Queendom of Death. These walls were smooth and white, without defect. The blanket that pooled around me as I carefully sat up was warm yet thin. I couldn't make out the threads that were used to create it. Even the furniture, the bedframe and the wardrobe to the side, while elegantly made, didn't reflect dark skies and freezing oceanic winds. They spoke of someone homely, the delicate gold designs inlaid in the wood telling me their owner had a good eye.

My eyes caught on my Weapon, Cynthia, who rested in the shadow of the wardrobe. Her staff and blade showed no signs of the fall. I slowly stood and grappled for her, the pain in my body leaving me feeling unbalanced. I curled in around her, comforted. She seemed to groan in relief as I relied upon her, both of us releasing a deep breath.

I should have expected you'd be fine. You were never hurt during my trainings. My hand strayed to my wing as I compared the pain of my mother striking me on the back when I would fall to now. *I can do this.* My hand tightened on the scythe, and her wood was still beneath me. *I have to do this.* The need to survive thrummed in me as I contemplated my captor and what it would take to escape.

My eyes turned upon the simple wooden door in the room. *Who could have taken me?* Options ran through my mind as I slowly approached the door knob. *Clearly not anyone who has heard of the recent news.* I grimaced as I left the room as silently as I could. *I'm certainly not worth anything as a bargaining chip now.*

The corridor was strange. The fabric beneath my feet seemed as though it grew up from the earth like grass. My bare feet welcomed it despite how it tickled. I slowly walked down to what seemed to be the main room, passing doors on either side of me that were built with eerie, exact edges and straight lines. *Does such an artisan exist?* The Castle of Death was created generations ago by my ancestors and showed their zealous attention to detail, but this was beyond even that.

I gripped Cynthia with both hands as I leaned forward and peeked into the main room.

No one rested in the sitting room. The furniture here was not wood, but rather seemed to be cloth that was expertly stitched together. I wandered closer in confusion as I examined the glass table in the center of the room and the odd glass fixtures standing around the room and on the ceiling.

I flinched back when I heard a hum come from the next room. A feminine voice drifted towards me, hidden by another flawless wall. "Are you sure you want to be up and about right now? You were rather damaged when I found you."

Damaged? The odd word choice registered lowly inside me as I opened and closed my mouth. *I don't want to give myself away — or does she already know who I am?* Sweat started to gather at my hairline as my insides cramped with stress.

I jumped out of my skin when a woman with tight, dark curls and no wings emerged from the open doorway. She held a tray with cups and a steaming tea pot. "At least have a drink. My name is Max," she looked at me evenly, and I felt myself quake down to my ankles. *Does she know who I am, what happened to me?* I swallowed nervously. *Is she going to kill me?*

My feet stepped around to avoid her as she slowly approached and set the tray onto the table. From a distance, I watched as she set the table. Her eyes closed as she poured us each a cup. She inhaled deeply, as if enjoying the aroma, but my eyes narrowed at the clear, steaming water. *It's not tea,* I decided. *There's no color, smell, leaves.*

'Max' slowly sat on the furniture opposite of me. She crossed her leg over her knee before she looked at me evenly. Her eyes were crystalline. They reflected a multitude of colors, many more in number than the absence of emotion she showed.

"Sit down," her voice was a touch warm as she invited me and gestured opposite to her. "The davenport is not for show," her lips twitched as if she was remembering an inside joke.

"The davenport?" I looked uneasily at the human-centric sitting furniture I had stepped defensively behind.

"The couch," she clarified. Her calm body language spoke volumes.

Rather than question the foreign terms, I slowly stepped around and sank into the seat opposite of her. I leaned Cynthia against the back of the furniture within my reach.

Max softly smiled at me. "There. That wasn't so hard, was it?" She asked rhetorically while I glanced at the hot water she had poured me.

The mostly empty glass sat in front of me on the table. Water droplet fell down its sides. A small amount of clear, sparkling water remained. I blinked and swayed back as an odd sensation cleared from around me. *Did I drink that?*

I looked up and found the woman sitting before me. She looked at me expectantly. "I said, I found you in the forest. How did you get there?" *What happened?* My foggy mind unwound itself as I tried to grasp at something that didn't quite exist. *Has time passed?* I looked to my right out the 'window.' I looked back down at my hands. *And why am I so relaxed?*

I gulped and suddenly wished that I hadn't finished my drink already. The tea pot she had brought out was nearly dry. I wet my lips, and I pressed my hands together and wrung them as I slowly started to explain. "My name is Phaedra," I began after a few false starts, "Princess of the Queendom of Death. I was banished by my mother, Queen Mara." The words were whispered, and the woman leaned closer to me as her eyes betrayed her sharp mind.

I continued, "I saw her kill someone close to me. My best friend, Liraz. I — I knew she was going to kill me. She's never been pleased with me." Speech came easier now, faster. My hands became red as they worried each other. "I ran. I took the secret exit, the one behind Cynthia in the armory," I explained as if she knew which one that was. I didn't stop to think about how preposterous it would be for a lowly human to be in a castle of angels. "When I arrived at the throne room, she told me to kill her or be banished." My lower lip wavered. *This woman,* my thoughts bumbled into each other, my emotions a mess, *why do I trust her so much?*

The woman reached across the table to grip my hurried hands to hold and calm them. Her hands felt cool, a refresh from the crosswinds brewing in me. "You didn't want to fight her," she reasoned.

I shook my head slowly. "No, that's - that's not it. I couldn't fight her," I sagged into my seat, pained in my heart. "I'm not strong enough," I whispered. "I didn't want to fight her." I squeezed my eyes shut as I gripped her hands back at the admission. It was so easy to picture this woman as Liraz, her curls replaced by looser waves and a sun-worked complexion. *I want to stay with this woman,* I realized. *She reminds me so much of Liraz.* The thought of leaving behind a connection to Liraz was painful.

My heart thudded in my chest. A pressure built inside me at the thought of never seeing her again. Tension slowly grew in me as I resisted my sudden nausea. The woman was quiet as my breath shortened and I gave into sorrow. A tear worked its way out before I could think to stop it.

More slipped out as I bit down on my tongue to stop the ugly gasps I knew would come next. The woman let go of my hands and there was some shuffling as she did something. I pawed at my eyes messily before I let my hands drop down as anger bled into my emotions and gripped my glass.

Crack!

I jumped with a gasp as I looked down to see I had accidently broken the cup underneath my now bleeding hands. "I'm — I'm sorry," I gasped out, panicked that I'd no longer be welcome in this woman's home, be sent out with nowhere to go. What remained of the tea mixed with my blood in the deep cuts and simmered in me. *Mother would be furious with me!*

Everything within the castle had been precious to Mother. *To break something is to rob our children, our children's children, and their children, of it,* I recalled her words as she stood over the ashes of a burning book. Keres had been shaking in the corner, the torch she had brought to the library extinguished at her feet.

"Let me see," the woman's commands were gentle and caused no resistance inside of me. I presented my hands to her, and she wrapped them in a bandage, likely what she had shuffled around for earlier for me to wipe my eyes with.

She looked over my minor injuries after they were gently wrapped. The leftover sparkling tea bled into the fabric. "What will you do now?" She looked up at me as she gently released my hands.

Now? The question hadn't occurred to me. I was no longer bound by the laws of my queendom, no longer a servant of any higher purpose. No longer a friend. Liraz's face jumped back to the forefront of my mind. A hot iron rested in my chest.

Liraz had been my single friend for many years after the Queen had forbade the others from 'distracting me from my training.' Without her, I had no purpose. I had long accepted I'd never be queen with my weak body and mind, especially in comparison against my gifted sister, Keres. I'd also presumed that after Keres took the throne, I'd be free to roam the queendom in search of new books and writings to read and learn from.

Now, that presumption of the future was shattered, thrown away in the face of reality. An outrage burned inside me. My future had been stolen from me. My friend had been taken away from me, from the world, from her loved ones.

"I need to learn how to survive," I contemplated the future.

"To survive," Max echoed to me as she leaned back from the table. She rested her arms on her crossed legs while she looked at me evenly.

"I don't know how to hunt," I explained, nervous. "I've never cooked, cleaned, traveled," I trailed off, struggling against the daunting mountain of things I had yet to attempt.

"Your royal education lacks grip in your new life," Max surmised.

"It does," I breathed out. I rubbed my new injury and wrapping while I processed. "I need someone to teach me." Ice formed inside me as I realized I couldn't learn these things on my own. "I'm going to starve otherwise," I mumbled as my attention started to withdraw further inside of myself.

"I'll teach you," Max blinked at me once slowly.

"What?" My fingers interlaced tightly at her suggestion.

"I said I'll teach you." A barely-there note of tension subverted her words. *She doesn't like repeating herself,* my mind began to mark down what was safe and what wasn't.

"But why?" *Why would this stranger, who gathered me off the forest floor, suddenly want to teach me how to survive?* My feathers fluffed out as distrust swam in between them.

Somehow, Max's calm face flattened further emotionally. "I live alone, as you see." She gestured around us, from where I had come. "It would be nice to have some company," she explained slowly.

Company? I shifted uneasily.

Apparently content with the resolution, Max gathered the drinkware and teapot on the tray and returned them to the kitchen.

My attention lingered on her empty, wingless back as she turned away. *Could a human teach an angel?*

The sound of a brook surprised me. *A river in her home?* Cautiously curious, I crept towards the kitchen. I peered around the edge of the hall and saw Max standing before a counter, long drapes off to the side with sunlight beaming around them, and a table pushed against the wall. *Clean*, I noted. *And spotless. She does this herself?* I was impressed.

"That Weapon you have."

Max's voice made me jump back from the corner before I took a half step into the room. *She hasn't seen me,* I noted. *Can humans sense us?* I had not had prolonged contact with one before. Realizing she was waiting for me to respond, I said, "Yes?"

"It is quite dangerous," Max sighed as the sound of the brook quieted before it disappeared. I frowned, unable to see around her. *Where is the stream?* I wondered. Max turned to look at me and placed her hand on the counter.

In the face of her confidence, I wavered like a ticklish fern. "Yes," I admitted quietly and averted my eyes.

Max watched me patiently before she responded as if to make sure I had said my piece. "Does she talk to you?" She questioned.

"Talk to me?" My fingers fidgeted as I first tried to wrap my arms around my waist only to drop my arms by my side.

Max waved me off as she turned to approach the drapery. Behind her, I saw a metal object that had been fused with the counter. Small spigots rested in the back of the human device. *A well, perhaps?* I wondered. *Our sinks are just scraped out of wood,* I admired the craftsmanship. Sudden light in my eyes made me flinch and wrap my arms around myself as I squinted at the source.

"Come this way," Max instructed me as my eyes adjusted painfully. I slowly walked forward and paused. *A window-door?* I admired it briefly before a gust of wind kissed me on the nose. I sucked in a breath as my eyes focused farther in the distance.

Max stood with her arms crossed in the deep grass. Around us, great natural stone walls rose into peaks. Heavy, bowling winds flapped our hair. *Animals?* Shocked, I watched a distant herd of deer meandering thoughtlessly.

"The Key Stone Mountains."

I turned to look at Max. "They're hollow!" I told her breathlessly.

Max gave a small smile. "This is the most important place in Ouranios." Her eyes seemed to reflect a rainbow of colors. Each gleamed with pride despite her cool exterior. "This is a good spot." She looked farther into the undermountain and I followed her gaze.

"A lake!" I marveled.

"There's a few different terrains here," she started to walk down, and I trailed behind a safe distance. "The real world isn't made of brick and flat stone." She advised me with a twinkle in her eye as the ground began to grow steeper towards the water.

My feet slipped on the lush grass as we made eye contact. With a gasp, my legs split and I began sliding. Max gracefully cleared the way as my weight sped me up. I grunted as I dug my fingers into the earth, wings flapping against the ground as I tried to gain air for leverage.

I huffed as I slowly slid to a stop before the water. I froze as Max's feet came close to my hands, but she merely stepped around me. "The grass can be slick," she warned from behind me.

I rolled onto my back to get her in my vision while my inner thighs complained. Max ignored me while she watched the lake. I followed her eyes and saw only the far stone wall. "Does it rain here?" I asked quietly to not disturb the nature around us.

"Would you like it to?" She half turned to look down at me, and I shivered under her examination. I forced my breaths to keep even as she stared into my eyes. Max's emotions reminded me of a treasure chest, locked away, closed, existing but absent.

Apparently content with whatever she saw, she turned away from me and back to the lake. "Your body needs time to recover. You could seriously injure your wings," she informed me.

A human doctor that treats angels? I kept my tongue still.

"You want to train in here?" I grasped my elbow with the hand I had wrapped around my middle out of anxiety.

"We will train in here," Max affirmed to me. She stood with her thick hair tied back in the center of the living room. The furniture had been shoved against the far walls to make plenty of space for us.

Wouldn't one of the other rooms work better? I held my question in. I hadn't inquired about all the closed doors, and I hadn't explored the spaces. *I can't just invite myself into another's home.* I stared as Max spread her legs and slowly fell into a stance.

"Do you know what this is?" She asked, her posture straight and her eyes bright.

I chewed my lip as I looked through my memories. I've read so many texts on fighting, but they didn't have pictures. I squeezed my middle harder as I grew tense.

"It's okay if you don't know," Max informed me easily as she moved into another stance. "What about this one?" Her arms were above her head as she breathed slowly, deeply.

"It's okay?" The ignorant question fell out of my mouth. *Mother would never!* The admonishment wanted to breach my lips like a sudden hurricane, whether it be meant for me or Max or both of us.

Max looked at me evenly. "You won't be able to succeed without the proper tools," she explained to me as I considered the idea more than the stance she held. "The tools are available to you. I'm just making them easier to find," she explained as she demonstrated a lower stance.

I observed how her back curved as she took an almost predatory step forward, her body close to the ground.

My nails, which had begun to dig into my elbow at some point, slowly released as I took a deep breath. *Is this what it means to start a new life?* I wondered as I slowly tried to copy her stance. Max watched me patiently as I fought for balance. *She's not going to get mad at me?*

"A proper stance is important," she informed me and changed her footing and shifted. I tried to copy her. "Not only will it strengthen your muscles over time, but it will increase your flexibility." She glanced over my twitching back as I extended myself. "You will grow stronger," she assured me.

"Every weapon is unique," Max handed the spear to me. I accepted it, my toes curling uneasily in the small sandy shore that encircled the lake. "They each have advantages and disadvantages." She twirled her own and drew a hand from the base to the tip. She squeezed it and then looked at me. "While some are similar, each needs a unique strategy. There are many ways to accomplish a goal," she continued. "Rather than a straightforward path."

I feel like a child. I looked down at the dull weapon. "I have sparred with Cynthia before," I assured my mentor.

In response, she tossed her spear up before she elegantly caught it with the same hand still extended. "Successfully?" She stared up at her weapon as if measuring how straight it was.

I was thankful for the small privacy she afforded me. "No," I whispered.

"Just take a moment to feel the spear," she instructed me and lowered hers. She balanced hers in front of her while I straightened mine out somewhat awkwardly. *Where am I supposed to put my hands on this stick?* "Feel how heavy it is, if it curves one way more than the other." She ran her hand along hers once again. I copied her, eager for praise.

"You're eager to return to your Weapon," she stated. "This is the same height and width." She nodded, confident. I swept my feet out in a side stance and dropped lower, eager to begin. Max's eyes twinkled with excitement as she raised her staff above her head. Her hair, untamed and down, crowned her gloriously.

With impressive speed, her staff feinted as it came down to strike the middle of mine and instead smacked me loudly in the side. I scrambled as I was thrown a small distance into the nearby lake. The deer that had been meandering nearby stared at us emptily, unafraid.

I floundered in the water, my wings weighed down dangerously as my legs kicked futilely. I tried to grasp at the surface, but I was swallowed whole. A hand curled around my upper arm, and I latched around it as I was brought up. I gasped into Max's side as she half dragged me to shore.

"Didn't know you couldn't swim," her quiet observation fell on deaf ears while I dry heaved onto the sand.

"I'm sorry," I spluttered into the sand. "I'm sorry." I whispered as she crouched next to me. A soft pressure on my head made me gasp and freeze. *She's...petting me?* I looked up at the strange human in confusion, my face an overexerted red. Max's empty eyes stared back.

She looks a bit...more intense than usual. I observed a fleeting thread of emotion on her face, too fast to read. My wet hair pooled onto the ground and myself, and I shivered.

"A bow," I found Max outside after she hadn't been in the two rooms I'd always found her in; either staring out the window in the living room or staring around the back door into the undermountain. On her back was a simplistic quiver full of arrows, and in her hand a beginner's bow.

"Today is a good day to start archery," Max agreed as she looked over towards the herd of deer that had meandered closer than usual. "They're getting used to you." She handed the bow and a quiver of arrows to me. I swung the quiver over my shoulder.

I examined the simple beginner bow as I contemplated the animals. "I'm going to miss, and then they'll run," I said. Experimentally, I raised the bow and brought it back. The loose tension allowed me to make sure my feet were in the correct spot. I aimed at the deer at the head of the pack and released.

Pwing!

"Ah!" I hissed as I grabbed my forearm. The bow string had split in the middle and snapped against my bare skin. The deer scattered at my exclamation, and I dropped to my knees. Defeat, embarrassment, and shame mixed within me.

"Most bows break if you release it without an arrow," Max crouched next to me and grasped my wrist with her thumb and pointer finger. I displayed the red, angry skin for her to see.

"Why?" I grunted as she released me to stand.

"The force travels into the arrow and propels it forward," she answered easily. I looked up at her in confusion. *What is she saying?* Max stared at the backs of the retreating herd.

I looked at the broken bow I had dropped. *At least she won't yell at me,* I shivered from the memory of Mother's angry voice. *I'd take her babble over that.*

"Stand up," Max didn't offer me a hand, and I sighed as I rose. "Try again." She brought around another bow from behind her. *Was that there the whole time?* I stared down at it. "This time," she pressed the weak wood into my palm, "try and hit that tree." She nodded forwards.

I breathed deep. I scrambled to awkwardly retrieve an arrow from my quiver. "Dinner might be a bit tough tonight," I remarked.

Max hummed as she stepped up behind me. She helped me guide the bottom of the arrow to the string. I noticed it was notched slightly, and I took advantage of her thoughtfulness. "Fresh meat isn't my preference," she spoke quietly, her breath tickling my ear. I tensed as she spoke, my limbs almost stone as she pushed my arms up.

I breathed easier when she stepped away. "This uses different muscles than sparring. It's a unique skill," she offered before she fell silent. I let out a slow breath, aiming with both eyes open this time, and I released.

The arrow sang a short distance before it stuck in the ground, bottom over front, some distance from the tree. Without a word, Max retrieved it and handed it back to me. When she stepped back, I aimed again, higher this time. *She doesn't get mad when I fail.* I released the arrow, and the distance it flew doubled. It burrowed more deeply in the ground this time.

I accepted the arrow from Max with thanks. *She explains things as many times as I need,* I realized as she once again raised my arms with her hands. *She's giving me the tools to survive.* The confidence I had in her and the confidence she inspired me to feel about learning these skills had shaped me into quite the adept, eager learner. *Is this how Keres has felt? Mother always seemed so pleased with her.*

"You shoot better in my absence," Max noted as she judged the arrows sticking out of the tree. I fidgeted as she strode over and began to yank them out. She gripped them easily, her voice rising to breach the distance. "Why is that?"

I bit my lip only to receive a warning look from Max. *Right. She doesn't like it when I bleed,* I coached myself. "I get nervous," I looked away and started to pick at the bow.

"Nervous?" Unblinkingly, Max stared into my soul.

An odd sensation fluttered deep inside me, uncomfortable. It felt like bubbles coming to the surface, a great fish hiding below waiting to strike. "I don't want to be reprimanded," I almost whispered.

Max's human ears caught the words easily. "My rules are simple," she sighed and closed her eyes. "I've not gone to the point that —"

"Mother — Queen Mara, she did," I stumbled over my words as I interrupted. I grasped my hands together tightly with the bow in between as I stared down at them.

My shoulders hunched as Max approached me. I tensed as she passed by me only to drop the arrows at my feet. She continued on, and I focused on keeping my breathing silent as I heard her enter our dwelling. The back door slapped shut with a bit more force than was necessary.

She's not Mother, I took up an arrow and drew my bow back. *I never have to see Mother again.* Liraz's smiling face, her hair gently swaying as she shook with laughter came to my mind. The backdrop of the library, my place of solace Keres wouldn't follow me into, was warm. The comforting memory soured as I considered not being able to see those places again. *I'm so far away from you, Liraz.*

The strange sensation of the monster beneath waves that had risen up inside of me diminished as a soft wind embraced my feathers.

Cynthia struck Max's spear loudly. She was a warm and familiar weight in my hands. Max overpowered my strike and threw Cynthia to the side. I kept my hands connected to Cynthia and directed the rebound to dig the base of her into the ground. I shifted my hands as Max made to strike my ankles.

I used Cynthia as leverage to jump up and over her strike so that it instead hit my scythe. I used my momentum to strike Max on the head with my foot. Max hissed and jumped back after I struck her. I let myself drop back to the ground and flapped my wings in satisfaction.

"Happy in your worship, Princess?" Max smiled menacingly as I showed my growth. She darted toward me with terrifying speed and struck me in the stomach with an open palm. *I should never have told her this is how some fairies pray!* I regretted.

I grunted, the air knocked out of me. Max's crystalline eyes gleamed as I grabbed her wrist and swung Cynthia's blade towards her face. Max laughed as she ducked down and swept my legs out from under me.

The ground met me too quickly, and I was sprawled out on my back. Max's spear went high before she struck down towards my face. I shrieked and scrunched up my face, my hands flying up to protect myself, but no pain arrived. I hesitantly peaked between my fingers, my body curled up in anticipation, and saw Max staring towards the dwelling. The spear had stopped moments before my face.

"Someone is here." A touch of frustration showed as Max tossed the spear up, caught it by its middle, and impaled it into the dirt deeply as she turned her back to me and left.

Who is it? Worried, I got up and brushed myself up. *Death angels?* Cautiously, I crept to the backdoor. I held still as I listened to shuffling, then quiet. *It's been quiet for so long,* I counted my breaths. I jumped when, after several minutes, there was more shuffling. The backdoor sliding open next to where I had been just out of sight made me jump.

"Come in," Max, exasperated, ushered me in. I looked over to see the bowl she had gathered fruit from the undermountain trees was now full of salted meat. I swallowed hungrily as I was ushered to the living room to sit. Max sat opposite me as I twisted around to see if we were alone.

"Just a lost traveler," she assured me. Max paused, and I forced myself to relax as I saw she was thinking something through. "Word is that Queen Mara is attempting to take the Fire Sphere." Max dropped the bag of new spices she had garnered from the lost trader on the table.

I looked up at her in shock. "Take another Queendom?" I gasped. Max sat on the opposite davenport and uncharacteristically leaned back and relaxed. Her eyes closed as she sighed. "She can't do that!" I tried to rouse a reaction from the calm woman and waved my hands.

"You're strong now," Max slowly opened her eyes. Her crystalline gaze bored into me like a hand tool. "Go and stop her."

I slowed and quieted. "Alone?"

Max's face didn't betray it if she felt surprise or disappointment at my odd question. "You're strong now," she assured me. "You have bloomed into a true camellia flower."

There was silence while I thought. *I don't want to leave Max.* I sighed as I leaned back, frustrated. *I'm not even associated with the Queendom of Death any longer.* I began to frown. *Although if Mother were to start a new war, it would make things harder for me.* The idea of trying to disguise my black feathers so passersby wouldn't notice almost made me chuckle.

Max stared at me easily, unblinking in that uncanny way I had become accustomed to. In my mind, it was easy to overlay her features with Liraz's more gentle, emotive expressions. With the news swirling in between us, I was brought back to that night.

"The idea of Mother striking down others," I averted my eyes to the floor as they wetted. I'd not discussed much with Max of my childhood, my background. It was a heavy weight inside me, a weight I had to bear alone.

The weight of Liraz's corpse weighed down my soul. Envisioning her cold shell of a body upon Mother's floor made my heart beat fast, my limbs shake. Sweat began to dance across my forehead. But above all, anger had gathered inside of me. The core of the emotion sat heavily in my heart, large in a way that I had to maneuver myself around it. It strained my heart as I tried to survive around its burgeoning waves.

"I'll ask you one more time," Max proposed to me. "What will you do now?"

"I'm going to kill the Queen," I decided. "And take revenge for Liraz,"

"How?" Max questioned me intensely.

"If Queen Mara conquers another land, wouldn't she want to claim it for herself?" I answered. "Such a thing has never been done before. She'd be the first." *She places her own achievements on a pedestal.*

Max stared at me for a heartbeat before she stood. "You'll need proper clothes," she murmured as she walked into the hall. I half turned to watch her go. I heard one of the doors open and curiosity took over me. As I stood, the door was closed and Max reappeared. She offered a bundle to me. I took it, confused. "These are traveling clothes," she informed me. "What you are wearing now is too thin," she warned.

I looked down at the clothes Max had presented to me. "Oh," I looked myself over.

"I've included a cloak as well. It is dense and will keep you warm," Max explained, and I was quick to thank her. "Do you know how to tie it over your shoulder?" I looked at her in confusion, still holding the bundle. Max pressed her hands together and looked at me with expectant eyes. Upon seeing my confusion, she took the bundle and extracted the cloak, and set the rest on the table. "Like this," she began to wrap the cloak around me in a strange manner.

Max peered outside of the entrance of what had become my home in such a short time. "It's fair weather to depart," she remarked.

"Yes," I was eager to agree as I stood awkwardly outside of the borough. My feet wanted to carry me back inside to where I was safe, to where I had found a companion.

"The map will show you which way to go," Max turned to look at me. Her features, as always, were difficult to read. "And the compass will help," she reminded me.

I nodded. We stared at each other in silence, and I wondered once again what was happening inside her when she observed in this way. "I don't want to go," I slowly admitted. I maintained eye contact, desperate for some emotion, some semblance that she cared for me, wanted me to stay.

"Life is never permanent," her kind tone couldn't stop the wrenching of my heart. I no longer wished to see Liraz in her. I wanted to run far, far away from this feeling. "Things come and things go," Max told me.

I grimaced at her before I caught myself. I lowered my body in a small bow and spread my wings to honor her. "Thank you," I directed my words at her feet to hide my face, "For everything." I looked up, and Max was silent as she easily stared into my soul.

My feet were carried away by difficult emotions as I made to leave. My face caved somewhat from the pain.

"Phaedra," Max's voice stopped me. I stilled but didn't turn around in an effort to hide my wet eyes. "Don't fly. The others will see you easier if you do." Max warned me.

"I won't fly, Max," I promised her.

Traveling alone was a lonely and difficult affair. The fire starter Max had given me worked well and was reliable. But it was summer, and I had enough dried meat and fruit to last the entire journey. I passed by several others on my way through the confusing lands and landmarks on my way to the desert. Quick to steal away and hide, I was confident none of them had noticed me.

On the edge of the desert, that changed. A small caravan, just past where the greenery suddenly cut off into golden, diamond-like sand, had planted their temporary roots. I observed from a distance, jealous of how their wagons encircled to create a windbreak, and noticed a piece of forgotten paper blowing towards me.

Eager for kindling for my own meager fire that, hopefully, was kept hidden around a small hill, I snatched it from the air as it tried to escape me and wile out of my grasp. I spread it and read from my tiny firelight.

"Feathered wings," I whispered to myself, shocked. "What's the reward?" I wondered out loud. *If they're recruiting this way, then they don't have a large enough personal army,* I reasoned from my strategy textbooks. I folded up the paper and snuck it into my pocket before I curled around my pitiful, small, safe fire. *If I join and survive until the end, I'll be able to see you,* I embraced the dark sensation curling in my gut, *Mother.*

May it please Your Majesty.

Thank you for your letter. Our nations have been quite close since trade began on our waterships, and I am quite eager to create this bond. I am prepared to offer five of our fastest waterships as well as the Flat Claws to you. I would also offer the Noxious Waters, but I fear it may convey insult.

I look forward to your reply.

The King of Fire

Chapter Three

The trenches were scratches in the earth and did little to keep the mauling sun off our backs. Far behind us, the Castle of Fire rose out of the flat terrain proudly. The red rock castle and its lofty walls gave off shimmering heat waves. My black wings ached to the bone in the punishing heat, strapped tightly to my back and hidden away in clothing. The fire fairies around me were none the wiser as I strung my bow, aimed at the incoming death angels flocks, the incoming enemy.

My clothes covered my paperwhite skin, protection from another burn as well as something to hide me among the rich russets of my comrades. I loosed an arrow to the sky and it found its mark in someone who had once called me Princess Phaedra as they flew ahead to lead the charge. *The flock leader, their echelon.* Their body fell and the shiny metal of their Queendom of Death armor glinted in the beginning of another sunset. I pushed the bile back down inside me.

Death angels had been attacking the Sphere of Fire for a time now, to what end was starting to become obvious to even the humans that had long since scattered. *Queen Mara sought control of the Sphere, their territory, and may soon have it. But why?*

My thoughts popped as the fairy next to me spoke. His red, dusty, butterfly shaped wings twitched as he released an arrow that missed as the angels adjusted to their secondary leader. He disturbed the thick layer of dust that rested atop his black tresses and umber skin when he went to grab a nonexistent arrow from the quiver on his back.

"You're a good shot," he complimented me as he grabbed free arrows from the runner's back bag as she ran down the trench. These runners supplied to the fairies that desperately needed help. "Name's Egan. Who're you? Did you train with the Queen's Guard?" He asked innocently, trustingly. The large flock of death angels overhead began to break up into smaller squadrons as they began their tactical assault.

My bow cracked in my ear as I let another shot free. I aimed for where the new leader of the closest death angel squadron had swooped down to throw spears at fire fairies who dared face them with swords outside the trench. The new leader had guided their small flock back up when my arrow struck them where their wing met their back. My eyes tightened as I missed the shoulder I'd aimed for.

"No," I answered simply in an effort not to give myself away. My anger at being forced to kill innocents, at innocents going to a war they didn't start, loosened my lips. I whispered to myself, "We're taught not to swoop like that." I recalled someone other than the Queen teaching me to fly, but I don't recall her name. She had used a long, biting stick to bat at me when I had done that same swoop maneuver. It had the possibility to tear your wings muscles.

"Runner!" I threw my head over my shoulder and yelled, looking for the young girl from earlier that was manning our section of the trench. I grimaced and shielded my eyes as I looked for her. My bow lowered.

I had to hold out in this land of wanton and senseless death until the Queen herself made an appearance. Queen Mara would surely come once we whittled her forces down enough. The fire fairies had been steadily losing ground until I arrived, but these past three days, we had managed to hold this trench firm.

The runner appeared in my sights, and I flagged her down. Her wild, feral eyes pinned to me as she sprinted, mouth open as she gasped for air. *Tonight, we will turn the battle. We will keep this trench firm.*

She stopped in front of me, still gasping, and opened the bag at her side as I grabbed a spindle of arrows off her back. She produced bandages for the archer next to me to wrap his hands before she started sprinting to the other end of the trench. As I unwound the rope that gathered the arrows to each other, my sleeve inched up to reveal my normally pearl skin had painful sun kisses across it, blisters that I had to be careful not to burst. *I can't afford to need treatment and have my cover blown.*

I fixed my stance. I drew back another arrow and slowly trailed the death angels in the sky. There were fire fairies in the sky that engaged with the numerous death angel flocks. Each side wielded bows, arrows, swords, and shields while they flew. With the distraction of the fire fairies, it made it easy for the ground soldiers to pick off the angels. Although, it seemed as if the grounded fire fairies were unaccustomed to using bows or at least using them on flying targets. Arrows littered the battlefield below the flying angels, waiting to be picked up come sunrise to be used again.

My grip weakened on the arrow in my bow as a group of death angels came between the trench and a group of fire fairies. They were trying to cut them off, to divide and conquer. I watched with narrow eyes as I looked for a good shoulder shot. My eyes kept me hesitating as they unwillingly trailed to their faces. I looked for someone familiar to make sure I wouldn't shoot down anyone I had once known.

A hand on my shoulder jerked me around, and I gasped and dropped the arrow in surprise. My bow snapped, empty, between the fire fairy soldier and I as she stared into my eyes with unbridled fury. "You," she snarled to me. Spit flew into my face. Her other hand gripped the scarf that I had wrapped around my face and neck to disguise myself and tightened dangerously.

How did they find out? The air whistled out of me as I saw she stood in the place Egan had stood earlier. I bit the inside of my mouth as two guards flanked her. All three wore brilliant red armor that matched the rich, ore filled earth around us. I could see my reflection in their breast plates as the guard that held me commanded, "Take her to the King. He'll want to see this," she let go of my throat as her two lackeys grabbed each of my arms as well as my wings. The two slits in the back of my cloak were defenseless against their grip.

I reflexively tried to duck away, the sensation of strangers on my feathers uncomfortable. But their grip hardened and hurt before I cried out and gave up struggling. None of the other soldiers that shot arrows off around us noticed, too focused on trying to protect their territory and loved ones. It was a small blessing that they hadn't also come down upon me.

They began to march me down the trench and toward the center of the fire fairy forces. The trenches slowly gave way to ground level, and when night overtook us, I found myself being stood before a decorated ruby red tent. Yellow banners flew in the wind. More guards surrounded the tent. They looked like they had not yet spent a moment on the frontlines, the same as the clean guards that hauled me. I held in my scoff as we entered the tent. I had been no different not that many nights ago.

I stopped short as I entered. A guard shoved me forward before the red flaps fell in their faces. I stumbled and fell on my knees. I kept my gaze on the floor, and shook lightly as I realized I was in deeper than I thought I had been.

Shoes on the edge of my vision through the legs of the grand table before me led up to the King of the Fire Sphere. His great, long black locks were braided around the golden, jewel-encrusted crown atop his head decoratively, his umber skin not burnt by the sun like me. He wore regal red furs despite the heat, and a delicate, golden scepter rested in his large hand. The King's wings were large, and others moved expertly to not graze them. His deep yellow butterfly wings melted to red at the edges. A third color, white, spread just over his shoulder.

King Cole and I had never met, and I doubted he would recognize me from tales alone. Other well-dressed fairies surrounded him, members of his cabinet that helped him plan the next maneuver in the war on the table above me. There were two guards at the entrance of this tent. More stood at each leg of the tent, I assumed, and surrounded it completely.

I could almost tangibly feel the smugness of the three that brought me here as I attempted to shrink down and make myself smaller. *There's no easy way out of this.* I controlled what little I had left, my inner narrative, and forced myself to remain optimistic.

New feet stepped in front of me too close, and I flinched. Their owner grabbed at my black cloak, at my scarf, and pulled them off of me violently. Several of my feathers were pulled out with the quick, unforgiving motions, and my breath hissed. I raised my head to ensure they didn't pull at my throat, and my porcelain hair fell into my face. I shook my head to clear my view. I found myself looking up at someone who could be none other than the Princess of Fire.

Fira, the Princess of Fire, shared her long locks with her father. They fell to her waist in twists, their dense and glossy texture not weighed down by the heat. She dropped the clothes at her feet before me, before her hands tightened into fists at her side. Her locks were still as her face slowly twisted at me. She slowly took in my black wings. Her reddish-brown, sepia skin slowly turned more carmine with anger as her ruby wings beat angrily. I made sure to keep my wings close to me in an effort to appease her obvious indignation.

Her hand shot out, and I gasped as she took Cynthia from the sheathe on my back. The advisors in the room cried out as she gave the scythe an experimentally swing and nearly nicked one of them. She switched her grip and dropped Cynthia's blade so that the sharp edge of the blade faced up as well as the snath. As she glared at me. the bonfire in her soul grew larger and larger, and she held Cynthia close to my throat. I wanted to swallow reflexively, to shake, but her unforgiving blade had tasted me willingly many times.

"I'll kill you," the Princess of Fire whispered to me, the quiet words loud despite the advisors huffing and puffing over her actions to the King. "I've heard of this Weapon before. What does the Banished Princess of Death want with us?" Her mouth pulled tight into a scowl as I became tinder to her inferno.

So my story has reached even this far? The idea startled me into silence as I imagined the whispers going over even to the death angel's enemy lines. Her face flashed as she gave me a solid kick to the stomach, and I keeled over. I gripped my stomach as my feathers curled in pain.

"Your Majesty!"

"Royal Highness!"

Two guards yelled as they ran into the tent. They both panted as I slowly sat up fully. I used an arm to support myself as they spoke and used the moment to gather my air back. "The death angels have taken the line!" One said urgently and the room gasped at the news. My eyes turned to the Princess. I tried to look through her to see the King's reaction.

"All the lines are gone, My King! Please, it's not safe here!" The second soldier said in a rush, his wings beating in fear and stirring the tent. *Were we the farthest back trench?!*

"We need to move," the guard who had first grabbed me spoke behind me, her voice calm despite the dire circumstances. The advisors in the tent quickly filed out. Those who wore clothing that could hinder their wings stripped it off just outside the tent and dropped it before they took flight. They turned into a mass of red butterfly wings as they fled.

My heart thudded in my ears as the King spoke. "Yes, we need to leave. Take Princess —" the King interrupted himself as the Princess of Fire stepped aside so he could look at me. "Take this death angel with us," his large eyes betrayed no emotion.

I jerked back as a cloth was then pressed to my mouth and nose from behind me. I had forgotten about the other two guards that had brought me here. My vision blurred and my thoughts swam as I breathed in the odd scent. *Does this mean...my mother is coming?* A painful, sharp sensation in my heart was the last thing I felt before I closed my eyes.

Liraz...

The cell was windowless. I ached for freedom. My body remembered the pains of being transported better than my mind. I scrambled on the bare, dirty stone floor as I came to and recalled where I was. The stench clung to my skin like bogwater. My fingernails cracked against the dry stones as I tried to stand. I threw my head around until I saw the bars of the cage.

Someone stared at me from the other side. I felt feral. The urge to grab them and tear at them just because they were free and I wasn't showed in my bared teeth. I slammed my head on the grime caked stones in front of me in an attempted threat. Instead, the loud slap was muffled by the sound of fabric. *My cloak!* I quickly put it back on. *I didn't realize they'd tossed it in under me.*

I blinked my eyes rapidly as they adjusted to the low light of the weak torches, and the figure moved away from me and left me alone. *Who was that?* My head throbbed sharply as I recalled what led to this situation. *Are we in the Castle of Fire?* Death angels flew into my mind, their spears sailing from above to below and into innocent peasants. Death angel arrows struck home in my growing guilt. *I couldn't stop them. How did they overtake the trenches so fast?*

A metallic clanging accompanied by soft whispers and footsteps diverted my attention and halted my racing thoughts. I shrank back as two large guards stopped in front of my cell. One dangled keys in front of him but did not say anything. My feathers raised in anticipation as the guard tossed the keys up and caught them by grabbing one specific key before they fell.

The lock was quick work for the rusty piece of metal, and the door was quickly opened. I jerked back, unable to help my fear response, as they rushed in and grabbed me by my arms and wings. I hissed at their tight grip but obeyed their nudging towards the door.

The guards led me from the dungeon to the upper part of the castle. The Castle of Fire was massive. The hallways were large enough to fit several flocks of angels and a few flutters of fairies comfortably. The red stone exterior of the marvelous construction gave way to a warm interior of warm ochres, maroons, and sandstone. The steps of the staircases were awkwardly large, and I stumbled as I stretched my legs uncomfortably to keep pace with the guards. Despite our similar sizes, they took the stairs with practiced ease.

Windows, however, seemed to be sparse. The first window I saw was a tiny one that showed only a sliver of blue sky high up a spiral staircase. I jerked towards it and thought I might be able to fit through if I broke the glass before the guards dragged me backwards, and I almost fell back down the stairs. The scare quieted my want to flee, to survive. As my eyes darted around, I noticed that all of the windows wouldn't be able to fit even a child.

I remained calmer until we reached what I could only call the war room of the Queen of Fire. The Queen herself wasn't present. She likely had more important duties. Instead, King Cole stood in the back of the room. He stared at a map on the wall surrounded by the same people that had fled the tent. The large room was grandiose, and their elaborate yellow, red, and brown outfits fit in much better.

On the floor rested a quilt larger than life. It reminded me of the quilt that rested in the library in the Queendom of Death that depicted the two goddesses and the Goddess of All in harmony as they created our world. The blocky, ancient thread technique in both was lost to us all now. This quilt instead showed one goddess, her form pure white and angelic, as she attacked the Goddess of All. The fine fabric almost sparkled in some places and showed the petals falling from the Goddess's body to our world, Ouranios.

"Sire, we brought the captive," the guard to my right spoke and pushed me down to my bruised knees. I looked up at him to glare, and I was surprised to remember clearly that he had been one of the guards that had captured me initially. *Where's the woman they were with?* I looked at the other guard as if he would answer my question and saw he was the same as before as well. My memories were still unclouding.

"I see that," King Cole's voice, despite being rough with lack of sleep and stress, made me still. The authority in his tone was natural. Despite not being the leader of this sphere, he was still in charge, and all would obey him.

May the Queen save me. I looked at him and tried to keep what little blood was in my ghostly skin where it belonged. If I went too pale with fear, they might think me dead and toss me out. The small hope of Her Majesty made me relax a tiny amount.

"Banished Princess of Death," he looked at me evenly, and I strangely saw no judgment in his eyes despite the black feathers littered above his fallen comrades across his territory. "Why are you here?" The King's question was simple, short.

Nonetheless, a drop of sweat spilled down from my face. It was warm right now, but not warm enough to cause the chest thudding, mind racing anxiety I felt. I felt as if the air was going to smother me, and I gaped like a fish as my mind turned slow as molasses. Despite being nothing like the terrifying Queen of Death, the way he stood before me, above me, was enough to remind me of how very small she made me feel. The King of Fire seemed to tower above me as she had.

"I'm here to end Queen Mara," the truth brimmed over my tongue unwillingly. "And take revenge for the fallen." Red fairy wings flitted across my mind, fresh as Liraz's blood inside my memory.

The others in the room grew silent at my revelation. Some stared with distrust, others with wide eyes. Some feigned to ignore me altogether and snuck looks at me over their shoulders. They bored me just as the court back home had.

The King's eyes had laughing lines. But the laughter was gone, and he studied me critically for some time. I shifted uneasily. The guards squeezed down on my wings tighter, and I started to sweat noticeably through my cloak.

I sucked in a tight breath when the King turned around to look at the war map. I followed his gaze, and my face fell at what I saw. Red ink crossed out many towns and villages and travelers' rest points on the map. The red ink had been allowed to dribble down before the vengeful sun dried it. Despite none dripping onto the Castle of Fire, as the Queendom of Death was to the south, the marks came closer and closer.

"Word from the front!" A woman burst into the room, and the door behind us slammed open. Before it had hit the wall, she had half flown, half run to the map, picked up a brush, and marked off the closest village to the castle. When she turned around to explain what had happened to the now lost village, I blinked and saw that it was the same runner as before. *How thinly spread are we?*

The King made a motion to the side of the room, and I looked over and saw the Princess of Fire. She stared at me with a deep hatred, and I shrank back involuntarily. I had been so caught up in the presence of the King I hadn't noticed her. Her cheeks had begun to blossom cardinal in anger as she obeyed and approached.

The King put an arm around her shoulders, and she crossed her arms over her chest in a standoffish manner as he pulled her around to look at the map with him. The runner bowed as she finished her report and made her way to the side of the room to wait for orders. I avoided her keen eyes as she looked at me with curiosity.

Instead I watched as the Princess drew back from the King as if offended by something he had said. The King released her and pointed at the map as he explained something, his tone low enough that I couldn't hear. The Princess shook her head, livid, and I could see the King's shoulders slump for a moment before he recovered. The King turned to face me.

May it please Your Majesty.

I am glad to hear from you. We would request trading rights in Wreden's Opening at a reduced tax than Fire Wing Bay.

No insult is taken,

The Queen of Death

Chapter Four

THE CONFIDENCE IN HIS voice carried the order easier than it would be to accomplish. "You will travel with Princess Fira and Royal Guard Egan to the Realm of Earth and win over their help. I do not believe we can win this war on our own."

"Your Majesty!" "Sire!" "King Cole!" The others in the room, including the lowly guards, startled at the King's admission. My heart fell deeper in my chest, a rock in a stream pulled under by the current.

"I have heard your story. You fled the Queen of Death to survive. So you will help my Princess and my sphere to survive," the King stated. I slowly nodded my head and assented. *It's only natural Queen Mara wouldn't reveal the weakness of her throne's heir to the outside world.* His commanding tone raised hairs on the back of my neck. I had to fight to keep my feathers smoothed down. *If I disagree, he's going to make sure I die here.* The thrum of the need to survive sang in me, and I felt as if I would lose the lunch I hadn't eaten. *This is my only chance to stay out of that cell.*

"With your experience with the enemy, and they are your enemy," he paused and I nodded. Both of us were aware of my fate should I be captured, if them not putting me down like an animal immediately wasn't already an order, what would happen. "You will ensure Princess Fira's safety so that she can convince Queen Dunia to send aid," the King paused and looked me up and down. "If you're willing, of course," his tone lightened, and his eyes smiled at the guards.

I couldn't help but bristle. "Of course," I kept my tone neutral, not letting out the verbal bite I wanted to at the thought of what they had planned for me before they thought of using me. The ancient trade alliance between the Sphere of Fire and Earth Realm has long fallen by the wayside, but it never involved death angels. My life hung on a string that was supposed to keep this bolting-horse-of-a-situation tame.

"I refuse," Princess Fira announced, arms crossed. "I'm not going to abandon my people when they need me most. I can fight," her eyes pinned him like prey at the edge of a knife.

The King didn't back down. "No. Queen Fiamma has already ordered it. The decision is made," his tone didn't betray if he thought differently than his greater, the Queen of Fire.

"Then why don't you show me the document where she wrote this order herself?" The Princess demanded, and I winced. Even I know a Queen is never to be questioned. Princess Fira stepped forward imposingly, but the King didn't back down.

Instead, his eyes flashed at her dangerously. "You would rather stay and sacrifice yourself needlessly, putting your pride over your people?" His tone was low, but his curled lip showed his distaste.

Princess Fira blinked. The sound of teeth gnashing was quiet as her wings beat behind her in agitation. After a moment, her head dipped and her expression was hidden by her locks. I watched her face redden further with rage and felt something inside me shift uneasily at the thought of traveling with her.

At her silence, the King drew his stature up farther. "It is decided," he reiterated. "Egan," he called the boy's name loudly, and the door behind me opened. I looked up at the fairy who sold me out and tried not to glare.

"Yes, Your Majesty," Egan bowed deeply. His eyes used the motion to lock onto mine. I hoped my citrine windows didn't betray anything that would show my anger. *I'm angry at myself for slipping up. He did the right thing.*

"Ready the Princess, our guest, and yourself to depart at once by land. You will be working with our guest," the absence of my title was heard when he paused before my name, "Phaedra, to travel to Queen Dunia to ask for reinforcements. Give her this." From his fine clothing, the King produced a scroll. *By land?* I pictured the King's fleet of boats in the harbor. *Queen Mara would anticipate us traveling by water and have prepared for it,* I concluded. *They wouldn't expect anyone to flee across the desert.*

"Yes, Your Majesty," Egan accepted the scroll with another bow. "I will fulfill your orders exceptionally." I noted how his hands shook as he held the scroll up as if it was his most precious possession.

"Good," the King nodded at him before he turned back to the map. I distinctly heard the fast steps of another runner from the open door behind me. I mused over another escape attempt by throwing myself backwards to try to get to the window again.

Should I help Princess Fira? The Queen of Death is winning this war, so she won't appear on the battlefield. I looked at the map, at the buildings in the city and the harbor. The thought of the ships that rested in Fire Wing Bay at her disposal made my soul harden. The Fire Sphere truly was in more dire straits than their soldiers had been led to believe.

If I can't get to her directly, I'll have to pull in the earth fairies to whittle down her forces until I can.

"Dismissed," the Fire King waved his hand over his shoulder as we were ordered to leave. I looked at Princess Fira as I rose from my knees. My wings had begun to ache from being pressed against my back so tightly.

Her brown eyes carved through me, a butcher knife against my rabbit soft skin. I shivered, intimidated, before I averted my eyes. The guards released their hold on my arms and wings, but I still wasn't trusted. One walked in front of me, guiding me somewhere new, and the second followed closely behind.

The royal guest quarters were much nicer than the dungeon. I had been given an opportunity to bathe and change clothes, and my well-loved black cloak had been replaced with a sturdier, simpler one. Ladies in waiting helped me put on fire armor, and I kept having to ask them to readjust the straps. The weight of the fine metal was heavier than what death angels wore, its make more crude, and it would slow me down. But if I could figure out how to balance it on my body without it slipping in flight, I should be able to fly in a straight line.

"This should be fine," I pushed at the vambrace on my arm experimentally as the three women stepped back. Their eyes shifted to one another as if I was about to eat them, and their wings flitted nervously. *My mother certainly would have devoured them. They'd all be terrified if anyone knew what Queen Mara dined on.* The armor didn't move, and I resisted the want to do the same to the cuisse and greaves I wore to not startle them.

I nodded at the ladies in waiting. They politely dipped their heads and curtsied before they filed out. The guards in the room straightened as they left, and I obviously examined the armor in an attempt to put them at ease. Fire armor, while heavy, was high quality despite its inferiority to death angel war armor. To my knowledge, it hadn't been out into real battle until recently and instead was commonly used to protect those who mined for minerals within The March mountains and the Flat Claws.

If we can return in time with Queen Dunia's forces, we'll be able to retake the place your materials were gathered from. I noted the stamp on my armor in several places, a triangle with a lone line through it, marking that this metal had been gathered from the Flat Claws.

The door opened again, and I dropped my arm to my side and saw Egan. My Cynthia rested somewhat uncomfortably in his hands. Behind him entered an old man. His white and gray locks spilled almost to the floor.

"Ah, so it is true," the elderly man remarked to Egan. I stood taller as the white haired elder approached me. "I thought my newest creation might not fit an angel." As he circled me, he examined how I wore his work in detail. My chin lifted, daring him to find fault, before I realized myself and backed down. My feathers flattened out. He returned to my vision, and I found it easier to relax when I could see where he was staring. His cloudy eyes made me question if he could see much these days.

"I was worried that this piece wouldn't be great enough for a vessel of the Goddess," he mused to himself. *How far has news of my being here spread? It could complicate leaving...*

"If the Goddess walks among us, it's certainly not as a death angel, especially one causing so much misery to the Fire Sphere and its people," I reassured him, familiar with the old myth that the Goddess had abandoned her realm to walk among us peoples of the world as the rulers of our lands.

The old man chuckled and gripped at his hip as if it was hurting him. "The Goddess is in all the royal bloodlines, and she does not account for the petty emotions of the living," he clucked at me, annoyed.

I tried to defuse the situation, not wanting any more incidents. "A goddess fades and dies without worship and a warrior the same without armor of this high of quality," I complimented.

The man scratched at his scalp, looked at his fingers as if expecting to find something, and then agreed. "I am the King's Armory Master," the man introduced himself. "I normally would give my name, but I fear I am not long enough for this world for it to matter," he told me bluntly, and I blinked in surprise.

"Mas —" Egan interrupted, looking strained.

"No, it's the truth," the elder shut the younger down quickly and gestured for him to stop hovering by the open door and approach. "This war is working me to the bone." He looked at me from his side eye and explained as he waved again impatiently.

I nodded slowly, of the mindset I might be better off quiet. Egan stopped next to his senior and held Cynthia before him with the same tremble he held the scroll from earlier.

"This Weapon of yours," he turned to Egan and took the scythe from him, "she is light and well-crafted. Where is the wood from?" He made a show of holding her up and spun her in a circle with surprisingly dexterity, hurting hip forgotten.

"I don't know," I admitted, wondering if I would be allowed to hold her again. I wanted to run my hands over her, dig my nails into the smooth yet bumpy White Wood that made up her snath. I could almost see the shadows moving against her blade as if she was also looking at me, feeling the same. "Cynthia is a family heirloom. I don't know anything else."

"I see," the armory master twirled her once more before holding her out to me confidently. I accepted her gratefully and slid her onto my back. "She reminds me of a Weapon another wields here, a smoke pipe that allows the woman to breathe fire." He admitted, looking at me in a way that made me think he was forlorn I couldn't tell him more.

With her light pressure on my back, my curiosity peaked. "I've never seen another Weapon before," I admitted. I had read about them plenty in the library, but texts that explained anything about them were absent. Only great tellings of the powers they granted remained. *If I could learn more about you,* I looked up at her, *maybe I could become stronger.* The thought that had echoed in my mind since she was gifted to me reintroduced itself strongly.

The old man turned to Egan and looked like he was going to make a smart quip before a quiet cough from the door alerted us that someone new had joined us. The two men stepped back, and I sucked in air at the sight of the new lady in waiting.

Her hair was barely wavy, black, and her complexion was a beautiful sun-loved terra-cotta. "Liraz," I whispered to myself. I wanted to fall at this stranger's feet and beg her if she recalled me, the time we had spent in the library together, eating together, growing together. I wanted to hold her hand, tell her everything I'd been through since our unfortunate parting. But it was all I could do, to hold myself still as a leaf that trembled in the breeze. My eyes burned as my nails dug into my palms.

"The King has ordered you to depart shortly." she looked at me evenly without the warmth Liraz had always seemed to emanate, "after sundown. The enemy is more active after sundown, but the cold temperatures tonight will inhibit them." The lady in waiting bowed and left, politely closing the door behind her that the men had left open. I wanted to run after her, embrace her, convince her that her name was Liraz and not whatever she was called here. I wanted to hold her until I knew she could never be hurt again.

Egan and the elder both looked at each other.

"You should make sure Princess Fira knows. I have to return to my workshop," the older man rubbed at his chin, brows drawn tight. I shook my head as the smalltalk cleared my mind. *She's gone, Phaedra,* I firmly told myself. *There's no undoing that.*

Egan nodded. "And you," Egan addressed me finally. He paused, not sure of how to address me.

"Phaedra," I helped him.

"I know your name," he told me, and I felt my feathers begin to fluff with annoyance. "But I need to know if traveling with you — if you're going to help us." He struggled to get a full sentence out, and I noted how he picked at his chest pocket, the uniform too new for it to have loose threads yet. Seeing me look at his picking, he forced himself to stop. His red wings began to flutter behind him.

"I'm going to help you," I reassured him. "I have business with the Queen of Death." The sharp edge in my tone was natural by now.

Egan almost seemed to shrink into himself, his shoulders going lower as he retreated back half a step. He nodded. "Right," he agreed. His wings fluttered faster.

The old man, taking no interest in our conversation, called to Egan from the door. "Come on, son. Nothing's going to happen until you're out of eyeshot of the castle anyway." He reassured him in a way that sounded like he knew when a problem was out of his hands.

The door closed behind them, and I was left with the two guards in the room. I turned around to look out the window, no longer in the mood to try and make them comfortable. Their eyes had rubbed against my black wings every time I had been 'distracted.'

I pulled at my armor, the weight cumbersome. *If I wear this and fly, I'll be slower and become exhausted faster than normal.* I stared out into the desert, the tower I resided in conveniently on the side that didn't show any of the city or its military assets.

But we need to leave fast. I swallowed at the thought of being found in the open by a squad of death angels. There was only going to be three of us. With this armor, maybe the Princess and Egan will be able to keep up with me. I weighed the risk of the heavier armor versus us being able to fly in close quarters and maneuver as a group to avoid detection.

I sighed as a knock rattled my door. *I'll have to see how they fly before I decide.* The idea of running from Queen Mara again had bile rise up in my throat. With the added surprise of that lady in waiting, I felt ready to vomit.

KERES

The parched sand grated on my nerves as I shook it off the map. I laid the map back down on the table as I contemplated. "Here," I pointed to Commander Bruno.

He examined the spot and nodded. "Good eye, Princess. The ground there will be softer and easier to dig."

I nodded, sure of myself. "Take the troops," I ordered him as I straightened from being bent over the war map. "This will be the last trench. If they dig any closer," I glanced down and traced around the Fire Sphere's final bastion, "they'd risk the integrity of the structure."

"When shall we attack, Princess?" The seasoned leader looked down at me, ready to be thrown into the fray at once. It reassured my restless heart.

"Attack at sunset. The low visibility is better than burning," I hid my scowl behind a blank face as I felt the bandages on my back throb. I had flown here from the Death Queendom, ignorantly unaware of what happened to animals during the day in the desert. I had been seared like well-done life angel meat.

"Yes, Your Highness," Bruno held his arms at his sides, tight, as he quickly bowed and departed. I watched him go with dark eyes. After the flaps of the tent had settled, I allowed myself to lean lightly as I relaxed. I placed a firm hand against my back and pressed into my wound.

I hissed. *I wouldn't be here if it wasn't for Phaedra.* The thought of my dead sister made me sneer in anger, and my mind drifted towards my own hidden weakness. *If Mother knew about this wound, she'd be disappointed.* The idea made my veins go cold despite the overhead sun.

May it please Your Majesty.

A deal is struck! I shall send a committee.

The King of Fire

CHAPTER FIVE

PHAEDRA

PRINCESS FIRA COULD KEEP up with my more adept wings for a good while, but Egan always fell behind immediately. And so we walked, to all of our annoyance. I held my tongue, knowing it was unfair of me to admonish him for a difference he couldn't help, but Princess Fira hadn't held back.

Traveling through the desert of the Sphere of Fire was brutal normally, a fact which I had found when I'd decided to volunteer myself into their forces. But traveling this desert on foot was a near crippling experience. Egan, thankfully, was always quick to resupply our water skins with the precious resource from nearby plants he would cleverly cut into. Together, we would shoot arrows at small game as we walked along, one of us usually able to snag a small lizard or creature before we startled it. I wondered privately to myself if he was being helpful because he felt guilty he couldn't keep up, if it was because he was the newest member of the Queen's Guard, or if it was because Princess Fira was here.

Princess Fira, on the other hand, was also a valuable asset. She knew how to hunt the larger game in the desert, the drought-proof horses and the wild hounds that would hunt us back if we weren't careful. She could also find shelter expertly though wouldn't admit she had spent enough time sneaking out of the castle to master this skill. *You can't just 'happen to have heard of' all of these convenient restops,* I tried not to give away that my guess was correct.

Egan's issue was flying. My issue was my milky skin burning black given enough time. But Princess Fira seemed to lack issues physically. It was her personality that was the real issue. She had refused to talk to me the first evening and night before she realized Egan and I couldn't locate a cave or shade to sleep the incoming, unforgiving day away. And when she did finally deign me worthy to talk to, her answers were short and simple.

I tried to not let it bother me and instead used the time to observe what a real princess acted like. She carried the same proudness as my sister, her back straight and her grip strong as she wielded her sword and bow and shield. She also seemed to carry, if not the same then similar, anger as my sister did.

"I should have stayed to fight," she told me one night as I struggled to quiet my hurting feet. "You fought."

I looked up at her from my bedroll, shocked at her sudden, unprompted disclosure. The stars were pinpricks in an inky sky, and the black night dripped onto her tight face. Her eyes almost looked wet.

"We are fighting," I assured her. King Cole had been correct in his words. Had she stayed, she would have died needlessly if not by now then soon.

"This isn't fighting," she argued with me. The brittle stones in her hands snapped apart and disintegrated as she watched for danger.

"Fighting isn't always swords and shields," I scooted closer to the fire and drew my hair back. "Sometimes fighting is knowing things and gathering soldiers." I changed the words Liraz had told me once slightly.

"Fighting isn't always swords and shields," Liraz tucked my hair behind my ear from where I cried in the corner of the training room. "Sometimes fighting is knowing things and knowing when to be kind to others."

I peeked out to look at Liraz and sniffled. "Why is the Queen so mean to me?"

Princess Fira was quiet, and I grew suspicious as the silence dragged on. She would have said something sharp to Egan by now.

"Is it true you're the Banished Princess?" she asked me as her hands shook the dust of the rocks away and pushed it out of her lap.

"Yes," I answered. I rolled onto my back and stared up at the cave ceiling. The sun was going to rise soon. I almost wanted to suggest we should put the fire out now, but it was still so cozy and comforting.

Princess Fira began to snap more stones into pieces, and I resigned myself to checking my hair for her debris when I awoke.

KERES

"Princess!" Bruno's messenger called to me as he sloppily landed in the sand that night had spilled over. His feet dipped beneath the surface as he struggled not to fall. I sighed as he righted himself and came to bow before me. "Bruno's legion has taken the Fire Sphere. You were right!" He smiled while he looked at my feet respectfully.

"Did you think I wouldn't be?" I asked.

The nameless messenger faltered at my reaction. "I — I —" he trailed off.

I sighed again, frustrated. "Take me to their throne room," I sharply ordered and gave him a reprieve as he failed to answer. While he spun on his heel and clamored to obey, I gestured for my four personal guards to follow. "We're going to claim victory," I told them, a smirk over my shoulder at them. They smiled back at me as the nearby guards that protected the intelligence hub whooped. Milo and Kane slapped each other on the back while Koa and Griffith joined in on the yelling.

I shook my head, agitation replaced with exasperation, and easily took to the air from a standstill. My back burned, but I pushed through as the wind of the cold night sky soothed it. *If Mother finds out about my back...* Deep shame dwelt within me. I didn't glance back to know my soldiers had followed me.

As I passed over the trenches we had conquered with I and Commander Bruno's expertise, I glossed over the fallen bodies and looked to what remained of the equipment. Bows, shields, swords, arrows. "A ballista?" I questioned out loud as I passed over what had been their command center, a single, simple tent that barely stood on its own. The ancient creation was made of wood and wouldn't look like it'd live to see the light of day.

I flapped and let myself hover as Koa caught up to me first. I reached out and grabbed the lance he had found and wielded as he flew past and chucked it at the ballista. Milo and Kane stopped short midair as they avoided being struck. I laughed and ascended over the walls of the Fire Sphere.

The throne room was not impressive. The carpets and drapery that held the insignia of the Fire Sphere as well as its history were of poor make and didn't have the same sleek and clean look of the throne room drapery back home. Before the throne, a man knelt, his head tipped so that we could not see his face.

My guards greeted the other death angel soldiers in the throne room excitedly but quietly, happy over my conquest in Queen Mara's honor. I approached the man. I flattened my expression and observed that his hair had been messily cut short and his attire had been roughed up.

I stopped before the defeated king. "Who touched him?" I asked, icy, as I saw a large crown on the throne. Made of gold, the jewels that had been burrowed into it weighed it down farther.

"I will find out, Your Highness," Bruno stepped into the throne room through the main doors. I turned to look at him.

"See to it," I ordered. *I had wanted to uncrown him myself.* My eye twitched as I held in my poison. I stepped around the King and approached the throne slowly. *With this, I have fulfilled her orders.* I pictured Queen Mara standing before me, her face obscured as she flattered me and recognized my skill.

I stepped up to the throne and turned to examine the death angels and singular fire fairy that gathered before me. The previous King turned to look at me over his shoulder but paused and turned back. His resistance made my stomach tighten as my soldiers began to chant, "Princess Keres! Princess Keres!"

It's only through her high expectations that I made it this far. I looked at the small, singular glass window above the main doors. *So small,* I thought, curious.

"Your Highness," Bruno joined me on the left as the soldiers finished. "What shall we do with the King?" A heavy question.

I looked down upon the hunched back of the broken man. "Keep him alive. But lock him in the darkest dungeon for resisting," *we need to keep him alive to extort his people. We can't expect them to share the technology Queen Mara desires willingly. We need to prepare for the incoming life angel attack from the Domain of Life.*

PHAEDRA

Fira, as she requested I call her now as we were both royals, was softer after we had talked. She was also kinder to Egan which led him to try and please her more by beginning to scout ahead for large game and possible threats. But the moment I noticed a touch of green on the horizon, I knew that the larger animals likely weren't anywhere near here. We had seen our last game some days ago.

The border between the Sphere of Fire and the rest of the Ouranios was quite stark. There were a few small, dead grasses before a tidal wave of lush, green wildgrass took over. We paused on the edge, and I realized that I wasn't beginning to overheat and hurt despite the rising sun.

I cupped a hand to glance up into the sky before I looked around us. "We made it," I announced.

Fira paused with me, and Egan began to move ahead faster, likely to scout again.

"Watch out for the wild chickens, Egan. They lay in the grass," I tried to warn him, but he simply flapped his wings a few times and rose up before flying away to avoid walking through the grass that was taller than him. Trees also sprinkled the area but didn't seem to hamper the growth of the other wild things.

"Have you been here before?" Fira asked and plopped down in the not-quite-as-tall grass now that she didn't have to keep up appearances. Only the top of her head was visible.

I shook my head and sat down across from her. "I've just read a lot," I admitted. I watched her pull at the long grass experimentally. "Have you?"

"No, just heard about it. My mother told me about the world before she passed," Fira began to weave the blades together gently.

"The Queen is dead?" I asked quickly, shocked.

"So you haven't read everything," Fira pointed out somewhat playfully and avoided answering as she tried to hide a wince.

I laughed a little. "I might have missed one or two books."

"Your Highness!" Egan's panicked voice has us shooting up and out of the grass. We looked in the direction he had gone, ready to fly to him. He appeared before us suddenly, pushing the grass aside so we could see him. "Over here!" He called backwards to someone who we could now hear fighting the grass to get to us.

Another fire fairy emerged, looking extremely dirtied and unkempt. He had scratches all over him that he itched at. "Your Highness!" He almost doubled over in his attempt to greet Fira.

"You're a messenger?" Fira asked, raising her arms. One crossed over her chest and the other balled over her mouth, hiding her anxious, pulled back lips. I watched the color drain out of her face as her mind worked.

The only reason they'd send someone after us —

"Your Highness," the defeated, dirtied, desolate messenger raised up to look her in the eye, "the Castle of Fire has fallen. King Cole has been taken." Egan began to shake noticeably, turning pale. He began to pull at his short locks painfully as if to ground himself.

I averted my eyes. Rage washed over me as I pictured Queen Mara standing atop the Castle of Fire triumphantly.

Fira quietly drew in a large breath next to me, and I jumped when she screamed with all her might. Her roar reached the treetops and scattered the previously hidden birds. Her scream turned into a wail as I heard a thunk. I looked and saw she had fallen onto her knees, her fist pulled back as she punched the ground.

"That sick queen!" Fira yelled into the dirt. "She took my home!" *Punch.* "She took my castle!" *Punch.* "She took my — my —" she teetered off, gasping for air as her wings made a windstorm around her. Her wings slowed as she gasped, losing momentum.

Egan was at her side the second he could be. He reassured her, "You can take our home back," he told her, gripping her shoulders to my surprise. "It's your birthright. You are the princess." She looked up at him, her expression hidden from my view.

I listened to Fira take a long, slow breath. "What of my people?" Her tone was a bit shaky now. The screaming might have hurt her voice.

"Many fled, Your Highness, but many were also captured," the messenger's voice broke. "I fled," he admitted quietly, and my expression crumpled under the weight of his sadness as well as my own. I turned around but stayed to listen.

"It's okay," the grass rustled as Fira stood and approached him. "It's okay." Someone sniffled before small, muffled noises of the messenger's crying began. I stared up into the sky and pictured Princess Keres on Fira's throne. My stomach tumbled in every direction, and I had to close off my throat.

We made camp where we had learned the news, none of us wanting to move a pace. The news had burrowed deep into us, a parasite that would grow to consume us as the long grass ate up the earth beneath our feet.

The three of us were well away from camp to allow the broken messenger to rest next to the fire and sleep undisturbed. Fira had crossed her arms. Egan tapped his foot and pulled at his locks again. I pulled his hand away from his head. I had started to get a headache just by watching him give himself one.

"What do we do?" Egan asked, mostly looking to Fira for direction, his remaining great leader.

May it please Your Majesty.

Hello. I greet you by letter so that you may know me before we meet. I am the second son of the King of Fire, Cyrus. It is my honor to make the introduction. While I am the second son, I still hold many lofty titles in court such as Judge-Master, Keeper of the Flame, and Appraiser. I am proficient in swordfighting, politics, and trade. I enjoy a large, hot meal as well as star watching. Please ask to your heart's content.

Sincerely,

The Prince of Fire,

Cyrus

Chapter Six

"You're in the same situation I was," I told Fira, my voice a touch raw with honesty.

Fira was quiet and gave a long look to the sleeping messenger. "What did you do?" She asked me quietly and refused to meet my eye.

I hadn't expected her to ask me for help. "I was found and taken in by my mentor, Max," I admitted. "I laid low."

Egan started to pick at his breast pocket as Fira looked up at the stars. The song of crickets slowly crept in between us, and I felt, despite standing here in front of me, that Fira was worlds away. She had left to help her home. I had fled mine selfishly.

"She resides in the Key Stone Mountains," I whispered, the blanket of humidity an odd sensation against my skin after so long.

"They'll be looking for me," Fira said after some time. "If I go to my people, it will put them in more danger," she explained to Egan. "If the three of us lay low, then the enemy will be easier to overthrow. They'll get complacent." She looked at both of us, and I assumed the third person she mentioned was the messenger. Fira turned to me exclusively. "Would your mentor help us?" she asked me.

I paused to think. Max and I had spent a long time living together and training, but I had never even had the thought, let alone the option, of asking to bring someone else home. "She will" I answered confidently. *She took me in. She's compassionate. She'd never killed me during the time she trained me despite having many chances to.* I recalled training with Queen Mara, my small body on the ground from one of her heavy blows, as her scythe hovered above my neck while she contemplated.

Fira nodded and leaned back on her heels. "We'll break camp at first light. He might have been followed," she shrugged to the messenger. "I'll send him to the rest of my people with instructions to tell them that I'm staying away for their safety. They might be only hunting me," her tone was gruff, heavy. Her boxed away emotions were starting to leak out slowly.

I agreed with her and turned to leave to give them space. *I've been around them constantly since we left the Fire Castle. They don't need me right now.* A few paces away, I stopped when I heard a horrible gnashing sound behind me. I half looked back and saw as Fira walked in the other direction. Her wings flapped in anger as she worked her teeth together. "Had that wretched queen been killed long ago, none of this would have happened," Fira spoke to herself and flew away.

I watched her leave and squeezed my arms around my middle. *She's not wrong.* I made myself comfortable by the fire as Egan shuffled down into his bedroll. My hands played over Cynthia as my overactive imagination made a puppet show of whatever Queen Mara had decided to do with her new subjects.

Bile rose in my throat as I pictured King Cole, cooked like a chicken, on her table the same as the life angel she had forced me to eat the night I had left. Keres had been beaming at the delicacy, but I hadn't been able to stomach any of it. The messenger shifted next to me, and

I looked down at him. He looked so young while he slept. The dirt of the day gave him an innocent look.

Locating the entrance to Max's home was a struggle. I hadn't seen it except when I left for the Fire Sphere, hopeful to return but quick to leave. I was still worried that I wouldn't wish to continue my journey if I spent enough time in her comforts.

But the steep, treacherous mountainside, eventually, yielded a wooden door disguised by simple vines and wild bushes and berries. I pushed my wing into the barrier that blocked the outside forces from her abode, and the shield gave way. I slowly entered.

"Max?" I called out in question. I leaned forward to look around before I stepped in fully. The Key Stone Mountains were always cold if not downright freezing, and the warmness inside made me want to give my feathers a good shuffle to disperse the chill.

"Phaedra?" Max appeared from the hallway as she called, shock on her face.

"Max," I took another step in when her eyes smiled at me.

My mentor looked up and down at me despite the short amount of time not having affected either of us. "I didn't think you'd come back," she admitted and clasped her hands together.

"Something happened," I agreed with her. "And we're looking for refuge. I thought you might take us in." My voice grew quiet as I asked for permission, and I felt like a child.

"Your friends outside." Max seemed to twinkle as a star might as her lips pressed together in humor. *How did Max know they were there?*

"Y-yes," I agreed. I moved to look back to see if they were hovering in the doorway obviously.

"You can come in," Max's strong voice raised easily as she put her hand onto my clasped fingers. "You're always welcome here," she assured me, and I relaxed at her words. My feathers fell, relaxed. "Now come here. I want you to taste this new recipe," she directed me as I heard Fira say something demeaning to the vines as they caught in her hair.

As Max led me to the kitchen, she glanced behind me at my friends. *Have we come that far?* I followed Max's quietly intense and intrigued look at Fira. *Can we be counted together?* I looked back to Max as she pulled me alone to the kitchen.

I woke that night parched, and like countless times before, blindly strolled from my room to the kitchen for water. I paused on the threshold of the kitchen and listened to make sure what I was hearing was correct.

The sound of water running was bouncing off the fine, decorative stone in the floors and the plain walls. The water would begin and then suddenly stop as if being played with. I scrubbed a hand over my face and stepped out. My bare feet sounded heavy on the cold floor.

Fira jumped and twirled around, a guilty look plastered on her face before she saw it was me. The look faded and her eyes narrowed. "What is this?" She demanded, and I saw she had indeed been releasing the water and then closing the pipe.

"That is a sink and water faucet," I told her, my exhaustion making me unimpressed.

"Where does the water come from?" She asked me, turning it on and off again as if to prove a point. I walked up to her, took a mug out of one of Max's closed shelves, and held it under the faucet.

I gripped Fira's hand as she held the faucet and filled my cup before shutting it off with her help. "The water comes from the mountain," I enjoyed the refreshing feeling down my throat as I pointed up with my free hand. "Through pipes." I cleared my throat before I offered her the empty mug.

"And this one?" She touched the other handle curiously.

"Hot water," I told her. I opened the faucet, letting the water run out, and twirled the bar that gave us hot water. I held my hand under it, enjoying the warmth against the frosty bite that seeped in easily here.

Fira copied me cautiously. "I've never seen magic like this," she admitted.

"Max is gifted," I answered and closed the tap, sleep weighing on me welcomingly.

The next day, light streamed in through the windows and brilliantly lit up the simple and elegant living space. Small animals, unable to see in through the glass that had been enchanted to look like rockface, scuttled about. I sat off to the side while Fira sat across from Max. Egan sat close to his leader's side as Max nodded through our story.

Max leaned back into the couch as Fira took over to explain what happened after they discovered me. I shivered as Fira admitted the things that were proposed to be done to me, a supposed infiltrator and informant. Egan at least had the conscience to look at me with a sorry expression while Fira barreled on through the story without pause or admission of fault. Fira, having stood as her own words invigorated her, heavily sat down on the couch between Egan and I as she finally folded her hands in her lap and went silent.

"And so Queen Mara has taken a kingdom that does not rightfully belong to her," the fear that I had told Max of, that this might happen should the siege continue after she had told me it began, had come to fruition.

Max's crystalline eyes flicked to me as she thought.

"Even if you had told me earlier of the war and I had gone, I wasn't strong enough," I admitted and recalled how I had enjoyed my newfound strength after joining the Fire Sphere's ranks.

Max let out a small sigh. "The Queen of Death is a proponent of the old ways," Max looked up at the ceiling as she crossed her arms.

She looked as though she was reaching through old, deep memories to find one in particular. "That she would take another's Queendom goes against those ways," she murmured almost to herself.

"My people are suffering," Fira interjected. "And I find no cause except the Queen of Death's greed." She concluded, features firm and expression quietly dangerous. Her eyes jumped to me for a moment, something heinous swirling inside, before they leapt back to Max.

"I don't know why the Queen would do this," Max looked at the three of us once more as she came back mentally. "But I do know of something that will stop her." Max stared into Fira intensely. "What are you willing to do to take back what is yours? To protect your sphere?" Max leaned forward, arms on her knees, as she probed into Fira.

"Anything," Fira responded automatically, trying to sit up straighter and higher, perhaps unconscious of the effort.

"Anything," Max echoed, slowly standing as she rubbed at her chin. I watched as she went to one of the few book cases on the wall, the ones she had allowed me to look through in a limited capacity. "Anything," Max took a tome off the shelf, its ancient pages loud and dry as she flipped through it delicately.

"You know a way?" Fira asked, body tense as if she was ready to attack Max to secure the answer.

Max took a moment to look a page up and down with particular interest before she flipped to the next one. She brought the book to the glass table and set it down gently so that we could read it properly.

"Yes," Max answered Fira. "Here." Her long, slender pointed finger tapped against an aged map, the ink on the page heavy and oversat-urated. "This is the Dragon's Den." All of us perched on our seats as she explained. "As you may know," Max looked up at Fira through her eyelashes as she bent over to point better, "Your castle is built out of different rocks than those surrounding it."

Fira's eyes narrowed and she leaned back a bit. "What of it?" She asked. I pulled my memories forward and recalled that it had been a different color. It wasn't a noticeable shade difference until it had been pointed out.

"That is because, according to this book, in ages past during the Campaign of the Dragons, the dragons had the ability to ignite the rocks of your spheredom with their fire breath," Max leaned back. I licked my lips, dry. It was as if this book had stolen all the water from the room.

"Then all we need is a dragon," Egan spoke hopefully, his face lighting up with hope.

Max hummed, "Not so easy." We all watched his face fall. "They were hunted down and slaughtered, and that's how it ended, the war." She crossed her arms again and leaned forward from where she sat on the edge of the couch, her legs out straight. "But there is one last remaining dragon egg." Her eyes were transfixed on the page. "If you can get ahold of it, free it from the monster guarding it by sneaking it away, then it'll hatch."

"How would setting the Castle of Fire on fire help us?" Egan wondered out loud.

"Threaten them," I answered quickly. "Say if Fira can't have it back, no one can have it." I showed our hand.

Fira looked at me, unsure. "And if they don't buy it?" She looked back to the book.

"You'll be able to take anything in stride," Max tried to assure her. "Besides, the castle itself won't ignite. Everything around it will." Max clarified as she closed the book. "The last dragon egg is protected by a malicious, hate-filled creature," Max read from the text, her eyes skimming the page. "This creature is powerful, strong, and was once revered," she warned us. "You may not survive."

A dragon, walking among us? I couldn't picture it. I knew the old texts well, many of them filled with stories of the grand, grudge-filled beasts, but I couldn't imagine one alongside an angel. *And a malicious beast to defeat would have terrified the old me,* I realized with a start. *But now, I feel confident.*

"I'll do it," Fira's firm response made me blink. Her resolve grew, smoky, inside her until it spilled out of her eyes. "I'll do whatever I can," she promised. Egan nodded with her before he looked at me. Fira did not take her eyes off Max.

"I'll go too," I told Max as she turned to me. "I wasn't able to do what I set out to do," I admitted. "I'm not going to put your training to waste," I promised her, and Max smiled softly.

I'm not going to let our time go to waste, Liraz.

Egan gasped as Max pushed aside the gray drapes and opened the clear, glass door. "This was here the whole time?!" He nearly shrieked into my ear, and I flinched back as he marched out after Max.

Fira's eyes were wide and feet hesitant as she followed. I stepped out last and closed the door behind me as I enjoyed the lush grass against my feet. The sweet air enveloped the four of us as Max made headway down the small incline. The grass rustled loudly as the critters and creatures that resided nearby fled.

"We're inside the mountain," Fira stated as I turned back round to see her staring up at the inside of the Key Stone Max resided in.

I smiled at her. "I knew we'd be safe here," I resisted the urge to put a hand on her shoulder reassuringly, not sure if she would bite the appendage off, and followed after Max and Egan instead. I let out a laugh as Egan lost his footing, and he slid the rest of the way down the hill, sprawled out and sliding past Max spectacularly.

"Careful of the lake," Max chided after him as the deer startled from his dramatic entry. Their blue coats glinted brightly from the sun as they fled, and Fira's face twisted unpleasantly.

"He should have better decorum with our host," she admonished him as he sat up and shook himself free of whatever plants he had captured on the way down.

"Max doesn't mind," I assured her. I could still feel the cool mud up to my knees if I focused hard enough from the time I had been upset from training with Max. She had caught the downswing of Cynthia and had pushed me into a pit. It had startled me out of my anger, the frustration I felt about myself when I couldn't rise to meet a challenge immediately.

The memory of Max's chime-like laugh faded as we joined her and Egan by the lake. Max gazed over to where it met the far side of the mountain sprouted from the water before she turned back to us. "This place is my home," she explained. "I brought you out here to show goodwill," Max addressed Fira directly. I hovered, unsure of not being the center of Max's attention.

Fira dipped her head. "Thank you," she looked back at Max. "Is this where you trained?" Fira asked me. I nodded.

"You may train here, if you like. If you do, I would enjoy challenging you," Max proposed to Fira, a soft smile on her lips. "Phaedra was quite enjoyable." I blushed at her words and felt childish. I wanted to defend myself but couldn't think of anything before Max started to walk back to the house. The only thing giving its existence away inside the rockface was the clear sliding door. "If you should both challenge me, that would be interesting," she threw over her shoulder before leaving.

The sunlight filtered in through the ice on top of the Key Stone Mountains. Or at least that's what Max had told me when I had questioned how it was so bright. That same light now watched as sweat swept over my eyebrows copiously as I rested on my knees, Cynthia before me defensively.

Fira twirled the sword Max had given her, enjoying its light weight,as she waited for me to recover. I slowly stood and swiped at my forehead with annoyance.

"Again," Max ordered before us, her hands and body bare of armor and weapons. Fira and I both dashed at her, and I used the longer length and curve of Cynthia to make a swipe at the back of Max's ankles while Fira went for her throat. Max remained calm as she jumped up and back at the last moment, avoiding both of us. I pushed my hand against the bottom of Cynthia's pole to stop her from slicing into Fira as Fira took a few more steps to slice at Max's gut.

I stepped to the side and sliced up towards Max as Fira backed off for a moment to raise her arm for another strike. Max leaned back slightly and expertly dodged Cynthia. Fira struck out at Max from the side, and Max ducked down easily, looking unphased.

Twirling Cynthia, I sliced down at Max as Fira captured her momentum from her side swing and made to swing her new blade again the way it had come. Max's hand delicately caught Cynthia and pinched around her sharp blade. Max's free hand then stayed Fira's blade. *Her bare hands!* Max looked at us evenly, and I felt satisfaction at hearing Fira pant as hard as me from exertion.

"You're both doing quite well," she commended us, not letting go of the blades. "I think with a little experience, you both could cause a good amount of trouble together," she promised us.

Together? I eyed Fira's red, angry face. Her lips were pulled back threateningly, her wings sharp and beating to appear bigger.

Max stepped away and dropped her grip from the blades. She dusted off her spotless clothes, and my jealousy for Egan as he lounged carefree in the cool water of the lake returned. "That's enough," she told us. "I think you're ready to search out the last dragon egg."

May it please Your Majesty.
Thank you for your
letter. I fear mine shall
not reach you before
your watership departs.
I also enjoy star
watching. Do you enjoy
painting?
Sincerely,

The Princess of Death,

Mara

CHAPTER SEVEN

KERES

I HAD BEEN ORDERED to return home after news of my victory reached Mother. As we walked through the village there had been quite a fanfare. The village had grown quite significantly in my short absence. The merchants that supplied our weapons intermingled in the crowds with the tradeworkers who had built them as well as the families of our soldiers. They threw star flowers at our feet as they wished us fast recoveries and thanked us for our service to the Queen. New shops and other buildings had been created in our absence, our hard earned victory reignited the local commerce that had been falling into stagnation in recent years.

I led the top-ranked soldiers into the main hall of the castle, Bruno and the other flock commanders just behind me as I walked with my head held high. My feet wanted to run to Queen Mara as I saw her standing at the throne that overlooked the hall. Before her, large tables had been moved in and had been set. *A banquet!* The seared meats smelled heavenly.

I slowed to a stop before Queen Mara as she watched me. The Queen gazed at me, alert, but it felt as though if I were to reach out she would disappear into whatever great beyond she saw. *Untouchable, as a Queen should be.* I dropped to my knee before her, my wings spread out proudly. I spoke loudly and clear, "Your Majesty. I bring good news. We have secured the Fire Sphere for our own."

The soldiers cheered as they filtered to the tables and found places to rest. I kept my head low as a maid approached the Queen and then quickly returned to stand to the side of the room.

"Stand," Queen Mara ordered me, and I felt an excited flush up my neck as I rose. *Acknowledge me!* I craved her ratification of my work. "To the future Queen of Death!" She raised the goblet now in her hand as she looked over my head at her warriors. They cheered as my eyes began to well up.

PHAEDRA

Traveling all the way around the Key Stone Mountains felt pointless and boring. Max had instructed us to walk around them, not fly, because the air around them got so bitterly cold it could freeze your feathers mid-flight. The chill that hung around them even at midday made me wonder if her story was half true. But they were to our backs, and we currently squinted at a small map I had of Ouranios.

"Here," Fira pointed to a small path that went between two woods. Some things were shown in grander detail, such as the Castle of Death and the plains. Other things, like this route, were almost impossible to make out.

"Princess, I'm not sure this route is..." Egan trailed off, not wanting to admit he doubted her.

"It's where we're going," Fira looked at him firmly, and I quickly rolled the map up to avoid a fight. I also could barely see the route.

"It doesn't seem like a popular route. We can avoid others this way," I explained to Egan as Fira started to walk along through the healthy pine trees that grew around the Key Stones.

Egan hummed. "That's smart," he spoke up to make sure Fira heard him, but she gave no indication. He turned back to me and looked a little downtrodden. "There was a castle in those marked woods next to the trail." He pointed out and my lips thinned.

"I don't know what it's called," I informed him, not finding anything when I sifted through my memories of the books I had read.

Egan nodded, and I vowed to keep an eye out. This was the farthest west I'd been of the Queendom of Death. I had little idea what lurked in the world.

KERES

The fanfare outlasted me and Queen Mara. I retired to my rooms once I had had my fill with the soldiers, our jokes steering more crude as the drink kept flowing. Accompanied by Zelda, my youngest maid, I stumbled as I reached the royal rooms.

"Drinking in excess," Mother surprised me as she stood outside my door.

I looked up, my mind slow and my mouth open. "I was celebrating," I whispered, voice hoarse from the fun and games.

Queen Mara strode towards me and grabbed me by the collar of my shirt. "Not. Again." She looked at me with fury, and I felt myself shrivel as my wings pulled tight to my back to protect themselves.

I dumbly shook my head, my simple mind unable to keep up. She released me, and I put a hand on the wall to steady myself.

"Tomorrow," she whispered to me quietly, her words and expression a steel blade that sliced into me, "you will begin research on the Realm of Earth." This was an order, not a request.

My fear swelled. *It's not fair. I succeeded!* Queen Mara shook her head and turned to leave us. "I've only just arrived home," I whispered to her back.

Queen Mara stopped mid-stride and turned back to look at me. She looked upon me like a grotesque insect as she stopped before me once more.

Slap!

"Queens do not rest," she instructed me and left.

PHAEDRA

"I think the castle is abandoned," I stood in between Fira and Egan as we lined up to stare at the deceased, naked, crippled, and blackened trees that stood before us. There was a firm line where the healthy, lush growth behind us cutoff. Even the insects and birds kept a healthy distance from the divide.

"Let me see the map," Fira held out her hand, and I quickly produced the parchment.

"The path should be close," my hand latched onto Egan's collar before he could go off scouting. He stopped short and made a choked noise, one foot still extended. "I don't trust these trees. Don't run off," I ordered him and let go so he could rub at his neck.

"It's this way," Fira looked up and west, and I followed her gaze. It was still early, and a heavy mist coiled around the world indiscriminately. I couldn't decipher what she could possibly see beyond.

I held in my sigh and hoped silently we weren't about to get lost. Maneuvering around the Key Stones had been easy. But now we had lost the advantage of being able to fly up and see them. If we did, we might alert whoever or whatever was nearby.

As Egan and I ventured in after Fira dry dirt crackled under our feet. I looked down and felt a twisting sensation as I realized there was no grass growing. I looked back at the vibrant, lush pines and low grass behind us and hoped that Fira was indeed correct.

"Fira, please wait for us. Egan can't find his footing," I helped him up once again as her wings flicked in annoyance just at the edge of my vision. The fog hadn't let up at all and instead had begun to lap at my skin like some sort of sick creature.

Fira looked back at us and frowned. "I can hardly see you back here, Phaedra," to rejoin us, she flapped and flew above the gnarled tree roots that attempted to ensnare her the same they had Egan.

"The fog should have lifted by now," I looked up. "It should be close to midday." My voice was unsure as I looked around.

"Princess Fira," Egan spoke hesitantly. "I think we're lost." He whispered in fear of retribution.

Fira's eyes narrowed as she looked around. "I thought the path was around here," she admitted, and her shoulders sagged slightly.

"One of us should fly up and look around," I proposed. "I doubt anyone else can see in this fog. And if they do see me, then they won't be able to get to us in this." I volunteered myself. My wings would be able to take the slaps of the hidden, dead, sharp branches above us much better than theirs.

Fira nodded and put a hand on Egan's shoulder to steady him again as he began to waiver. "We'll stay here," she agreed.

I nodded and backed up a few steps, careful to watch my feet. I gave them a long look, hoping to memorize where we were in case I couldn't find them on my way down, but the fog laid upon the land and in the air heavily. My wings flapped, and I stirred up the wet air as I bent my knees to ready for takeoff.

I jumped up, and my wings caught the air. I flapped hard and slowly raised above the trees. I squinted. My canary eyes blinked against the wet that tried to blanket me. My muscles, sore from the awkward takeoff and ascent, protested in a voice that sounded eerily like Queen Mara's. I ignored it and put a hand over my forehead as if to block out the sun. A subtle outline could be seen against the bottomless fog.

"A castle!" I shouted down and pointed. I spared a glance down only to see that I couldn't decipher my friends from the gray void. Frowning, I scrunched up my face to make out the bare outline. Something lodged in my throat, and I coughed. I reached one hand back to grab at Cynthia to make sure she did not fall.

I slowly relaxed my muscles and drifted downwards, careful not to hit the ground that I couldn't yet see. Cynthia stirred in my hand. Her wood shifted silently against my skin.

An odd sensation bubbled up in me, pulling me towards the castle. I wanted to reach out and grab the building to drag it closer, by force if necessary. Fira and Egan appeared before me as my feet made contact with the ground.

"That was you, right?" Egan mumbled quietly, his shoulders hiked up in a show of what was supposed to be strength but came across as anxiety.

My eyes dulled over as I slowly decided how to answer. "Hope so," I blinked slowly at him for the effect. Egan swallowed.

"Of course it's her," Fira huffed. "Which way?" She bent her head down to look at her feet as she rubbed mud off her heels and onto a tree root. She looked up at me from under her lashes, quietly embarrassed.

I brought Cynthia around to my front and nodded behind them. "That way," I indicated. "I'll go first. Who knows what's in here." I lowered my voice as Cynthia pulsed against me. They parted for me and followed behind, our feet quiet against the alternating mud and cracked, dead earth. Hairs raised along my arms the deeper we went. My feathers slowly stood straight up, and my breath was silent as I listened to the world around me.

There were no creatures in these woods. Despite Egan's trampling attempt at secrecy and quiet, nothing startled out of the nearby feeble and bare bushes. No birds sang overhead. No rabbits sprang out from underfoot.

Cynthia pulsated again, and I felt a hot sensation wash over me. It began in my gut, a warm, mildly pleasant fire that turned into an overarching stream of magma the farther it crawled up. I stopped, a hand on my abdomen as I leaned over.

"Are you okay?" Fira's hand on my shoulder made me jump up in surprise. I hadn't heard her come closer.

"I'm all right," I assured her quickly and stood straight despite the sensation. She blinked in surprise, and I regretted my sharp answer. "I'm sorry." I looked away, not sure where the sudden anger was coming from.

"It's fine," she agreed tersely, and I forced myself to move forward. Our footsteps echoed louder and louder the deeper we went. My shoulder itched as if being watched, and I glanced to the side. The swirling vapors greeted me, playing ignorant of what hid inside them.

Inside... Cynthia pulsed again, and I felt as though now my feet were being yanked towards the castle. Each step threatened to trip me as they tried to run out from under me.

My eyes almost seemed to play tricks on me. The fog would come so close I would have to focus on not flinching. Other times, it receded so far I thought we had accidentally found the edge of this cursed place. I took a deep breath to gather myself.

I started talking and hoped the sound of my voice would ease both myself and the two behind me. "We used to play in this forest," I babbled. "It wasn't misty back then." I assured her. Cynthia pulsed in my hand in agreement. I spoke of how the forest had once been green and good, the land prosperous with trade and alliances. Humans weren't worthless, after all.

"Phaedra, stop," Fira's loud, booming voice startled me. "What are you talking about?"

Dear Husband,
My job as Mara's lady in waiting has tripled since her betrothed arrived. The boy has brought mud into her chambers (his own fiancee's!) every fortnight. He is clumsy, and he distracts her from her duties. I fear for the future of our queendom. I found them coming down from the roof last night — can you believe it?! The Princess is as bouncy and happy as she has ever been, despite these troubles.
Sincerely,

Zeltik

CHAPTER EIGHT

I GASPED AND BLINKED. Before me, a tall, stone arch rose. The stones were old and broken. Some had fallen away in time, and it looked ready to come crashing down. But farther beyond the arch, I could see a dry fountain and a courtyard. Mermaids circled the base of the fountain, their cups outstretched in eternal thirst.

"I'm fine," I gestured with Cynthia. "I'm just ready to rest here." I suggested.

"Phaedra," Fira's hand caught on my shoulder, and I shrugged it off unwelcomingly.

I fell silent at her behest and instead wandered the grounds as I had in my youth. The courtyard had fallen into disrepair, as was expected. No more did the thoughtfully placed flowers bloom. The ornate stone and glass paths were either buried under the mud or their rocks had been split over time.

The dark stones of the castle were cold under my hand where they had once been warm. I headed toward the greenhouse as the two fire fairies talked in hushed tones behind me. My fingers trailed along the castle wall, and I hesitated at the mural that still stood.

The art was still proud, though the colors muted. The tall woman with ocean blue hair and eyes of whirlpool still stood face to face with the smaller princess. The smaller princess's sunflower eyes gazed back at her lovingly. Behind the taller woman, the outline of a castle that was broken, ravaged. Behind the princess, a sword bathed in red paint etched into the bricks.

My mouth twisted at the reminder, and instead of going to the greenhouse, I ducked into the side door of the castle. The rotten wood fell off the hinges behind me.

"Hey!" The taller, more womanly fire fairy yelled after me. I heard them dash after me, a small commotion as they knocked into the tables and chests and other forgotten furniture. "Stop!"

I emerged into the throne room. The ceiling was low, but the stones here still held some warmth, some magic, long forgotten. I slowed down, my footfalls heavy in the large, empty space as I approached the throne. As I made to sit upon it, as I had so long ago, my two followers practically threw themselves through the entrance I had come from.

"Phaedra!" They both cried out in shock as they took the sight of me upon my throne. Their eyes were wide. Their wings beat frivolously from fear. They weren't reaching for their weapons.

I felt sympathy for them, their fear, their anger. The monstrosity that slept inside her, its power red as magma, ready to burst forth and burn the world around her. My body turned to look out the window that sat at eye level across the throne room.

In the distance, a large castle rose, its glass walls carved from the very mist that now protected this place. I spoke, my voice quiet. The echo of the room amplified it, brought it to their ears more easily. "I became a weapon, a warrior, to finish what I started. I became a Weapon to allow others to see and destroy things hidden to them as I did."

I turned back and stared at the Princess of Fire and took in her terrified expression. She was pale, her body gripped by fear as she shook lightly. I continued, "You have something hidden inside you. Would you like it destroyed? I can't see where it ends and you begin. It might kill you." I warned her and pointed into her chest.

The Princess of Fire was, for once, branded to the floor. Her servant and protector, however, was quick to draw the fine steel blade at his hip. He brandished it towards me as if to block my words. As the knight carefully stepped in between the princess and myself, my strenuous posture released.

I slowly blinked and looked around. I felt odd, dreary, and resisted the urge to bat at my eyes as I shook my head. "What — what happened?" My voice ached as if I had been screaming.

"Phaedra?" Fira's voice wavered.

"Are you okay?" I asked and found my feet and stood. I noticed Egan's blade as he slowly sheathed it. "What's happening?" The chamber around us was old. Cobwebs creeped into the center of the room as the spiders spun away in the corners. The stones beneath my feet were uneven, mossy. Faded relics from a different age rested around us.

"What's happening?" Fira echoed, her wings slowing in their beating as she relaxed. I stopped before her, ready to accept what her taut tone promised. I tucked my wings in tight as Fira spoke, her words hushed as she continued to both glance around us and look me up and down.

"I brought us here?" Confusion swam in me as I tried to recall how I got here. "The trees... I remember us entering the forest," I admitted. The forest's loneliness, held at bay by these stones, sent a shiver up my spine.

Fira gestured for Egan to talk as she frowned at me, and I shrank as I wondered if her reaction was out of worry, distrust, or anger. I swallowed nervously as Egan finished.

I cautiously looked at Fira before I spoke. "I don't remember that." My hands raised as I pleaded. "Please, I — I don't know what's going on." I grabbed at my cloak as my body shook. An imaginary hand teased the hairs on the back of my neck straight up. A ghostly breeze whispered through my clothes from the far open window.

"We need to leave. Now," Fira commanded, arms crossed as she made toward one of the large hallways that branched off of the room. I opened my mouth as she walked past me. I wanted to convince her I was truly innocent and had no evil intent, but her hand landed on my shoulder. Fira grounded me solidly, her hand a warm hearth in winter. "Come on."

I shivered when she dropped her hand and hesitated before I followed after Egan as he passed me. I glanced towards the open window as I passed by. My eyes squinted to try and see through the mist I knew would be there. But to my surprise, a high castle, clear yet colorful as if it was made of precious glass, stood very close by.

I heard a small commotion from the way my two companions had gone and quickly ran toward them, the magical sight banished from my mind. Cynthia pulsed once on my back as I rounded the corner. I ran after them and used my wings to propel myself down the spiral staircase and out an odd side door.

A large, rusted castle gate faded into the distance between the mist and the trees before we stopped for a breath.

I wrapped my cloak around myself tighter against the water droplets, "Did you see that second castle?" I asked Fira and Egan.

"That was the only castle around for miles, Phaedra," Fira frowned as she looked skyward. To try and see beyond the dead limbs of the trees ahead only led one to mist.

Egan and I looked up, searching, and I tried to orient myself and turn where I knew it should be. My breath was pushed out of my body as I felt a brief yet heavy weight on my back. Cynthia quietly pulsated, a low noise in my ears.

"We need to go," I urged my companions, unsure if they could hear the dangerous beat.

KERES

"The most accurate information would be in the Royal Library," Bex, my oldest maid, informed me as she brushed my hair. I had been trying to grow it out like Mother. Eigra readied my outfit for the day behind us, and Zelda set the table for breakfast.

The library, I frowned openly. "Anywhere else?" I asked, hopeful, as Bex expertly worked through a large knot.

"I'm afraid not, Your Highness. Unless you know an earth fairy far from home," Bex informed me.

I sighed.

"Your Highness?" Zelda asked, and I looked at her in the mirror. I ignored Bex as she stiffened under my gaze.

"Yes?" I asked impatiently.

"Why do you avoid the library?" Zelda asked unintelligently.

I rolled my eyes to Bex, who had put on her mask, before I looked back to Zelda. "Don't ask such questions," I nipped the behavior in the bud. The memory of Phaedra's burning book made my back twinge. The beating Mother had given me for setting the fire and destroying that knowledge continued to be sore through the years.

"Yes, Your Highness," she bowed, apologetic, and silently continued to watch Bex work.

PHAEDRA

The plains were deceitful and dangerous, their beauty great. The golden tallgrass swept up into a never ending sky, a promise that an angel could fly as high as they like as long as they don't mind being seen by everything and everyone for days around. And so we found ourselves rooted to the earth on our secret journey. Egan and I stood before a pair of humans, goods sprawled out before us.

Egan looked half glanced at me before I gave a subtle nod, and he traded some of the feathers I had shed for a bag of dried fruit.

"Sew them inside of a coat," I told the woman, my arms crossed as I leaned back into my heel. I felt that if we dawdled here any longer, the tallgrass itself might wrap around me and never let go.

The woman accepted the large feather gratefully and smiled at me. "Thank you. I've never been able to see one up close before," her shoulders were hunched as she ran a hand through the down and vane, her eyes wide. My eyes softened at her childlike wonder. "I remember a tale from when I was a child," she said softly.

The man grunted her name, his arms crossed like mine. "They want to be on their way," he told her.

"It's fine," Fira stepped up behind Egan and I. With the hot sun that bore down on my neck already, I felt as if The March had come to visit me personally.

"When I was a child, my mother used to tell me of The Banished Princess, of a death angel doomed to roam alone for eternity," she paused. Her hand settled against the feather as she finally looked up at me. "Is that — is that you?" She asked so quietly the gentle breeze almost ate her words.

I paused and wondered. *Could telling this human woman really be dangerous? I'm so far from home.* "My name is Phaedra," I nodded to her gently.

Her eyes were so large I feared they might fall out. "It is you!" she practically squealed. "I knew it!"

I shifted, uncomfortable, and bumped into Fira as Egan smirked at me, enjoying my frown.

The woman, thankfully, noticed this and was quick to calm herself. She then bowed before us, to my shock, and introduced herself. She grasped my hand and shook it as she spoke, and my mind trailed off quietly as I saw the gray in her hair, the love pleats on her face.

As Egan packed the new goods into his satchel, I watched the couple slowly pull away in their animal-drawn wagon.

"Make a new friend?" Fira asked behind me as Egan hefted the bag onto his back.

"I knew humans lived short lives but..." I trailed off, the stark black print of my books in the royal library echoing through me. "They sleep twice a day and twice a night. I wonder how they have time for storytelling."

"Have you not interacted with humans before?" Egan looked at me with disapproval as we turned back toward our heading. I let my feathers skate over the grass as we walked. It felt good to catch the breeze now that fire itself wasn't breathing down my neck.

"I have," I insisted.

"When?" Fira asked from behind me.

"Used to being worshiped?" Egan didn't relent from the teasing, and I sullenly looked at the back of his head.

"That's not real and never has been," I corrected him.

Fira hummed behind me to sound off her doubt.

Would the Queen of Death want that in my absence, an entire species on their hands and knees before her? I shivered as the breeze wicked at the sweat between my feathers.

KERES

The library held an especially unpleasant memory. But I strengthened my resolve and walked into the space confidently. Eigra trailed behind me at the proper distance. I had selected her to assist me with this task as she could read the fastest of the three.

"Begin by identifying all the sections that might contain references to earth fairies and their home," I decided to divide and conquer. Eigra bowed and walked to the other end of the library as she searched for the plaque that listed the sections.

I ignored her and went to the large north wall. *All the legends,* I softly touched their slowly disintegrating bindings. I noticed an odd shadow on one of the books. My hand tightened around its binding before I forced it to relax. I slowly drew it off the shelf.

No cover. I huffed as I slowly opened the book and flipped to the dog-eared page. *Who would dare fold one of the pages of the Royal Library?* On their own accord, my eyes slipped up to the delicate metal and glass table that sat in front of one of the many tall and thin windows that traced this room. Next to the table, a large quilt hung, its purple hues simple.

Of course she would. I went to free the page of its crease but hesitated. My eyes narrowed as irritation swam in my gut. I left the page dog-eared and slipped the book on myths onto the shelf. Alone, in the space my sister had once claimed, I contemplated. *Phaedra could never meet Mother's high expectations, so I had to.* The windows rattled as a small flock of angels flew by at high speed. I longed to take time to rest and enjoy myself. *I'm jealous of the lower expectations Mother had for her. But look where it got her.*

Dear Husband,
I will not return home as planned for Zelda's birthday. Mara has announced that she is expecting by her fiance. Her parents suddenly passed when she announced it privately. I hadn't been allowed to prepare their elevenses, Cyrus, Mara's betrothed, insisted he do it instead. I should have been there.
Sincerely,

Zeltik

CHAPTER NINE

PHAEDRA

THE DRIED FRUIT WAS a long forgotten memory of happier times. The peninsula was cold in a way that made bones snap and eyes go dark. It lashed at our faces and cut up our wings. Flight was impossible. The constant wind was like blades upon our flesh.

There were no animals here, at least none that were recognizable. The barren, rocky landscape was empty save for a few oddly shaped, scurrying lizards that had odd amounts of limbs and the small fish that had gathered at the shoreline, gaping at us with double heads. Our rations had run low, and we resorted to hunting the strange animals and eating them to try and survive our journey.

It was as if this land had been forgotten by humans, fairies, and angels alike, for good reason. Nothing could ever grow in this forsaken land. The words passed between the three of us were quick and always came out sharper than intended. Despite that, we attempted to maintain amity for all of our sakes. When the sun fell and the cold reached so far inside our hearts we had to huddle beneath my wings for a suggestion of warmth.

When we finally came to a stop just outside a stone structure, my heart thudded an odd rhythm inside my chest. I thought I might finally be whisked away by the wind and out to sea for good. Odd symbols and pictures were carved into the arch, faded as though a millennia had passed. I approached the structure first and pressed a hand against it, only to rip myself away with a hiss.

"Is it cursed?" Fira yelled above the wind, and I turned back to see her eyes ready to ignite me.

"Freezing!" I yelled back, my throat wet with blood. Breathing in the constant cold on top of screaming had left my insides cracking.

"Inside!" Egan commanded us. He marched ahead. A stone building stood before us, proudly impervious to the cold. As I followed after Fira and brought up the rear, the glossy stones had me gaze at myself. My eyes were sunken, and my black feathers reminded me of carrion.

I followed the other two into the doorway, and I whipped around on my heel to help Egan roll the stone door closed. When it had been rolled to a crack and then sealed, I pried my statuesque hands off the rock and collapsed to my knees.

The still air tried to fry me alive. I ripped off my extra layers, and I huffed with the pain of warmth as it filled my lungs so quickly. "Are you," I gasped and panted, mouth open, as I looked behind me at Egan and Fira. They seemed to be in the same state.

"We're okay," Egan assured me as he relinquished himself of his extra layers and bent over to rest his hands on his knees. He stared at the floor, eyes empty. "We're okay," he repeated.

I nodded and threw myself to the side as my bleary and blurry eyes took in the new setting. My breath slowly calmed down as my body began to hurt all over. A loud grunt, and I tried to bring my knees back up so I could push myself off the dusty ground. Fira waved a hand in my direction and I stopped. She kicked around the winter cloak she had dropped and made a small nest for herself before she sat heavily.

"We need to rest," she told me, eyes weighing on me in a way I knew meant this wasn't a fight I'd win.

I nodded and swallowed, my face drawn tight at the blood that went down my throat. The silence outside our loud breaths made my ears ring. It had been so, so long since the constant whistle of the wind had begun.

"You're bleeding," I blinked at Egan as he pushed his thumb into his lip.

I copied his gesture and my hand came away bloody. I smacked my lips a few times. "Couldn't taste it." Fira looked between us as Egan nodded at me.

Fira, not one to stay idle, grabbed Egan's satchel. "We need to see if they have supplies here," she said as she rooted around.

"Here," Egan brought a small cloth out of his chest pocket and handed it to her. "I was saving it for you." My eyes narrowed as he glanced at me quickly before looking away, his face somewhat red still from the cold.

"Thank you," she accepted it gratefully. She dropped the cloth, and I saw a small piece of aged cheese. Fira tipped her head back and swallowed it whole, not chewing.

I shook my head as I forced my legs under me and my body up. "I don't think anyone is here, Fira," I told her gently as my legs came back to sensation.

She looked at me suspiciously, not budging from where she rested.

I shook what was left of the cold off my body and gestured. "This place is just as forgotten as the world outside," I stated as I looked upon the heavy dust, the rubble that unceremoniously decorated the floor.

We were in a small room, a single dark empty doorway leading farther into the temple. *In a land so barren and painful, what kind of monster could await us here?*

"No one has come for us yet," Egan supplied, his eyes following mine to the empty doorway. The more we waited, the more I felt it was growing. An odd, living weight upon my feathers made my wings shudder behind me. *Unease?* My feathers start to stand up. This roused Fira into standing. Egan followed her.

"Did it eat them?" I lowered my voice as I glared into the dark. A shapeless mass, a writhing of claws, beaks, talons, and hooves danced just beyond my view. We had asked all we came across: *'What monster lay at Dragon's Den?'* And none could answer.

Fira took one of the feathers I had shed months prior from her pack and handed it to Egan. He held it so that she could strike a flame with a flint to it.

"We have to find the egg," Fira commanded as the feather caught flame. It was slow to burn, but the meager light was enough for me to see as she turned away from me and headed into the unknown. "I'll save them. All of them," Fira pledged.

I tailed behind Egan as he followed after his princess devotedly. My wings stretched as I entered the doorway, enjoying the freedom without the cold that pounded them down, and my feathers kissed the ancient stone before the shadows enveloped us. In silence, we walked. The telltale sigh of Fira's dagger ghosted ahead as the tight corridor relaxed.

I gasped as I stepped into a rotunda.

"What is this?" Egan whispered quietly next to me, his soft voice lost in the immense space.

"Dragon craft?" Fira whispered next to us.

The room was darkened more than any sleep I had ever experienced. I could not see the high ceiling above, but I could hear the glacial winds beat against it relentlessly. The walls bowed away from us with great force, a slight lean in that I could barely detect. The stones, their details hard pressed to reveal themselves in the light of a burning feather, were fitted together with such precisionI thought it impossible.

Our group jerked back, each of us spreading our wings and balancing on the balls of our feet, as a solitary light sprang up in what seemed to be the center of...*whatever this place had once been used for.* I frowned.

"The monster," I informed my companions. The living weight that had burrowed between my feathers and into my flesh when I entered this place made itself known, a strange smell ripping through the stale air straight for us.

"For the Fire Sphere!" Egan leapt into the air and beat his wings to gain some height before he drew his sword and plunged toward the ominous light.

"Egan, no!" Fira shouted and chased after him.

"Stop!" I followed with Fira, my wings pushing me ahead of her as my body shook with adrenaline.

I reached out and grasped Cynthia. I brought the lower and un-bladed part of her staff in front as I made to knock Egan backwards when I caught up to him.

My eyes adjusted to the purple light as we came up on it, and my throat constricted as I took in the monster. *The monster?* A lone woman sat hunched over on a gathering of pillows, blankets, quilts, and other assorted objects.

"Stop, Egan!" I begged his back as his sword rose, his body not stalling as he prepared to cut through her skull. *This isn't right!* I wanted to scream.

As I reached out with Cynthia's dull end, Egan's form changed and my eyes squinted. There was light shining through his stomach, and his feet hit the ground in a painful landing followed by a second *thunk*. I gasped in realization and back pedaled. I almost dropped Cynthia in my haste.

I gagged, and my feet hit the ground painfully as I dropped like a stone. I swung Cynthia into Fira and stopped her in her tracks. She dropped next to me, the wind knocked out of her.

"Egan!!" The blood curdling screaming left her lips as Egan's top half landed behind the woman.

"She cut him in half," I stated dumbly. My eyes jumped in between his legs, the woman, and where I had seen his raged face disappear behind her shoulder.

Fira screamed and struggled against Cynthia as she made to go to him. But I gripped her shoulder tightly to hold her back.

How? Circulated in my mind. *How? She has no weapons!* My eyes found her hand bloodied as I examined her, my heart beating faster than a rabbit. *Who is she?*

Her hand is bloody? The knowledge swept through me like a fever as Fira stopped struggling and dropped to her knees, hoarse cries coming out of her mouth as she stared at her shaking hands. I looked down at her, suspended in my battle stance, as I tried to make a decision. Any decision.

She cut him in half with her bare hand so fast that I couldn't see. A cold sweat broke out against me as I began to shake finely under the woman's odd eyes. Her whole complexion was unnerving. I felt as if I was staring at a forgotten story, a painting left to dry in an attic of a home long abandoned. Her white hair stretched down around her to rest on the nest. Her skin was odd, faded, as if she had forgotten what the sun was. Her eyes looked as if they had once been quite dark, but now were gray. It was as though her ink had been drained.

"I'll kill you," Fira's fierce whisper knocked me back into motion as I looked down to see her positioning herself to tackle the woman. "I'll kill you...!" She growled out and looked up, baring her teeth.

"Anyone sent by her would," the woman was calm, but her voice resonated like watercolors dropped in a pond in such a large space.

"What does that mean?" Fira stilled next to me, and I felt as though a string pluck would cause the tension to explode. My eyes slowly turned back to the woman, and I readjusted my grip on Cynthia so that her blade pointed towards the enemy.

"She sent you here to steal this dragon egg, didn't she? It's the last," the woman, unblinking, watched us. I swallowed as she looked me up and down but stayed quiet. *How does this woman know Max? Does Max know her?* Questions twirled around me like a carousel.

The back of my head began to ping slightly, a slight throb that made me tighten my white knuckled grip on Cynthia and listen to the woman. I was overthinking myself into a headache.

Not seeming either satisfied or disappointed with our non-response, the woman spoke. "This egg will never hatch without its mother's voice. My powers are the only thing keeping this egg alive. If I release this egg, if I let it go, it will die."

"You would have had to be here for centuries, since the time of dragons, for that to be true," Fira's words were meant to stamp this woman who murdered our companion. *No human can live that long!*

But the woman didn't seem affected. Instead, she extended her arm and waved it toward us. Fira and I flinched back at her simple motion. "Why don't you stay a while?" She nodded behind us.

My brows drew together in confusion as I angled myself to look behind. My eyes widened as my body went lax at the new sight before me. A grand table was behind us, lit with candles. Upon the table rested many platters of food, dishes that were both familiar and others that were entirely foreign. I swallowed as the different smells hit me. The unsympathetic winds that battled against this chamber suddenly seemed more booming.

"I would never sit and eat with someone who would take a life so carelessly," Fira stood fully. My eyes were quick to watch her heels for signs of movement should she choose to sacrifice her own life like Egan.

My eyes shot to his legs, but I forced myself to look away by physically turning before I could become sick.

"You were about to kill this egg, were you not?" the woman easily countered, and I brushed my hand against Fira's. She slapped me away and I flinched. "Even by accident, and send up a green flash through the heavens."

I averted my eyes from Fira as I tried to reign in my head pain. Fira was quiet at the woman's assessment. Our reactions seemed to have an effect on the woman, however, and she sighed, drawing my gaze back to her.

"I will tell you where someone is. They will be able to tell you when and how to stop the Queen of Death," she promised us.

My eyes narrowed. *She hasn't acknowledged Egan's corpse once.* Headless fury reared inside me at this and at the implication that someone so powerful would sit idly by while the balance is upset. *How does a human, who has supposedly protected this egg for centuries, know what's going on outside of here?*

Fira opened her mouth, likely to say another jab and question the woman, but the woman spoke over Fira. "Even though I haven't left for centuries, I still know what's happening in the world," she warned us.

With all the strange emotions warring inside me, rather than take a dangerous plunge and lose my life, I strode to the feast and began to pick over the food. I struck at the things that were easy to pick up and eat should I need to move fast.

Fira scoffed at me, and I ignored her. *It's freezing outside. And I'm not about to stay the night here.*

"Seek out the Prophet on Silver Top Island. They'll help you much more than a dead egg," the woman explained as I watched her carefully. The things she rested on were nice and plush, soft. The idea of taking some for our journey appealed to me. *But the idea of being impaled appeals less.* The idea was squashed.

My eyes spied a quilt she sat upon, mixed in with all the rest. Its design was grand, golden petals falling into angels and fairies that held hands. *An origin story of how the royal families were created*, I recognized. Fira said something sharp, and the woman merely stared at her, still unblinking, before Fira gazed upon Egan's corpse.

"What do you see?" The woman directed the question to me, and I came back to the moment. I blinked and made haste to swallow the unchewed berry I had chosen. But the woman continued.

"This quilt is one of many an old friend bewitched to appear in the correct order only to Mother," the woman's face crumpled slightly, the only emotion she had shown thus far. "I miss Mother." She spoke quietly and looked down to the corner of the quilt where intricate gold embroidery portrayed an eerie, white goddess figure looking at the petals as if Fira and I were no longer there.

Fira used the opening to dash over to Egan's remains, top and bottom, and place them inside the sleeping sack in Egan's pack. I made to grab him from her so that she wouldn't have to bear the burden of carrying her dead soldier, but she knocked her shoulder into my hands in a loud and clear denial. Fira didn't look back as she moved towards the way we had come from.

I glanced back to see the woman watching us, still unmoved. "Give her my regards when you see her again," she gave me a wisp of a tight smile before I turned to follow Fira, not wanting to be left behind. *This woman is unspeakably dangerous.*

"Ah!" Her voice stopped us both in our tracks. We both look back with wide eyed fear at her outburst. "My name is Minimum. Please call me Min," I looked at Fira and the Princess returned my look. Together, we half flew, half ran to the exit.

Egan was buried underneath a large pile of rocks outside of the archway. It was the best we could have done with the frozen ground. Fira had decided this location would be best so that she could return when she had saved her people and retrieve him.

"Bring him home," she had assured me.

Now, I stared at her back as we trudged back the way we came, the villain and the victim we left behind hastening our steps. My hands bled slightly from handling all the sharp rocks, and the tears had frozen to my painfully reddened cheeks. Fira hadn't offered me Egan's cloak, opting to wear it herself, but I wouldn't have accepted it if she did.

"We should have never come here!" Fira screamed at me as she whipped around on her heel.

I couldn't find myself to disagree with her.

She landed a solid hit on my cheek, and I fell with a loud thud.

Dear Husband,
I will return home shortly
for respite. Mara has birthed
a sickly girl heir. The child
has white hair and yellow
eyes. She's so tiny and pale. I
fear a curse has fallen over
the royal family. The late
Queen and King's funeral
was a damp and cold affair.

Sincerely,

Zeltik

Chapter Ten

KERES

A time after I found an old map of the Earth Realm while I shuffled through the books and presented it to Queen Mara, I was called before her and the other commanders.

"We're going to attack the Earth Realm?" I quoted dumbly. *Is this why one of the commanders went missing, she objected to the war?*

"Yes," Queen Mara impatiently rattled her thin pointing baton against the table, and my eyes fluttered as I resisted a flinch. *Is that okay?* I could almost hear her ask as she mocked my ignorance. She took my stunned silence as a challenge. "Now that we've conquered the Fire Sphere, it's only natural the Earth Realm will attack," she promised.

Bruno and the others nodded along with her as they watched her every move. *Hawks,* came to mind. I closed my mouth and approached the war map. It was detailed and large, more so than the map we had depended on to take the Fire Sphere.

"This is the Agee Tree, their source," one of the commanders pointed out the large tree that did not appear on other maps. "We believe this is where their water source is approximately," he continued.

We're going to take the Realm of Earth. The prospect did not rouse my ambitions. Rather my bones felt heavy, weighed down by the idea of more restless nights full of worry and concern for my success and standing.

"Keres," Queen Mara placed a hand on my shoulder as she leaned in. "I'm impressed with your work at the Fire Sphere." My heart stuttered as I soaked in her praise. "I'm going to have you lead the frontline in this defensive maneuver." My breath stilled as I took in what she said.

"Yes, Your Majesty," I responded as my training kicked in. *I want this to stop,* I desperately wished. *I'm tired.*

"Good," she affirmed and shook my shoulder as she gave me a happy and pleased look. "I know I can depend on you," she admitted, and my insides somersaulted.

PHAEDRA

"There's no hope," Fira sat across from me. We sat at the fire together. I was thankful the cave offered us some warmth. The last time we had substantially spoken had been when we left Dragon's Den. The mountains that blocked off the forgotten peninsula had offered us a cave for the night as well as a reprieve from the blinding cold.

I listened to Fira as I stared into the fire. *Will she continue to travel with me?*

"My sphere has fallen. Everyone I was close to is dead," she seemed so sure of this. *Eliminating high ranked officials of the enemy will help prevent organization,* my mind unhelpfully meted out.

"Egan," Fira's voice broke as she hid her face behind her raised legs.

My chest cracked at this. I had hurt for her every day since it happened, watching her silently, trying to reach out only to be pushed away or ignored. "We have hope. We'll find the Prophet," I tried to put certainty into my voice, tried to give her faith.

"It's all your fault," Fira looked up at me, and I was taken aback more by her bubbling eyes than her harsh words, "for leaving in the first place." She accused me.

I remained silent and thought of how similar her words sounded to Keres. Keres had always made sure I had known how weak I was, how I had been given Cynthia because I required the scythe's power. *Is it my fault for leaving?*

"I'm sorry, Fira," I told her. "I'm sorry," It was all I could say.

Fira, hearing my words, began to cry. Her body quaked, and I instinctively went to her. My arms wrapped around her like Liraz had done to me so long ago. I stroked Fira's hair as she reluctantly gripped at me.

The humans had quality goods. It was clear they had made many of the products themselves. The two women beamed at us as Fira paid them for the items we required and the nicer, more seasoned meat I had wanted. I stared off into the woods in the distance and hoped to see some game to hunt so we could make our new supplies last longer.

"I wouldn't go in there," the shorter woman told me as the taller one accepted Fira's payment. "Those be The Telling Woods. They're cursed." She told me ominously. Her wiggled fingers were enunciated by her few teeth.

"And beyond those, the Nothing Woods are also cursed," the taller woman smiled at her counterpart who clearly enjoyed the scary stories.

"Angels have been found recently looking like something had eaten them," the shorter nodded to Fira and I. We shuddered at the thought.

"Thank you," I told them earnestly. I did not need to hear any more stories about haunted woods to know staying clear was best.

"An odd duo, huh?" The taller one asked me, curious why an angel and a fairy might be together and so far from our lands. *Or maybe she means the two woods?*

"How recent?" Fira asked the taller woman as she put away the items.

"Oh, recently," the woman supplied helpfully. "The death angels that come through, we heard them say they found..." She paused for dramatic effect, and I could see that Fira was clearly irked. "A life angel!" She told us with wide eyes as she jutted out her hands for show.

My head drew back and I flapped my wings, startled. *A life angel?* My memory scratched against me as I recalled the execution that had been going on in town the night I had left. *Surely it's not the same angel.* I crossed my arms as I contemplated.

"They was real terrified," the shorter woman told us. "I reckon he haunted them." She nodded at me knowingly, and I tipped my head to her.

"Let's go," Fira brushed against me as she turned to walk away.

I glanced at both the women before I followed her. I stepped next to her side. The humans have been kind to Fira and I. They haven't been afraid, unlike the ones closer to the Queendom of Death. These humans from farther lands were genuine and unfearful of angels.

"The Agee Tree is on our way," Fira unfurled the map we had been given by Max.

"We should stop there," I agreed. The earth fairies held no alliance with Queen Mara, and they might have goods that we won't find elsewhere. *The Agee Tree held an alliance with fire once upon a time. It's where —*

"It's where Father sent me, originally," Fira echoed my thoughts. "They might be able to help," she rolled the map up tightly and signaled the subject was closed.

My wings flicked behind me anxiously as Fira struggled to control her occasional shudder.

This isn't right.

A colossal tree stood before us, its branches and leaves corkscrewing into the sky. The bark of the tree was dark, and the chill cast by its protection seemed uneasy in the quiet.

Fira and I stood closely at the corner of an empty house on the outskirts of a vacant village. Baskets had been forgotten here and there. Some still contained goods. But there was no one here.

While I crouched down to touch the trodden down path and the footprints, Fira kicked a basket that was next to us.

"These are fresh," I side eyed the blankets and clothes as they landed farther away.

"They were evacuated," Fira bit out, and I looked up at her as she stepped heavily along the path with no look back.

"Evacuated?" I asked her.

"They didn't take the non-essentials," she barked back at me. My eyebrows furrowed as I looked back towards the basket, and I saw a small piece of paper with some scribbles on it. I leaned down to snatch it up before I caught up with Fira with a flap of my wings. She didn't look back at me, and I found myself staring at the child's drawing. My insides wrenched.

The City of Agee melded perfectly into the surroundings. Homes were grown out of trees, walls were shaped from stone and mud. There were small paths that would sometimes lead to bigger roads that looked more frequently traveled save for the current lack of people. To my untrained eyes, it was difficult to pick out what could be a house or a shop, let alone differentiate it from the surrounding leaves and wild growth.

As we approached closer to Agee Tree, the forest around us grew more dense. The limbs stretched above us close to the ground, and we had to duck and try to avoid scratching our faces as we made our way through. My wings shuffled at the idea of needing to fly in this, and I realized I couldn't.

"You there, stop!"

Fira and I stopped some ways away from the hollow of the tree and the only fairy life we had seen for quite some time. The guards rushed around the hollow, carrying in supplies from the last few remaining wagons. The guard that had called out to us was slowly drawing his sword as he stared us down.

The other guards looked up from their duties before looking back to their work. They did a double take as they realized my wings. The wings of the earth fairies were large and awkward, made for gliding as opposed to long flight. Their hues shifted from light brown to dark green.

"Enemy!" one shouted and went for his blade. My eyes narrowed as my arm twitched to grab Cynthia and whip her around. I held the inclination back. The guard who had stopped us stepped in front of the others and in front of the supplies, his face full of rage.

"Why does a fire fairy accompany a death angel?" A booming voice commanded obedience behind the guard, and I felt the tree roots preserve me solidly in place.

Is that — is that —

The guards jumped as Fira straightened. The initial guard scuttled to the side. From farther into the hollow came a tall woman, her deep hair hanging down almost to the ground. Her eyes were as dark as black dahlia, their depths swirling with power and righteousness.

Mom? The tiny voice in my head sounded so young.

Something yanked on my hand, and I dropped to my knees as I stared. "Phaedra!" Fira hissed to me, and I dipped my head and swallowed. My eyes were wide as I examined the dirt below me.

"Speak," the woman commanded again.

"Your Majesty," Fira took the lead next to me, "We come from the Fire Sphere to seek your aid." The soldiers quieted and forgot their work as their booted toes appeared on the edge of my vision. The woman's fine green dress swayed just out of reach as she stopped in front of us.

"Your Highness," I found my voice as I slowly looked up at her. My feet quaked at the angle. "Why are you preparing for war?" I asked quietly lest my voice break.

"Why indeed?" Her eyes dropped to me, her expression unreadable. "With me," she ordered and turned on her heel. "We have much to discuss and little time." I blinked as she headed into the Agee Tree. Iron left my lungs as I relaxed.

"Phaedra, are you okay?" Fira put a hand on my arm as we stood up together. I nodded at her and swallowed before I made a point of looking down where we were still connected. I gave her a little smile. Fira huffed in annoyance at being caught showing me affection and released me.

"Get back to work!" the Queen of Earth yelled at the soldiers, and I felt poison re-enter my veins.

The grand hall bustled. People rushed here and there, their arms piled high with linens, weapons, scrolls, artifacts, and children. Items lay everywhere, either dropped or forgotten. The Queen herself sat atop her throne, the two smaller thrones next to her empty. She took a deep breath as she measured us silently. The hubbub did not seem to pierce her thoughts.

"The Queendom of Death, Queen Mara and her daughter, Princess Keres, your mother and sister, march upon us to claim our home," the Queen of Earth stated. She measured my reaction on her grand seat. Her throne had been trained from the tree we stood in, a connection to the soul of their land.

My eyes widened as her words descended upon my ears from her lofty seat. *Here? They're coming here?* My thoughts revolved in circles as my heart started to pound. *I — I don't know how to stop them yet. They can't!* My bottom lip trembled as the memory small picture I had collected earlier weighed down my breast pocket as an anvil might.

Her long fingers tapped her armrest. Her sharp nails dug into the wood. I watched her hand uneasily as I started to sweat. "And you dare to claim you come to seek aid for a sphere that has fallen?" The Queen of Earth turned to Fira, and I watched my companion from the corner of my eye.

Fira held her own, her chest still held out proudly. "I have come to request aid. We are traveling to Silver Top Island to find a way to stop Queen Mara," she said. She was even keel against the Earth Queen yet grimness swung from her words and face.

The Queen of Earth raised a hand. "That journey is impossible without a boat made in your homeland," she stated, waving the idea away. I frowned.

The Queen of Earth's eyes riddled through me, maggots in the muck. "You must be well-acquainted with the spirits for you look so pale and to not know their army is coming for us," the edge of her lip raised up as she humored herself. "Just before you arrived, we caught and killed one of their scouts," the silence of her nails abusing her chair was prickly.

Could I have known them? The idea made me sick and anxious. *I've only ever seen one death angel who* — Liraz's smile shut down that train of memory.

"The Banished Princess's impressive scythe and footwork will help," Fira interjected. I shook myself a little as I looked over at her. I tried to hold in my surprise. "Both of us hold a life grudge against the Death Queen and the Queendom of Death. They stole my sphere, my people, and Queen Mara stole her companion." Fira held a hand out towards me, and I agreed with her. "We want to fight," Fira gazed upon the Queen with conviction.

We do? Besides a few instances with humans, I've never fought anyone before besides Max.

As Fira spoke, a short man, his outfit the same as the Queen's, entered from a side door and took the throne next to her. A few moments later, a younger person who could only be their daughter, the Princess of Earth, took the final seat. The Queen looked the duo over, and her King nodded toward her.

The Queen gazed at us for a long moment, and I struggled not to move under her evaluation. "The Death Queendom's host will arrive late tonight or very early tomorrow. You," she turned to me, "Will not be permitted to fight. I can't trust those feathers, but until I can prove you're a spy, I won't be too cruel to you."

I couldn't help the deep breath that came into me as I heard this. I felt as though the Death Queendom was already here and that I was standing before the Queen of Death, her critical gaze judging me harshly for another failure.

I was pulled back by the quilt that hung behind the thrones, the centerpiece of the room. It was excellent quality and looked thick. I examined it to calm myself. Golden thread depicted angels and fairies with petals inside of them holding hands in a circle. Inside their circle was another circle with many elaborate designs on it. In the corner of the tapestry, silver thread depicted a woman with long hair staring at the figures with jealousy.

"You will stay the night at your own risk," the Queen finished before she stood. Fira and I bowed as she then turned to the princess to say something and left the room.

ELA

The Agee Tree was not prepared for war. But still it marched to our doorstep. The clank of the death angel armor resounded from our nightmares into the waking hours. *It's natural they'd come here,* as I waited for Ma to tell me why she called me here. She was wrapped up with our top soldiers as she tried to create defenses from nothing. *The Queen of Death wants to avoid a war on two fronts.*

As the soldiers left, I stepped in front of Ma. *A pincer attack on fire and death,* I thought idly, *would take more swords than we have ever had.* Ma looked down at me, the stress lines on her face permanent.

"I need you to see to our new guests," she instructed me rapidly. "It's the Princess of Fire and the Banished Princess." I jerked in surprise.

"What?!" I asked in alarm, my hand covering my mouth.

"Fire has fallen," Ma reminded me of our informant. "They're here to seek aid."

I slowly nodded.

Dear Husband,

Something is wrong. I finished preparing the tea that Cyrus began for Mara on their anniversary, and I noticed he had accidentally put spotted fern into it. He can be so helpless. No wonder him and that new maid are always sneaking around — he can't do his own buttons! I believe her name is Liras. She's come down with child from her husband, and she told me she intends to name it Liraz. Who will help Cyrus then? Not me!

Please see to it my garden is properly wrapped for winter. Those plants will carry us through the cold season,

Your Wife

CHAPTER ELEVEN

PHAEDRA

"I APOLOGIZE ON BEHALF of Queen Dunia for the shared quarters," the Princess of Earth, Ela, tipped her head to us as we stood in the center of the room. She raised her head and looked at us. "The attendant will bring you food in two hours. I have to leave to finish the preparations," Princess Ela curtsied to us.

We thanked her, and she softly closed the door behind her, her brown fairy wings that brought out her green eyes pressed tightly against her back.

The room was tiny, more of a closet than quarters, but we were thankful for the chance to clean our weapons and preen our wings away from prying eyes.

As we settled into the one bed, Fira and I lay tightly next to the other's feet. I propped my head up on my arms and stared up at the single window that let the night air in.

Everyone here has a role to fulfill. The smell of the bread and chicken broth they had graciously given us faded quickly now that the attendant had taken away our well-cleaned dishes. Distant shouts for reinforcement of a wall here and supplies needed there were soothing despite the incoming threat. My fingers tightened in my hair as my mind wandered.

I imagined for a moment that I was in my quarters in Death Castle, that Liraz was tidying a few things before she left for the evening, that I was ready to rest after a long day of advising the various counsels of what was best or maybe of defeating a monster that had attacked the town. The fantasy relaxed me, a warmth in my chest that was separate from the heat Fira always gave off. *As if Keres would ever abdicate willingly.* I scoffed.

Princess Ela, I thought of earlier, *she knows what she needs to do without being told.* The admiration in my gut tasted sour. *Must be nice to not fail.*

Could I be someone like that?

ELA

The Banished Princess, Phaedra, and the Princess of Fire, Fira, did not look pleased at being handed the last available accommodations in the castle. I apologized to them and promised to send food, but I couldn't sacrifice my other duties to wait on them hand and foot.

I bowed and left, my mind growing new, lush ideas. *The Banished Princess could still secure the throne from Queen Mara.* I looked out a window as volunteer soldiers picked out their weapons. *Could we stop this war?*

PHAEDRA

The silence was suffocating. It slipped down my throat, crawled into the hollows of my eyes, and licked in between my fingers. I found myself stirring, but no matter which way I turned my head, I couldn't hear anything. My hand batted down the blanket between us, and my eyes met Fira's in the dark.

She slowly looked towards the window, and my hands rested high on my chest as I also turned. I watched as she quietly extracted herself from the bed and crept to the window. Her wings pressed down tightly as she cautiously peaked out without revealing herself to the courtyard.

Fira returned to me. Her hands moved the blanket as tension strung anew inside me. "They've killed the two guards. They're sneaking in," she told me, voice deep with sleepy disuse.

"We have to raise the alarm," I told her. I wobbled as I got my feet under me while I grabbed Cynthia from under the bed.

Fira grabbed my mouth and held it shut, making me waver. She glared at me. "No! If we tell Queen Dunia, we can surprise Queen Mara," Fira smiled, her teeth shining in the soft light menacingly.

I nodded and blinked as my mind fully settled into being awake. Fira's look made my bones tremble. She looked hungry as she replaced her daggers and the armor that still depicted the Fire Sphere symbol proudly.

I followed behind her quickly, thankful I had been uneasy enough here to not remove my cloak and traveling clothes. We left behind our packs, not wanting the extra weight to drag us down in flight.

As we left our room and proceeded down the corridor, we had to watch our footing. This castle, this monument, had been created by the Agee Tree itself. It grew in these twisting patterns, confusing to an outsider, but natural to earth fairies. The bark floor and walls were strong, impossibly so, but not completely flat.

My eyes flicked up when I heard Fira hiss under her breath as we rounded a corner and encountered a fairy in armor. Despite the fire that backlit him, I could see the brown in his wings. *An earth fairy.* My hand snatched at Fira's arm to stop her from going to her dagger as she leaned toward the figure, and she paused in my grip.

Will she ever look at me like that? Fear quietly swirled in me as I took in the menace that her eyes harbored.

"They're here," she whispered to the guard. The guard's eyes widened, and his wings beat in surprise.

"This way," he urged her while he shot me a distrustful look. He turned on his heel and followed a different path. He held his armor, wood from the nearby forest based on its color, and was quiet as we passed empty hallway after empty hallway.

He led us some way up the tree before he finally stopped in front of two large and ornate doors. He knocked on the doors. The soft sound boomed in the silence that continued to sneak around us, and a soft voice from inside bade us entry. The guard slowly pushed open one of the doors and blocked the view from us with his body purposefully. A gasp from him made me jump.

"Your Majesty!" The guard whisper-shouted as he rushed into the room, hand on his sword. Fira rushed in next, and I cautiously brought up the rear, cognizant of my black feathers and how they might startle. My hand tightened around Cynthia as I thought of having to defend myself from the people that hosted me so kindly.

As I rounded the corner of the door, my eyes widened, and my Weapon fell slack in my hands. Before me stood the Queen of Earth standing over three corpses, a common sword in her hand as she panted. She had a cut on her shoulder, and blood soaked upwards on her dress.

Death angels. Their corpses were lax, as if sleeping. Their wings stuck out at odd angles as they rested.

"Your Majesty, are you okay?" The guard panicked, making to take the sword from her, his hands flailing somewhat. My stomach twisted painfully as my dinner started to float up.

The Queen grunted as she shook off the guard and calmed herself. She ran a hand down her hair as her hard eyes drilled into him. "There were six assassins. The three I couldn't catch went after the King who is still searching for our son." Her lips curled in anger.

There was a choked noise from the doorway behind me. I quickly stepped to the side as the Earth Princess slammed both doors open. Princess Ela's whole body shook, but she stayed rooted upright. To see Princess Ela, a strong princess who knew what her people needed and did what they needed, upset shook something in me. I wanted to reach out and assure her it was okay. Princess Ela's watery eyes turned to me, and I swallowed when I realized the crushing weight of the Earth Queen was ready to trample me. I shivered as I looked at Queen Dunia, who seemed to have been speaking to me.

"I believe that you won't betray us, that you truly have been banished. How could any self-respecting queen assassinate another of royalty?" The Queen stepped over the bodies, not looking down as her foot crushed the woman assassin's hand. I averted my eyes as my stomach felt like I had fallen asleep while falling and dropped below the clouds accidentally. "Do as we previously discussed," the Queen directed her daughter and the guard. The guard bowed to the Queen as Princess Ela nodded. The Queen, unhurried and somehow calm, waved a hand at us to follow as she left the room.

The halls started to come alive with noise as the Queen led us farther up into the Agee Tree. She walked us through several busy sections of people distributing weapons, her head held high as her people made way for her. Many of them stared at me and met my eyes in challenge when I watched them back. The farther up we went, the brighter the corridors became until the tree branches twisted up into leaves.

It was here the Queen Dunia led us, a plateau at the top of the trunk of the Agee Tree. The Queen stood at the edge silently, her arms crossed, as all three of us looked down upon her realm. We could see small skirmishes breaking out below in the city around the tree. The thick woods around the Agee Tree hid anything more from us. In alleyways behind houses, small streets here and there, death angels marched along until they met earth fairies. My eyes skittered over every black wing as I looked for someone familiar.

KERES

The frontlines of war were much different than the cushy command hub. I numbly walked forward and dragged my heavy sword behind me. Small bodies rested on the ground around me. Blood, more red than a rose petal, leaked from their bodies and intermingled to make the air too sweet.

"Your Highness!" Kane shook my shoulders, and my eyes slowly settled on his blood smeared face.

"You're hurt," I observed, surprised.

"The King of Earth is just ahead!" He shouted over the militaristic wildfire that roared just outside this school. "We got him while he was trying to get his son!" He laughed.

I winced. *It has to be done.* Queen Mara's warm assurance of being able to depend on me rattled around in my empty mind as I strode deeper into the school.

I picked up my sword and held it ready. *Surely this can't be right?*

PHAEDRA

Fira put her heel on the edge of the plateau. Her wings spread behind her as she unsheathed her dagger.

"Wait," Queen Dunia commanded her. Fira stepped back and her hand squeezed her dagger and her eyes roiled silently. "This tree was planted by those who wished for peace between dragons and people, long before the dragon fortresses were built. It shall survive the night," she didn't glance at Fira as Fira shook her head and sheathed her dagger.

"Dragon fortresses?" The words left my mouth as a whisper as I stared down. The more we waited, the more death soldiers flooded into the city. Their black armor made them melt into the dark. There was a significant lack of earth soldiers but also a lack of earth fairy citizens.

My mouth tightened as I spotted a solitary earth guard thrown to the ground by two death angels. The smaller fairy scrambled to get back up. My foot inched forward as I contemplated what I could do, what might happen. Then suddenly, through the thicket of plants, trees, and wild rock that hid the small foot paths throughout the City of Agee, sprang earth soldiers. They seemed to come out of the plants themselves. Their armor disguised them expertly as they weaved through fairy made tunnels in a way only someone who was born and raised here could.

The sudden influx of the opposition startled the death angels who had just been starting to flood into the town as more flanks were released from the death army to attack.

"They're being overwhelmed!" Fira raised her voice in hope as we watched the earth angels form small groups to fight rather than take on the death angels alone. "The angels can't fly in this forest. Their wings are too big!"

"Look there," Queen Dunia redirected us, and we both looked to her and then where she pointed. My breath stalled as I tried to understand what I was seeing. At the edge of the woods, red armor began to emerge from the greenery, more reflective in the dark than the death angels' armor.

"Fire fairies," Fira's quiet words were spears through my chest.

"She's forcing them to fight." Dunia stated, and I was unsure if she was trying to comfort Fira or hurt her.

My eyes narrowed as I watched them approach and began to fight earth fairies. Their swords clanged as they fought on the ground. The fire fairies had cleaner footwork than the death angels, likely being more used to not traveling by flight.

We watched as a group of earth fairies gathered around a smaller figure in particular before they raised their swords and charged at the new flank of warriors coming to take what didn't belong to them.

"Princess Ela!" I turned and told Queen Dunia. I expected her to send out guards and recall her heir. I looked the Queen up and down when she didn't respond but simply held her fist over her mouth. I turned back to the Princess of Earth as she faced down the enemy, her sword being pushed back as she fought against an expert swordsperson.

The steps her enemy took, the aggressive swings of the sword and the feints, had me take a half step back.

No.

Fira looked at me with disgust as she made to jump off the edge again. This time, Queen Dunia gripped her arm harshly. "They won't realize you're an ally," the Queen gently ordered her to stay. She seemed almost sympathetic.

"I know those warriors," Fira pleaded with her and looked up at the tall earth fairy with wide, red rimmed eyes. Her voice shook, and I stared at her, my world slowly whittling itself down to one thing. "I'm disgusted she would make them fight," Fira looked to me as if she wanted my help, but my eyes turned back to the cloaked swordswoman who Princess Ela fought below. "She had to have threatened their families."

Princess Ela would not be able to stand up to her. Princess Ela was only incapacitating her enemies, and this enemy would require much more than sympathy to defeat. *Princess Ela is so kind and polite. She's strong. She's lasting so long against her. She's intelligent. She's countering these moves that she's never seen before. She's commanding those around her so well.*

She's the perfect princess, I realized.

Princess Keres had not changed since last I had seen her, despite the battlefield, despite the blood that covered her that was undoubtedly not her own. Keres brought her sword down on Princess Ela quickly and used her wings to get past the Princess's guard. Princess Ela was struck on the arm, and I watched as she collapsed. My feathers shuffled in anticipation of flight as my feet tried to decide what I would do next.

An earth fairy jumped in between Keres and Princess Ela, and another soldier helped Princess Ela away as Keres was distracted. I breathed a sigh of relief as I saw Ela disappear into one of the many tunnels, but my blood chilled as I felt Keres' eyes turn toward the three of us.

From where we were, I could see Keres turn her head up. She pointed at us, and I physically jerked back. The other two looked at me and watched as my wings flapped. At the simple gesture, my body felt as if I had been plunged into a lake of frozen ice, alone and scared.

Like before. My inner voice chittered and chattered as the cold swathed around me.

KERES

The King's crown dug into my arm and shoulder as I expertly mowed the inexperienced earth fairy soldiers down. "Have they never fought before?!" I called to Milo as he fought alongside me. He either ignored me or didn't hear. I looked up at the gargantuan tree we approached.

What? In the upper branches, a pale white figure stood amongst others, fallen snow in a mahogany battlefield. *Phaedra?* I cut down another soldier with ease as I sneered and pointed at them. The sounds of battle filtered into my ears as I thought of my deceased sister. *I wouldn't be here...if Phaedra hadn't failed!*

I struck down another soldier and looked up to see the figures had disappeared. *I'm losing it,* I realized coolly. *The crown of Queen Mara has bled insanity into us,* I gasped as I leaned against a wall for a momentary reprieve. My soldiers continued on without me.

PHAEDRA

"Your Highness!" We all turned to look at where we had entered. Princess Ela limped towards us, half carried by her soldier.

How did they make it up here so fast? I turned to look back at Keres, but my sister had disappeared.

"Go get a healer," Queen Dunia commanded the man who quickly headed back down the tree. The Queen was bent over her daughter, who now laid on the floor of the tree. I watched as the Queen's hands examined her injuries, a soft hiss as the Queen saw the extent.

A horn blew behind us, and I spun on my heel as the Queen's head shot up. Her eyes briefly met mine in alarm. I gasped as I observed the town below start to change color. Black and red invaded by air as well as by land. The fire fairies were able to fly through the thicket easier and gathered at the enemy's front line. The death angels flew in small spurts, hindered by the plant growth, and fought behind the fire fairies as the troops pressed forward.

"Another host," I realized with horror. Their armor shined as the moonlight struck them. It revealed their swinging swords and daggers as they began to mow down anyone in their path. Townspeople cried out as they were dragged from their homes, and earth soldiers were separated from their brethren and struck down easily.

There was a small scuffle behind me before the air shifted. "No," Queen Dunia's thoughts slipped through as she stared down into the bloodbath. "They divided the host in half? We've only been fighting half of them?" Her mouth trembled as I watched her become pale with fright.

My head swung on my shoulders as I heard an uncoordinated racket from where the soldier had left and we had arrived. "Fira," I warned her, and she drew her dagger as I swung Cynthia around. This seemed to bring Queen Dunia back to the moment, and she turned as two forms emerged onto the plateau. *Please don't be —*

Fira grunted as she sprang forward, her dagger plunging into the chest of a death angel who wore leather armor. I took advantage of the two enemies' surprise and stepped forward. I brought Cynthia down onto the head of the second soldier. He collapsed loudly, his metal armor drawing attention. I jostled Cynthia to free her from the soldier, my insides twisting and revolting. I squeezed Cynthia with my now clammy hands as I listened to the screams from farther within the Agee Tree.

I need to survive. I have to survive.

The red blood moistened Cynthia's blade. She stirred in my hands, a cat stretching after bathing in the sun. Her purr was a playful sensation on my palms. *I need to fight,* I realized. A desire, cloaked inside of me, brought itself forward as I swallowed nervously. *I want to fight.*

Fira and I stepped away from the stairs that led downward, and I half looked back at Princess Ela. The Queen had thrown herself over her daughter, covering her with her own wings and limbs, to try and protect her. Princess Ela herself watched us, but she didn't seem to comprehend what was happening. The princess was too pale, and her mouth opened with every breath. *She won't live long,* I guessed.

"She can't escape on her own," Queen Dunia met my eyes as she pleaded. Fira looked between us, her grip going lax on her weapon. "Protect her. Please take my daughter and flee," Queen Dunia extracted herself from where she protected her child. She remained on her knees in front of us. Princess Ela's blood marred her face as her eyes began to water. *I can't fight if I take her,* the conflicted sensations of bloodlust and empathy tangled inside of me.

Footsteps coming up the stairs made Fira and I turn back, both of us ready for the incoming enemy. I shifted my footing as I saw the guard that had left earlier return, followed by an earth fairy dressed in all white. They looked up at us, and our weapons slowly lowered, to Cynthia's dismay.

The soldier glanced at the bodies at the top of the stairs as he avoided them. The nurse stepped over the bodies without grace before she laid eyes on the Princess. Without a second thought, she rushed to her and began to care for the large cut on her arm. The guard stepped up to the Queen and helped her up. He trembled noticeably.

Queen Dunia ignored the guard. Her eyes pinned me to the spot. "You got away once before. I need you to do it again," the Queen ordered me, her tone leaving no room for question or error. *She's ordering me to run?* At my silence, the Queen continued. "You two," she directed the nurse and soldier, "take the Princess and follow our guests."

There was a thumping in my chest. It felt as though my heart was trying to say, *'Here, the Banished Princess is here! Stop her!'* My wings felt heavy on my back. My hand tightened on Cynthia as the distant smell of those cobweb filled, stone corridors of the Death Queendom swam in my nose.

The strong memory blew away the bloodlust that had billowed up inside of me. *I need to save her,* I decided rationally. *All this bloodshed, and I have a chance to help a survivor.*

Dear Husband,

I will return shortly. The entire staff has been purged. I returned to assist Her Majesty with preparing for bed, and I discovered her holding a bloody scythe above Cyrus. He has passed. I think she killed him. I asked her what's going on, and she said he attempted to assassinate her! I always knew the Fire Sphere was no good. I should have never trusted him. Her Majesty believes he poisoned her parents with spotted fern. On the day of her announcement, no less!! My happy, bouncy little princess has turned to a cold queen of death. Oh, fate!

I have a sneaking suspicion Liras's Liraz is not her husbands. The child's hair is glossy and twines finely.

Please see to it I arrive to fresh linens,

Your Wife

CHAPTER TWELVE

FIRA LOOKED TO ME and our eyes met briefly before I addressed Queen Dunia. "I'll get her out of here," I promised.

Queen Dunia nodded once to me, her eyes strong. "Get them out of the city the old way," she ordered the guard who then bowed to her. The nurse and the guard gathered Princess Ela up so that the nurse could continue to treat her and wrap her injuries while the guard carried her.

"This way," the guard didn't look back as he led us across the plateau to where a large pile of leaves, tree limbs, and smaller things had been thrown. I glanced back at Queen Dunia as Fira and the nurse cleared the pile. Queen Dunia's hands were tight fists at her side, and the emotion had been purposefully washed from her face.

Why would they be prepared for someone to take their home? I was the last to step down into the revealed staircase as I tailed tightly behind the others. *Queen Mara's vile treachery against all these lifetimes of peace.*

"Watch out!" Fira hissed in front of me as I missed a step and slid into her made my wings flap in surprise. "Good thing we don't have our packs," she grumbled.

"Quiet!" The guard stopped to look back at us, his form barely visible in the dark. We had foregone lanterns and fire opting instead to use the small light that peeked through the tree limbs to see. "We're here," he told us. We gathered around to the edge of the staircase.

How are we already on ground level? Before us rested a thick drape of vines, leaves, and flowers. I peeked through, and I was able to see the courtyard on the other side. Death angels and fire fairies rushed around, corralling earth fairy citizens and soldiers. The guard tapped me on the shoulder, and I gave him my attention. He jerked his head towards the edge of the courtyard, and I frowned as I looked.

I looked back at him and shrugged, not understanding. He looked at Fira to help and she shook her head, her eyes not straying away from the enemy for long. The soldier shook his head, clearly agitated, and crouched down somewhat. Princess Ela pressed her lips together, and I was relieved to note some color had come back to her.

The guard waited and watched where I knew the enemy was, and I watched him. I bent at the knees as he had done and waited. "Now!" I whispered as he shot through the natural drapery and into the court-yard. He didn't look back at us or over at the enemy as he moved forward, his legs working overtime to compensate for the extra weight.

The courtyard was a mess. We had to avoid forgotten pieces of armor, weapons, and slick pools of blood as we ran to the other side. As we reached the goal, I was dismayed to see the guard had led us to a large empty spot in front of a building.

A trap?!

I watched in shock as the guard took one more step and angled himself so that he slid down. The nurse did the same. Fira stopped and I caught up to her before we hesitated. A large, hollow root was before us, the bottom unseeable in the dark night. Fira clapped me on the back as she took a step and did a controlled slide in, and I copied her before my heart leapt out of my throat.

I brought my hands up to cover my face as my feet hit a small pool of water. I felt a yank on me, and I followed and stretched out my arms to feel my way through the darkness. I blinked as the group came into sight, and we paused under a grate to look up.

"Aqueducts," the soldier whispered as he pointed up. My eyes followed his finger, and I saw how it was not a metal grate but rather trained tree roots stretching across the small opening that let in the torchlight. Fira started to say something next to me, but the death angels that ran over the grate above us made her mouth click shut.

My head turned as the soldier, closely followed by the nurse, continued to make his way farther into the aqueduct. I put a hand on Fira's shoulder to urge her to follow, but she shrugged me off before she continued on.

These aqueducts continued all over the city, it seemed. As we followed the soldier well into what I had thought was only the forest, earth fairy homes appeared before us. Their architecture was synchronized with the environment in a way I had only ever read about. But still, above us, earth fairies were rounded up. Terrified and pained screams, the piercing cry of infants, and the shouts of death angels carried to us with undeniable ease. Every now and then, a splatter would fall in around us, fresh blood from an earth fairy as they were overwhelmed. Every cry felt like a heavy boot on my back.

There was a light source up ahead that wasn't a drain. I watched as my companions were slowly outlined, and I felt a pang in my chest as my eyes tried to search out Egan. As we neared the exit, the guard held up a hand and we halted. Voices floated down from the last drain above us, and I looked up with wide eyes.

"I thought I saw her," Keres' voice grated against my ears. Her anger made my heart beat louder and my forehead perspire. *I'm scared,* I recognized my body's tells. *But,* my hand twisted around Cynthia, *I want to fight her.* My own ferocity startled me. "I sent two guards that didn't return. The four I sent after that returned with her head and this," the group flinched as something heavy was dropped on the grate.

My eyes narrowed at the object, a soft glow emanating from it. *Queen Dunia's crown!* My face contorted with silent horror. There was a prolonged silence before whoever Keres' was talking to asked quietly, "Isn't that good news?"

A small scoff from Keres as she retrieved the crown she'd tossed before her light footsteps, followed by the soldier's, faded away. They were headed back to the city. The soldier quietly made his way to the end of the aqueduct and peeked out. He turned to us before he stepped out into the forest.

"We should make our way to the closest Tooth Pike and then head directly to Wind Mountain," he told us.

"We need to take the fastest route," I agreed, my eyes going to the ground to search for footprints. "We need to stay ahead if we're followed,"

"We can only hope that Wind lets in all those who have escaped," the soldier muttered as he stepped out under the deep green canopy.

"The alliance between our nations is still new," the nurse fell in step beside me.

"It was a smart move," Fira remarked behind us.

This forest that we walked through was different from where the Agee Tree slept. These trees were smaller, their branches more prone to break, and their leaves sharp against our faces. Little animals ran about in the tallgrass between the trees, and rocks tripped us up as we chose speed.

"How long have you been allied?" I spoke as the sky slowly lightened, the stars bidding goodbye to the atrocities they'd watched tonight.

"Since Fire fell," the soldier spoke over the nurse as she began to answer. *His arms must be going numb.* Princess Ela slept in his grasp.

"We didn't think the host of the Death Queendom would travel so far," the nurse admitted to Fira and I, side eyeing my wings for only a moment. "The Wind Territory is also allied with the Life Domain," she tells us.

I picked my footing as the trees started to break away from growing closer together to being more spread out. Death angels told their children the horrors of life angels as bedtime stories. But, as I had seen in the town square the day I had been banished, those horrors are very real.

But are we any better? I recalled the final dinner I had had that same night before I had left. Me, alone at the dinner table, trying to choke down the cooked entrails of the second life angel that had been caught by the guards. *"A royal feast!"* I recalled Queen Mara had said as she forbade me to leave until I had cleaned my plate.

Are they even so monstrous to begin with?

I stirred at the rhythmic sound that approached. My eyes struggled to open as the sun pierced me. I shook my head and disturbed Fira, who had fallen asleep on my shoulder against the rocky outcropping. I listened, my feathers spread out in anticipation, and I held my breath.

Marching footsteps.

"Get up!" I hissed at Fira and shoved her painfully. She fell over and scrubbed a hand over her face.

"Get up!" I urged the soldier and nurse. The Princess was propped up between them, still asleep. The soldier slowly opened his eyes at first before they sprang up. "Where —"

"They're almost here!" Fira whispered to him and grabbed the nurse's hand to haul her to her feet.

The soldier gasped before he gathered Princess Ela in his arms and stood. He swayed, and I looked him up and down.

"Do you have her?" My hands went out to steady him as he started to make towards Wind, wavering somewhat.

"I've got her," he gritted out to me and flashed a glare.

My eyes narrowed at his stupidity, and my promise danced around my mind mockingly. The footsteps continued to approach, and we ran.

After we ran for some time and the footsteps faded behind us, Fira pointed something out on the ground. "What's that?" I glanced down with the nurse at her question. The ground had been scuffed up here and there, and I felt my stomach turn at the small marks in between.

"They probably belong to a child," the nurse said aloud, and I kept my eyes straight forward. The trees thinned the closer we got to Wind.

After we had run to the brink of exhaustion, Princess Ela having been transferred to Fira's back, we arrived at the river that signaled wind fairy territory. There were a few, maybe five, wind fairies that wore official leather armor that helped earth fairies cross the river. We were all beyond exhausted, and the river came up to an average waist. *Surely we would drown without their help.* I glanced back at Fira and saw how she eyed the water.

I was in no better shape. The rapids were strong and greedily claimed most of the possessions that the earth fairies had been able to carry with them. Across the river, horses and carts stood ready, people loaded on as unnecessary supplies were dumped.

The soldier who accompanied us waved as he walked to the river, and a wind fairy looked up as a name was shouted. They greeted each other merrily, and I watched as the soldier pointed to us. The wind soldier stared at my wings, and I held them tightly against my back. *I can't afford to be taken hostage again. Not with Keres bearing down on us.*

A small sputtering distracted me. Fira made a noise as Princess Ela began to struggle in her grasp, and the nurse quickly began to whisper things to the Princess.

"Where —" Princess Ela's voice was raw and exhausted and shook.

"You can't move. You can't sit up," the nurse urged her to stop squirming as the two soldiers came back to us. I watched from the corner of my eye as the wind guard and the earth guard approached us. As Fira settled Ela and the nurse began answering Ela's questions, I was scrutinized.

"You're sure about her?" The wind soldier asked, his eyes steely.

"Mmmm," our earth guard agreed, watching his Princess.

"My patrol and I are lucky to have found you and the others when we did," the wind soldier's hand fell onto the plain sword at his hip. His wings buzzed behind him. I stared at his wings. Wind fairy wings were thin and long, their elegant style and flexibility impressive. As the man shifted, the light reflected in rainbows on the glossy surface in a way that wasn't possible with angel feathers.

"The Death Queendom is not far behind us," the nurse stepped away from Ela and Fira. "They're approaching on foot." The nurse's wide and wild eyes reflected our exhaustion.

The wind soldier nodded and looked Fira up and down. Fira frowned and adjusted her hold on Ela as they leaned forward slightly. "We'll help you across the river," the wind guard nodded to himself before he glanced at me and turned. "This way is the most shallow," he guided us.

A particularly sharp bump from the wagon made my eyes pop open. I swiped at them to clear the sleepy fog and gathered what happened around me. We were still in the carriage, our group packed in tightly with other earth fairies that had managed to make the crossing before the wagon was full.

Despite all the warm bodies, I noticed that the earth fairies shied away from touching either Fira, who had leaned into my space to sleep, or myself. They also gave a semblance of space to Princess Ela.

Ela's green eyes lanced through me in the crisp night air. My breathing slowed as I felt like a tallgrass chicken that stared down a hawk.

"Are you really the older sister of the angel that defeated me?" Her hushed tone barely crept over the noise of the turning wagon heels and the horses clopping.

I hesitated. "Yes,"

Ela's eyes relaxed as her shoulders dropped. Her fingers played with the braid of the sleeping earth angel next to her. "Thank you for saving me," she looked back at me.

"It wasn't just me," I assured her, and Ela smiled warmly at me.

Ela's eyes subtly shifted as she gazed upon Fira. "I heard she was sent away by King Cole before her sphere fell. I'm thankful I was able to fight for mine," her hands gripped at the rebandaged wound on her arm. "But I'm also glad I didn't kill anyone."

Keres' blade flashed in my mind. I slowly shifted, in an attempt to not wake Fira, so I could better talk to Ela without disturbing those around us. Ela watched my lips as they started to move and form whispers that I barely heard myself. As I began whispering, the darkness closed in around the wagon.

ELA

My body hurt tremendously. But I looked up at Phaedra as we rested in the unforgiving wagon. "Are you really the older sister of the angel that defeated me?" I questioned. They looked so similar yet so different. *It's all in the eyes,* I decided.

"Yes," she hesitantly answered.

My fingers fidgeted in the hair of the earth angel that slept fitfully next to me. I slowly relaxed. "Thank you for saving me,"

"It wasn't just me," she shared the responsibility. I felt an instant camaraderie with her because of her recognition of others.

"I heard she was sent away by King Cole before her sphere fell," I looked upon Fira. "I'm thankful I was able to fight for mine." I would much rather sacrifice my body than have my mind eaten by guilt and insecurity.

Phaedra started to whisper to me, and I listened keenly. I was relieved when she shared her goals and ideas of how we could stop this war. *There's hope,* I put my faith in Phaedra. *I just need to have faith and everything will be okay.*

Dear Sister,

I've been promoted to wait on Her Majesty. I hope you are proud of me. Please see my enclosed bonus. It should stretch quite far. I've also been moved to the room next to Her Majesty for ease. I share it with other privileged maids. They tell me Her Majesty has had a strange visitor over occasionally. I asked because I saw her tonight, a human woman with crystalline eyes. So odd. I'm glad Her Majesty has made a friend but wish they wouldn't stay up training so late. They're noisy!

Sincerely,

Hazel

Chapter Thirteen

The Mountain of Wind was a sight to behold. It stretched far into the sky, larger than its numerous peers. Between the mountains, small patches of grass inconsistently flourished. As we approached the mountain, the small ravines and rivers between them shrank and became tighter, and a constant wind whipped at us. It was among the shoal rocks at the base of the mountain that we were ordered to disembark.

Fira and I stuck close to Princess Ela as she accepted a hand from her soldier as she floated off the wagon, her wings barely moving. As the guards started to direct some earth fairies to a wooden platform that rested in the grass, an odd amount of rope hanging from it confusingly, I subtly flexed my burning muscles.

"You both must fly to the entrance yourself," the wind soldier from before stopped in front of Fira, Princess Ela, and myself. "Princess Ela, please follow me." He bowed to her and continued to side eye us before he led her away, her soldier in tow.

"Fira, do you see an entrance?" I looked at my companion. Fira nudged me to look towards the earth fairies that had been directed to stand on the wood. They were sitting now, and the wind fairies had each gathered around to grasp the pieces of rope around it.

"Are they going to carry them up?" I asked, dumbfounded, as the nurse we had traveled with came to stand next to us.

"I don't know, I've never been here before," she murmured, a hand over her mouth as the wind fairies started to beat their wings in unison. We watched in awe with the earth fairies who had been deemed able to fly as the platform slowly lifted and swayed under the effort of the wind fairies. Their wings beat faster than my eye could see, and it looked as if they suddenly had two or three pairs of wings each. The vibration in the air faded as they slowly ascended higher and higher.

Fira and I exchanged a look and nodded at each other.

"Excuse me." I stepped away from the nurse as she chittered with shock towards the steep, unclimbable wall of a nearby mountain.

"Hurry up!" Fira's voice from up above spurred my legs into a long jump towards the side of the mountain. Pivoting before I fell, I used the sharp angle of the rock to propel myself into the air before I unfurled my wings and flapped hard. They burned as I awkwardly dipped one wing down and turned in a circle to avoid running into the side of the opposite mountain. I flapped in what little space I had as I circled upwards tightly. Fira joined me once I had been able to straighten out and fly upwards safely.

"Dizzy?" She mocked me, her ruby wings not needing as much space.

I huffed at her, annoyed and flustered over almost crashing in front of everyone. Fira snickered at me.

The wind grew sheer at the proper entrance to Wind Mountain. It buffeted us and threw itself against my wings. It dragged me off course as I made a dive at the entrance. I scrambled as the slick, carved stone came closer, my hands trying for purchase along with my feet. I heard

Fira grunt as she landed hard on her feet. The wind pushed me once more farther into Wind Mountain before it let up on me.

I shook my head as I sprang up, my hand on Fira's shoulder for balance. She questioned me with a look, but I shook my head before I let go. Some wind fairies bustled inside their home. Most attended to the group of earth fairies that had just arrived. Others organized weapons, and still others eyed me darkly.

The wind soldier from earlier rounded a corner and saw us. "This way," he stopped before us and pointed farther in. I slowly followed his direction, and Fira hovered behind me. This home looked to be carved out of the very mountain itself. The passageways and stairs that we took were created of harsh lines of natural stone. The whistle of the breeze could be heard no matter how deep we went. The doorways and staircases were small, barely enough space for a wind fairies' wingspan.

I won't be able to fly in here. I'll have to rely on my feet. I glanced behind myself at Fira, my eyes briefly meeting the crabby guard's as he brought up the rear. She nodded for me to look forward, and I saw we had arrived at the healing area.

Many beds had been woven from dry looking plants and rested on soft sand. The sand had been scooped into a frame that had been carved out to give a notion of comfort for the ill. Wind fairies scuttled around as they bandaged fresh wounds and treated the earth fairies with charity. Only one bed held a wind fairy, earth fairies having taken the rest. I spied an additional bed that had been brought in. It looked to have been hurriedly weaved with the same dry materials. Princess Ela was in the bed farthest from the entry point, her face towards the far wall.

"Fira," I started, my feet starting to carry me to Ela, but the back of Fira's head had already entered my vision. I followed after Fira quickly, conscious of the sound of my feet on the cool raw stone floor. Fira knelt in Ela's view, but she did not shift. I sat gently on her other side, not wanting to rouse her.

"She's sleeping," Fira murmured. Fira stroked Ela's hair behind her ear and brushed her wings as if she was looking for a wound that still needed to be cared for. My chest clenched as I looked down at Ela's sleeping form, purple and black peeking out from her bandages.

"Your Majesty!" A startled gasp came from one of the wind fairies, and I turned to look over my shoulder. A tall man entered the room, his long hair slicked back efficiently and his wings held against each other tightly. Long, blue robes decorated his slight frame and gave him volume.

The man paid no attention to anyone in the room. His eyes roved until they landed on me. I scrambled up and offered a hand to Fira that she ignored. As the man strode toward us, whispers of, "King Notus," followed. The fairies bowed to him, earth and wind alike.

As King Notus halted in front of me, I tipped my head and bowed, my wings lowered and spread behind me with deep respect. His hand waved in the corner of my vision and I rose up.

"Queen Aethra has summoned you. All three of you," he looked over and behind me easily before he looked down at Princess Ela, her form still. "The Queen is currently preoccupied, but if your treatment is complete, you may come and wait with me."

"Thank you," I breathed out at the much taller fairy, intimidated by his height as he turned and strode away.

"I can come," Ela's quiet voice behind me made me take a half step to turn and watch as Fira kneeled down next to her. "I'll go," Princess Ela told Fira firmly before Ela turned to me. I nodded and offered her a hand to stand. Fira gave her her arm to hold, and the Princess slowly stood between the two of us while our guide watched.

"You'll stay," Princess Ela told her guard, who I hadn't noticed, who had risen from where he rested in the corner. "They need help treating our people," she calmly ordered him. I watched as the earth fairies that surrounded us relaxed as they heard her voice.

Queen Aethra entered the drawing room as a storm. The large doors bounced off the walls behind her as a small group of servants and advisors followed her. King Notus tipped his head as Fira, Princess Ela, and I rose and bowed politely. When my head rose, I looked up and saw the servants had flanked around the room, their eyes averted politely and heads tipped as they waited for orders.

Queen Aethra looked down at us. Her small eyes and closely cut hair made the severe expression on her face more intimidating. Every moment she stared down at us, which her tall height made easy, more blood slowed inside me from the feet up.

"The forces of the Death Queendom will attack my city at nightfall unless you stop them," Queen Aethra's eyes held mine painfully tight as she spoke loudly.

Fira and Ela shifted uneasily behind me as my feathers shifted uneasily. "What?" I asked. *All of them?*

"I have spoken to Princess Keres of the Death Queendom. Your sister informed me that if I give you to her, they will leave," Queen Aethra's tone remained firm, but her volume softened at the end.

"You can't!" Fira's outburst surprised me. I could hear her wings beat in agitation.

"Which do you prefer, one life lost or the many lives of my warriors wasted?" Queen Aethra pinned Fira with a poisonous look over my shoulder. A moment passed, and Fira let out a breath as she restrained herself and calmed. Queen Aethra turned back to me. "I cannot order someone who is not my vassal to go to Princess Keres. But I ask you to go," her hands tightened into fists, mostly hidden by the swells and falls of her elegant dress.

My eyes shifted around the room. We were surrounded mostly by servants with a few guards that stood around inconspicuously. *She could order us to leave her city and tell Keres which way we headed.* My core felt brittle as a dried twig, ready to snap. My insides shook as I contemplated my newfound confidence in my abilities. *I'm strong.* My faith in myself was a rock. *Rather than running away from Keres, I'll run towards her!*

"Keres' forces are likely exhausted and weak now," I turned a half step to address my companions. "Many would have had to remain at the Agee Tree to ensure the complacency of the earth fairies," I rationalized to them. *You would try to stop me otherwise, wouldn't you, Fira?* The Princess of Fire nodded along to me, and Ela looked at me with faith.

"You have never had to explain to a child why their parent will not be returning home," Queen Aethra's cold voice caused me to shiver. *I doubt Keres would allow anyone but herself to apprehend me.* I weighed the possibility of what Keres would do if she failed.

Cynthia thumped heavily on my back, eager. I took a step forward. "I'll fight," the Weapon began to pulse.

"You can't!" Ela gripped and pulled my arm so I'd face her. "It's too dangerous!" Her wide eyes begged me to change my mind. Fira's silent presence made me unsure if she approved of my choice.

"I have to," I put a hand over Ela's and untangled her from my traveling cloak. "It's my duty." I looked to Fira for reassurance, but her dark eyes and calm face offered me none. "I'll be okay," I promised Ela. My hand soothed over her arm before I turned to Queen Aethra.

The Queen grimly informed me, "You will leave in one hour."

We had been temporarily given spacious, connected quarters while we waited. I sat off to the side on one of the chairs while Ela sat at my feet. Fira stood, pacing occasionally, to my other side. I shifted uncomfortably. *Why would they decide to carve furniture from stone?*

"I told you it'd be uncomfortable," Fira snapped as she began to pace again.

"The floor is cold," Ela spoke up.

I'd rather be in this heinous chair than risk being in your path, I watched as Fira stomped on a small bit of gravel in the center of the room. The constant whistling of the breeze through this mountain refuge was starting to grate on my nerves. I rubbed at my ear, annoyed.

"Does your ear hurt?" Ela asked innocently from where she had begun to stack small, circular stones into a tower.

"She's going to be bloody soon. Why do you care?" Fira growled at our new friend.

"Fira," I warned, and she turned away with an upset noise.

"I can't believe you're turning yourself over," Fira's shoulders hunched, and I wondered if her wings would bristle had she been born with feathers.

"We don't have a choice," Ela defended me, voice soft.

"We can run," I couldn't hold in my gasp at Fira's statement. *The girl that always wanted to fight wants to run?* I blinked as Fira shot me a look over her shoulder. *And now I want to fight.* I watched as Fira leaned against the nearby stone table.

"No," I disagreed. Fira raised her eyebrow at me as Ela looked up. "I'm done with running." I looked down at my hand and made a fist. I held it out to show them. "I'm strong. Capable," my voice carried confidently, "And I'll be able to defeat them." I tried to raise Fira's spirit.

"All of them?" She looked at me skeptically.

"Keres won't let the others touch me," I relaxed my fist and looked down at my palm. "She's too.." I trailed off, unsure of my words.

"Cruel" Fira supplied.

"Masochistic?"

Fira and I snapped our heads to look down at Ela. "What?" We echoed each other. *How does she know that word?* We gaped at the innocent princess.

"Don't use that word," I told her brusquely.

"Who are you to order her around?" Fira strode over and grabbed a chunk of my hair. She began to yank on it repeatedly.

"Ow!" I complained, more annoyed than anything else.

"Stop!" Ela sprang up and tried to smack Fira's hand away from my hair. Instead, Fira hung on, and my head cracked as it hit the back of the chair.

"Ow," I stated, staring into nothing as I resigned myself to whatever was happening.

"Stop!" Fira complained as Ela, for some reason only the Goddess knows, lunged at her and bit her on the front of her shoulder.

"Let go," I insisted as I watched Fira cry out and start to yank at Ela's hair as well as mine.

Ela growled as Fira made to bite Ela but failed due to the angle.

"Ow," I reminded them, slowly becoming more invested in whatever their actions could be called. I made a startled noise as Ela reached up and grabbed Fira across the face.

"My eyes!" Fira finally let go of me to grapple with Ela's hands as they fell to their knees.

I gathered my hair around my shoulders as Ela wrapped around Fira with surprising dexterity. Fira clamped her hand down on Ela's side and Ela made a pained noise as her wings flapped frantically.

Fira instantly let go as Ela grasped at her side. "Sorry," Fira apologized.

"I'm fine," Ela insisted as Fira stood. Ela's big eyes turned to me while she stayed on the floor.

Queen Aethra and King Notus stood directly behind me at a distance. They were flanked by their personal soldiers as well as Fira and Ela. Behind my friends, the army of the fairies of wind stood in organized lines, armor and weapons ready for bloodshed should I renege on the deal.

Keres stood before me. She still stood shorter than me. She had not yet reached her full height. Her black wings, perhaps now greater in span than mine, were open wide in challenge as her yellow eyes split through me. Before her, I felt as weak as I had before, unable to lift my scythe. A child doomed to die by her younger sister's hand if not her mother's. I reached inside myself and tried to pull out that ominous figure that had appeared to Fira and Egan in the forest. Surely such a strong figure could support me.

I shivered. She smirked.

"I didn't think you'd come," her even tone was betrayed by the excited sparkle in her eye. She reached into the heavy, metal armor she wore and pulled forth a large black feather from behind the symbol of King Cole.

My mouth twisted as I recognized my own feather. I said nothing.

Keres' laughter was a bell in the wind at my reaction, and it pulled to the surface a distant memory of Liraz crouched next to me as I tried to hide in a corner, her hand soothing my back as she consoled me. *Keres had tried to take Cynthia then,* I recalled.

Keres' long, black hair was blown by the constant wind and passed over her face.

Reckless! I judged her loose hairstyle as I dropped into a crouch. My hand twisted around Cynthia, and I brought my weapon to slash at Keres as I lunged forward.

Keres' gasped and struggled to draw the traditional sword at her side. Cynthia was checked by the edge of the heavy blade. The mark of the Death Queen that had been stamped into the blade met my eyes.

I jumped back as Keres took a step forward and slashed at me, only able to because I had let up on Cynthia. Keres followed after me, obedient to the rage on her face. Every step she took, she thrusted her blade forward to try and pierce me. I continued to fall back and held Cynthia up and down as I used her to knock away Keres' blade.

She's living as the princess. Useless thoughts crowded my mind as Keres backed up a few paces and began to flap her wings for takeoff. I followed suit but thrust Cynthia into the ground for leverage.

I let go of my weapon as my wings caught the wind. Keres rose slower into the air than I did, but she was quick to fly between Cynthia and I. She tried to spear me again as I curved gracefully in the air, my feathered muscles allowing me maneuverability.

Keres growled after me as I flew higher into the sky to try and bait her away from Cynthia. The clouds were quick to greet me as they rested low today. I turned to see her flying after me, Cynthia in her free hand as she sheathed her sword. My eyes went wide with anger, and my feather bristled. A few more flaps, and I was above the top of the low clouds.

My lip curled as I suddenly flipped onto my back and held my wings out wide. Keres gasped at my reckless maneuver as she narrowly avoided flying into me. As she flew over me, her flowery scent forefront in my nose, my hand shot out and curled around Cynthia.

She's living the life I was born to have. Cynthia seemed to respond to my grasp and pulsated.

"Stop!" Keres screamed as our bodies became entangled when she refused to let go. The air felt heavy as we careened back down to the unforgiving ground. "Stop!!" She pleaded as we twirled around each other in a circle, her eyes shut tightly and her face scrunched up. "You'll kill us both!!"

My heart beat wildly in my chest as the ground approached. "Just let go!" I screamed over the wind at her.

"No! It's mine!" Her eyes abhorred me as she forced them open a crack.

I growled at her and beat my wings helplessly. Cynthia harmonized in our hands with the blood that sang of fear in both our veins. I let go of Cynthia with one hand and instead made a grab for Keres' sword. I unsheathed it through our tangled limbs and flapping wings. I sloppily plunged it into her side.

I gripped at both Cynthia and her as I spread my wings. I caught the wind, and I righted us just as the ground came up to meet us. My legs shook as I landed heavily, and I dropped Keres to the barren dirt and stone. Her hands slipped off Cynthia as she cradled her side. Her own sword still stuck out.

An odd, jealous pang in my chest echoed as I looked at the stamp on her blade. I stepped back. The sight of my sister left me conflicted. Her eyes looked up at me for a moment before she scrambled up and ran back to her host. Her army, halved in number and exhausted, stood messy in the far distance. *How much could they see?* My eyes burned as I watched Keres' shaking back and limp. I rubbed at my face, and my hand came away wet.

KERES

I stood before my new and improved army of fire fairies and death angels, my eyes and expression deadpan as I watched my deceased sister approach me in the distance. *The feather is true.* The red tint when held up to light was unique to her. As she approached, I saw how she had changed in her absence.

She was no longer that scared, terrified child that feared retribution. Instead, Phaedra had found her confidence. Her dark wings stretched out larger than mine, and her wild white hair was untamed as the wind grabbed at it. Her yellow eyes were calm as she took me in. I couldn't stop the smirk I gave when she shivered.

I reached into my freshly cleaned and polished breastplate to remove her feather and showed her. I held it up, smug. Her mouth twisted, and I laughed openly at the nostalgia that hit me.

Phaedra attacked me suddenly without warning. Her strikes were difficult to deal with. She would strike hard here but light there, and I overcompensated several times as I tried to match her. *When did she get so strong?! Is this Phaedra, the one who couldn't lift a Weapon?* My fury bloomed. *I'm supposed to be the strongest!*

I recalled Phaedra's poor flight as a child, and I flew up for leverage. She matched me despite the difficult, standing takeoff. My eyes narrowed as I saw her grip weaken on Cynthia — *my Cynthia!* — and I quickly dove between them and tried to claim the Weapon for myself. I sheathed my sword expertly as I flew.

Mother would be so proud if I brought Cynthia home! I clung to the scythe as I chased after Phaedra madly into the clouds. *It's your fault!* My eyes watered at the change in altitude. *It's your fault I had to kill those* — small bodies flashed across my mind, and Phaedra twisted midair dangerously. As I avoided flying into her, she grasped onto Cynthia midair.

We began to careened toward the earth. "Stop, stop!!" I finally spoke and begged her. "You'll kill us both!!" I tried to explain to the idiot what she was doing. My voice sounded like I was a child again, and she had failed to obey Mother. I squeezed my eyes shut.

"Just let go!" She shouted to me, and I shook my head.

"No! It's mine!" I screamed as I forced my eyes open a touch to glare at her. Unguarded, Phaedra took the sword from my hip and thrust it into me. A warm, wet feeling expanded on my abdomen. I released Cynthia to try and grasp the wound, to try and force it shut. *Mother can't know I was hurt!*

I hit the ground hard and the air left my body. I struggled to breathe as pain surged inside me. *Did she...angle me upright so I wouldn't hit my head?* A deep rage guided me to grip the sword still in me and slowly go to my feet. *It's her fault,* I believed. *All her fault.*

Me and Phaedra's eyes locked for a moment. *She's going to kill me,* I realized as a cold wind pushed at my feathers. I turned tail and scrambled to return to my soldiers.

Mother, I held my breath as I ran to try and not disturb my injury, *this is all your fault! Phaedra, stop Mother!*

PHAEDRA

My heart slowed as my tears faded. Cynthia calmed as I returned her to my back harness. A heavy weight lifted from my shoulders, and my knees met the ground with a loud thunk. *I beat Keres.* I could almost feel Liraz's comforting arm around my shoulders as she fussed over me.

"I beat Keres." Liraz's eager eyes watched me. "For the first time, I beat her," I told my lost friend, a tear falling to the ground.

"Come on," Fira was suddenly there and next to me where Liraz had been. Her firm hands guided me up with kindness. I practically melted into her as she ushered me back to the wind side. "We need to get inside the mountain in case that woman decides to stay."

I looked up at Fira as we made it to the others and Ela supported my other side. *Does she still wish she fought Keres, now and before?* My knees trembled as my sudden weakness worsened. *Does she still blame me?*

I found that I preferred one victory to one victory and one loss, and I did not ask.

Dear Sister,
I walked in on Her Majesty naked with her human friend in bed. I'm shocked!!! I left and Her Majesty called for me shortly after. She introduced me to her best friend, Max, and said I am to wait on Max as if she were Her Majesty. I don't understand what's going on, but I'm happy to be of service. Please see my extra bonus below. I think it might be for my silence, so don't tell anyone!!

Hazel

CHAPTER FOURTEEN

FIRA, ELA, AND I stood before the Queen and King of Wind, our heads tipped politely. Their thrones, carved from the stone of the mountain, had intricate swirls carved into them to represent the constant winds and weather of the territory. Behind them, a great quilt stretched ceiling to floor in the grand hall.

The quilt, curiously, showed figures separating to different places as they cried and mourned. *How depressing.*

As a well-dressed wind fairy stepped through the many advisors that hovered near their royalty to stand next to her queen. The little person, newcomer and last to arrive, was small of stature and stood below the Queen's waist. Queen Aethra waved away the niceties before she spoke. "Thank you for driving away the horde of the Death Queendom." We tipped our heads at her acknowledgement.

"However," she began, the warmth she had led with now noticeably absent, "why were you two in the Agee Tree?" She questioned us and ignored Ela.

I stepped forward as I addressed the Queen. "I am seeking a way to stop Queen Mara. We need to cross the water to Silver Top Island." I kept my head down and my wings tightly folded behind me.

"Why?"

I blinked and slowly looked up at Queen Aethra. "Why?" I asked. I didn't understand.

"Are you trying to stop your queen because the Queen of Death wronged you, or because the Death Queendom has caused so much pain and hatred?" Queen Aethra asked, her eyes quiet as she reserved judgment.

I paused to think.

"Are you willing to kill your mother if it is the only way to stop her?" Queen Aethra's eyes narrowed.

"I — I will," I cursed myself as I stuttered. The idea of plunging Cynthia into my own mother — queen —

"You need to harden your resolve," Queen Aethra judged, thankfully interrupting my thoughts. "But I believe you are the best answer for our current predicament due to your knowledge." I watched as she glanced over to the advisors that crowded around the steps and quirked her finger towards one of them.

An elderly wind fairy slowly took the steps. His joints audibly popped before he reached her. His hand rested on his back as he leaned down so they could whisper. After a quick conversation, the man tipped his head and slowly returned to his station.

"High to the northeast peninsula of Lake Lakira reside a people, fairies that live in communion with water and the ocean. They left the land after they were attacked by a dragon in the Campaign. I believe they are your best option for crossing the ocean."

"If they still exist," Ela whispered behind me, and I flicked a wing towards her.

"They do," Queen Aethra countered Ela's whisper. "To assist you by leading and brokering communication with the water fairies, I will send my own, Princess Wren." Queen Aethra's hand waved towards the nicely dressed wind fairy who had joined us last.

Princess Wren stepped forward, her flowing gown caught in a gentle breeze as she tipped her head to greet us. I returned the gesture as I evaluated her. She had her father's dark long, slicked back hair. She had her mother's ample build and grand set of wings. Her clear eyes, the trademark of many of her people, were quiet. *She'll be a vital asset.* I concluded, *if she really can broker between us.*

"Thank you for preventing unnecessary death," Princess Wren spoke to me directly. "You are admirable." She praised me, and I couldn't help the small, pleased flap of my wings behind me.

"I suggest you wait a few days for the horde to leave," Queen Aethra advised us. "I cannot help you beyond my borders. I still obey the old border laws, even if the Queen of Death does not." Queen Aethra's final statement was heavy with disgust.

WREN

Mother's interrogation of the death angel and fire fairy was interesting to watch. I knew firsthand what it felt like to be peppered by her questions, but I reserved my pity. *For them to travel so far,* I looked at the dried blood on them, *things must truly be in dire straights.*

"To assist you by leading and brokering communication with the water fairies, I will send my own, Princess Wren." My face didn't shift at the Queen's sudden announcement.

Sending me away? I discreetly looked at her. *To spend time with other races?* I judged silently. *I miss when things were calm and we were separate.* I looked down my nose at the Banished Princess.

I suppose it would be dangerous to keep all of the ruling family under one roof should the enemy invade, I made peace with the Queen's decision as I pulled apart ribcage of her reasoning to look inside at its heart.

PHAEDRA

The Queen of the Wind Territory had caught me off guard when she asked me to join her alone in her rooms. The scent of wine hung in the air, thick, as her staff poured me a drink from one of the many open bottles. Queen Aethra lounged nearby as she watched me with keen eyes.

"I apologize for my barbed words this morning," she apologized. The smoke of her pipe whirled around her playfully, and a sweeter smell invited me closer. I chose the lush davenport and fell into the cushions.

"I took no offense," I tried to appease her.

Queen Aethra made a face as she took a long drag off her pipe. "Now, that's not truthful," she judged me, and I felt caught like a red handed child. "The questions were out of place. And I was out of line," she warranted as she poured me a chalice.

"I'm not sure why I'm doing it," I savored the bitter wine and contemplated if the smoke would improve the flavor.

"Does it matter?" She questioned. I twirled my wine as I thought. "As long as it gets done."

"If the motivation was nefarious," I decided, "it matters."

Queen Aethra chuckled at my response as she readjusted. She brought her feet to the chair and perched as she drank and smoked. "Are you nefarious?" Her pleasant tone, and the way she closed her eyes while the wine slipped inside of her showed she already knew the answer.

"Heartpeak Fjord," Princess Wren helpfully pointed out to us as we crouched some distance away behind boulders that had scattered down from the high mountains behind us.

"This is a tight shoreline," Fira looked distinctly uncomfortable at how close the saltwater was to the base of the mountain.

"There's no one ahead," Ela's voice dropped out of a whisper as she looked back at us.

My hands pressed against the graveled rocks as I tried not to slip down and get wet. "We should move on," I advised as I reached out and gripped the boulder with my overly dry palm.

"This is the only break in the river that lines the Wind Territory," Princess Wren advised us once again. "We need to be cautious." She crept on her knees so that she hovered tightly behind Ela and could peer over the large rocks.

"Then we'll run across to there," I pointed to the trees across the border as the others glanced back at me.

KERES

I sat heavily, exhausted, upon the Earth Queen's throne. Bruno chatted in my ear incessantly while I blankly watched our soldiers give reports about what we now controlled.

"Your Highness, the Queen wanted her to be put down," Bruno's statement made me stop short.

"Take their Queen?" I questioned. The Earth Queen, who I had ordered take a seat in the corner and watch some time ago, watched while I decided what to do with her.

"Yes, Your Highness," he assured me as he leaned down to talk quietly in my ear. "She will be so pleased with this seizure," his eyes held dark promise.

We must take away their children and their Queen? I hesitated. She was gentle and hadn't put up a fight. Resigned, she had simply done as ordered. *She reminds me of Zelda,* I finally put my finger on what it was. "Do it," I whispered back to him. He made a sudden gesture towards Kane and Griffith, her guards, and they escorted her from the room in a hurry.

I turned my mind away from the Earth Queen as I contemplated my wound and Phaedra. *Why was my sister in the Earth Realm and Wind Territory?* I rested my hand in my palm as the soldiers resumed reading their reports aloud. *Is she trying to stop Mother?* The new hope in my chest was alien and only added to how uncomfortable I was.

The throne was hard and wooden. It reminded me of Mother's stone throne in the grand hall. *I don't want the crown,* I jolted at the thought. I waved Zelda off as she started to come attend me from the far wall. *Not if it causes whatever is wrong with Mother. Taking these other lands has been a mistake.*

PHAEDRA

Our group stood before the Telling Woods. The thin trees and pompous colorful plants looked suspicious even in the high sunlight. The terrain was familiar, but the humans Fira and I had traded with before were nowhere to be found.

"We shouldn't stay near the Earth Realm," Ela's big, glassy eyes were trained in the direction of the Agee Tree.

"The humans told us there's an angel eater in there," Fira interjected as Princess Wren took a step towards the cursed woods. Princess Wren turned and seemed frustrated as the rest of us failed to follow.

"They're cursed," I agreed with Fira.

"There's a rumor that strange things can be seen in there," Ela murmured as Wren's eyes fell on her last.

"Those are just rumors and human fairytales," Wren dismissed us. Her hand waved. I could practically see Queen Aethra where Wren stood.

"Princess Wren," Ela gently spoke up. "I do not recognize all of these plants. What if the plants farther in the forest are dangerous?" She asked cautiously.

"Typical earth fairy," Wren scoffed under her breath, and I was surprised. *Fairies treat each other like death and life angels?* "It's faster to go through than around," the wind princess addressed me now, her palm extended toward me as she tried to reason.

I frowned and looked at the overgrown foliage behind her. "We don't have time to spare," I relented. "We don't know how long it will take to find the Queendom of Water, assuming there is still a Queendom and they exist as one community." I turned to Ela and put a reassuring hand on her shoulder. "We shouldn't stay near the Earth Realm," I agreed with her. Ela's lips curved at the approval, but the haunted look in her eyes and the heavy slump in her shoulders remained.

Wren nodded before she turned and pushed her way into the forest. She shoved aside large, colorful leaves that swayed behind her. Fira followed after her as my hand pushed on the back of Ela, who hesitated. As Ela followed Fira, I gave a hard glance behind us as I settled into the rear.

These woods are so strange. I scoffed as Ela dodged below a tree limb that Fira had pushed out of her way and let swing back to hit me in the face. Fira snorted up ahead, and I held my tongue. *The less I distract, the faster the progress.*

Below my feet, odd, alien plants crunched or withered or pulled away almost in fright as I followed Ela. Some plants were light shades of red, others yellow. A smattering of blue plants here, various orange and pink plants there. Beyond the colors, the shapes of the plants were a shock to all of us, if Ela's continuous murmur was an indication. Some were vine-like, others large flowers. Some took up shapes similar to precious gems hewn from the earth, and others looked almost animal-like as they climbed on whatever was closest to them.

I flapped my wings aggressively as brilliant blue vines curled around my primary feathers, my heart in my throat. "It's almost like it's pulling us in," my whisper shot to the front of the group.

"Scared of some plants, bookworm?" Fira mocked me.

My lip curled as I fell silent. *Something isn't right.*

As we progressed, a new reality slowly sank in as my head grew heavy. Odd, foreign insects floated around and in between us slowly, in no rush. Some glowed brightly, others muted. Small animals avoided us when they could and scurried away in the underbrush and up trees when startled. I was only able to spy small glimpses of fur colored just as brilliantly as the foliage that surrounded us.

Wren wobbled around a large plant that blocked the deer path we followed, and Fira careened headfirst into it. Ela offered a hand to help her up, Ela's stance wide as she braced herself. I stared at them. My brain slowly clicked away as my thoughts ruminated. "I think we need to stop," my voice cracked, and the others looked at me as Fira brushed herself off.

Fira huffed and sat right where she stood in the middle of the trail, embarrassed at her clumsiness. Ela cautiously looked around before she slowly lowered herself and sat tightly next to Fira, curled into her somewhat. Wren gave me a long stare and ignored the other two.

"Calm down. It's obvious something is affecting us," Fira raised a hand and sloppily missed at grabbing Wren's clothes.

"All the better we should leave quickly," Wren relented as her face turned skyward.

I followed her gaze up. The sun did not peek between the leaves of the overcrowded canopy above us any longer. A small sound of clashing rocks drew my attention, and I turned to see Fira set a small, nearby pink bush ablaze. The alien plant took to fire quickly, and the warm press against my legs made me sink to the forest floor.

As we sat in silence and the heavy shadows crinkled around us, Wren finally broke. "We should have gone around," her eyes looked lazy in the firelight and matched the slump of her shoulders. I let her statement soak in as I stared into the small flames. Ela nodded almost unnoticeably.

Fira's head whipping around to look behind her as her wings battered the undergrowth in agitation stirred me from almost-sleep. "What's wrong?" I whispered to her above the snaps of the fire, unable to see into the dark beyond her through the flame's light. Ela turned to look as well, her tight fists on the dirt ground. Wren's hackles raised as Fira didn't respond.

"I thought I heard a jingling sound," Fira whispered to us. Her wings slowed as she peered into the dark.

Slowly, Fira turned back to the fire and stopped looking over her shoulder. Ela half laid down next to her and enjoyed the heat as Wren and I slowly relaxed. Wren had brought a well-beaten pack of playing cards with her and had introduced me to a popular fairy game. I frowned at the cards in my hand as I contemplated how badly I was losing.

Crack! Jingle jingle.

My wings shot out in alarm as I dropped the cards. I scrambled up and threw the others into chaos.

"Something's here," I told them, my hand behind my back as I tightly gripped Cynthia's staff. My companions drew their weapons, Fira her dagger, Wren her sword, and Ela favored her shortsword instead of her bow. I drew Cynthia as I stepped forward, and I wobbled as I failed to find my footing in the starless night. Cynthia pulsed in my hand, excited for battle, as I squinted into the woods. Slowly, I began to make out shapes as my companions shifted behind me.

Small things wavered around us, their forms only a suggestion of an individual. They easily danced across the foliage without touching it, but no wings flapped on their backs. They came closer before they twirled away as if trying to involve us in their delicate movements. My eyes pinned one in particular that gracefully danced towards us. Its odd, formless hands reached out as if asking us to join. It swirled closer to our group in a large jump.

"Ela!" I breathed in fright as it made to land above her head. I swung Cynthia above Ela as she shrieked and ducked. Her hands flew up to protect her face as I got a good gash on the strange creature. The creature shrieked with a high-pitched voice that grated my ears as it ran away.

Wren looked around wildly, "Why didn't I see them before?!"

Fira dumped wood into the fire that she had scavenged nearby. "We need to leave now," she urged me with wide eyes.

I nodded at her before I turned back to the darkness. "As soon as there's a break, we'll make a run for it," I instructed the others as I watched the remaining dancers for an opening we could all take. The other creatures continued to frolic as if their sibling had not been attacked. *Are they even alive?* My heart stressed as I saw they had no faces.

Another bounded towards us.

As the sun slowly tickled through the canopy, the dancers faded back to wherever they had come. I slowly lowered Cynthia, not sure if we were safe, as I hollowly stared into the beginning of the day. I was exhausted. *The group is exhausted.* I eyed them. Ela had fallen to one knee sometime earlier, and Wren was wavered on her feet. Fira's eyes met mine, reminiscent of the way she had looked at me while we crossed her desert.

"We couldn't defeat them," I growled out to myself. *I should have been able to defeat them, even if I don't know what they are!* The frustration made my skin itch.

"I can't, I need to rest," Ela pleaded, on her last legs.

"We don't have enough stamina," Fira panted. "Is this what happens to travelers here?" She gasped out as she half bent over to rest her hands on her knees.

"They come in here, have to camp because of the size of the forest, and get killed at night," I realized out loud. My companions looked at me, their eyes varying shades of exhaustion, fear, and sheer defeat. "We have no choice but to move on," I surmised. *If we stop to rest, we'll have to stay the night in these woods again.*

"I can't!" Ela wavered, defeated, and I lunged to catch her as she started to fall.

"You have to," I told her. I grasped her chin and turned her face towards me. "You have to," I made sure she heard me.

"Over — over there," Wren's heavy arm pointed towards a small pause in the plants. Beyond was a more used path.

I let go of Ela's face and ducked my head. "Let's go," I coughed and tried to work the dryness out of my throat. I helped Ela find her footing with a hand as we tried to walk to the new path. "We should be halfway through," I told the others, my tone false with renewed hope, as my foot landed on the more firm soil. *My feet feel like they'll split any second.* "We should be out before nightfall," I promised them nervously. Ela squeezed my hand as she slowly followed after Wren, who had already walked through the foliage, letting the thick leaves and strong branches scrape against her.

"What were those things?" Fira caught her breath next to me as I watched Wren's strong shoulders.

My mouth opened and closed. "Something beyond my under-standing," I squeezed Cynthia, thankful for her perseverance through the night, and replaced her onto my back. My feet thudded heavily as I caught up to Wren, and we followed the straight path. Wren's ragged breath was more noticeable next to her, and she caught my eyes as I glanced at her.

"I can keep going," she told me firmly. I pointedly did not say anything about the small tremor in her shoulders.

As we traveled on and the light grew brighter we walked on in silence, too exhausted to talk. I, occasionally, glanced back at Ela in between scoping out the woods on either side of us. She looked ex-hausted, her face dark as she suppressed her emotions. Her expres-sion made my gut twist as my hand accidentally knocked into Wren's smaller frame. *There's four of us now. It'll be okay.*

As I looked ahead once more, my eyes tight with sleepiness. I fal-tered as I saw an odd dark form tucked into the bushes and plants aside the path. "Hold on," Fira grunted with displeasure at my order as Wren huffed.

"What is it?" Ela asked, her voice light as I crouched down and gripped the object.

"It's a bow," my brow furrowed as I scanned it up and down. It wasn't broken enough to be discarded as trash, but it was used. My fingers traced over the carved markings. The small wood feathers matched my own down undercoat on my back. My head raised from my examination, and my heart stuttered with fear as I saw something familiar in the undergrowth behind a nearby tree. My body stilled as my breathing came slower, quieter.

"What's wrong?" Fira asked from behind me, closer now as curiosity prodded her.

"A hand," I whispered cautiously, and I heard the quiet draw of a blade behind me. I flinched as a twig broke next to me, and the back of Ela's head blocked my view. "Ela, stop!" I hissed, my mother's voice flying out of my mouth as I bared my teeth in fright.

Despite the others whispering similar threats, Ela stepped up as the hand didn't move and slowly stepped around the tree. I heard her suck in air in surprise as her hands flew up to cover her mouth. "Everyone," her soft tone belied her wide, alarmed eyes as she stared at her discovery. I slowly rose, and my knees clicked from fatigue. Wren and Fira delved off the path and through the plants until they could see. Fira hissed in sudden surprise as Wren stayed silent. Wren's horrified expression made my stomach drop, and I frowned at their reactions.

I slowly stepped around to see and understood perfectly. "Impossible," I quietly murmured. Before us, a child rested, curled up, atop a corpse. The deceased angel sprawled out, supported by the tree. His white wings slept on the ground at awkward angles. *A life angel.* The rotting flesh had yet to fall off and rub into the juvenile's feathers. The black fungus had yet to stain her skin as an undertaker's. The wide, cloudy eyes of the man stared hollowly at the canopy, his head upturned as if to beg for help. His wings had crumpled around him in death and made a sort of shelter.

The young girl's petrified eyes kept moving among the four of us, but she did not shake. Rather than meet her eyes, all four of us openly ogled at her wings. Rather than the child be a death angel or a life angel, she sat before us with two wings, one black, one white. Her skin was pale as if she had been in the woods for some time. Mud cooled atop her head and disguised her hair. *A halfbreed?* The crass thought was something I'd never considered nor heard of. *This is impossible. Angels don't mix. There's life angels, and there's death angels. What is she? Is she real?*

"This is harebrained. It's another trick of the woods," Fira's agitated tone made the child flinch.

"No," Wren disagreed. "It can't be."

I opened my mouth to agree with Wren when a high pitched whistle noise came from farther down the path, the way we had come.

"Hide," a tiny, hoarse voice pleaded with us. I looked down in abject horror as the child spoke. "Hide!"

Fira yanked on me, and I fell into the undergrowth as Wren and Ela hid behind two nearby trees. *She talked.* I watched the small edge of the path that I could see through the large pink leaves as my thoughts collapsed. I flinched as something brushed up and pressed into my side opposite Fira, and my wide eyes saw the child shake as she wrapped her wings tight around herself.

Dear Sister,
Max visits frequently, at least once a season. Since I am her Appointed, I've been privy to Her Majesty's and her conversations. Max told Her Majesty that Princess Phaedra is ill and will turn out like her father. Do you know, did the Queen have a husband?

Hazel

Chapter Fifteen

A SMALL SHUFFLE ON the path drew my attention away from the child. My slowly blurring vision revealed first a cloak shuffling along the ground, then a single, dark foot as someone stepped in front of us. My brows drew together as I recognized the same eerie starlight quality the creatures from last night held. With extreme slowness, the creature raised its four-toed foot and made its way down the path as it whistled occasionally. I shivered as it passed from my vision.

"It's okay to be scared," the child whispered to me, barely audible. *I'm scared of you,* I wanted to stress back. *You shouldn't exist!*

When the creature had, eventually, made its way far enough down the path we could no longer hear it or see it, Wren made a show of emerging from behind the tree as Fira, Ela, the child, and I uncovered ourselves. "Who are you?" Wren's heavy tone made the little girl take a step back. She pressed her surprisingly frail body against me, her old dress sticky on my arm.

"I'm — I'm Twila," the little girl slowly whispered. She sounded as if she hadn't spoken in days.

"What happened here?" Wren glanced at the fallen, well-dressed life angel.

"He was an emissary," I spoke up. Fira's eyes pinned me with an odd undercurrent of emotion. "I don't know him. But his uniform is similar to the emissaries of Queen Mara," I tried to explain myself. Fira didn't react and instead turned, unblinking, to the child.

"But what happened?" Wren stressed and shifted uncomfortably.

"Did you come here with the army?" Ela's tone was warm and gentle as she tried to prompt the child to speak. Wren's eyes narrowed as the little girl didn't open her mouth. I crouched down and gently engulfed the tiny child's bony shoulders in my hands.

"It's okay," I reassured her as she turned to hide her face in my shoulder. "I've got you," my eyes wet as I imagined the stress she must be going through.

Twila shuddered in my arms before she whispered to me. The other three crowded around as the child spoke. "I...was traveling with Mom and Dad." A small sob. "We were walking through the forest." Her tight little hands scratched my arms and neck as she wrapped her arms around me. "And that thing attacked us," her voice went up in pitch as she shivered in fear. "It — it can't go off the path. But it got them," she sniffled, and my body tensed as I realized she was going to wail loudly.

Ela bent down to rub Twila's back comfortingly. "Where is your mom?" She asked quietly.

"A — a bunch of death angels took her away," Twila's nose wet my neck as she turned to look at Ela. Twila sniffed helplessly as Ela opened her arms to offer a hug. "They took Mom!" The child's wail was muffled as she accepted Ela's embrace, and Ela pressed Twila's open mouth into her shoulder. I pinched the bridge of my nose and looked down as I tried to hide my own emotions.

"We can't stay here," Wren urged.

"Mom didn't — Mom didn't move," Twila wheezed into Ela with painful gasps. "It got her." The child's knees buckled as she began to sway with exertion.

"We need to escape," Wren's statement urged me to stand and flap my wings to show my strength.

"Take us!" The child latched onto Ela as Ela started to stand. "Take me and Dad out of these awful woods!" Twila pleaded, her small fists locked into Ela's traveling cloak.

My eyes met Ela's, and I knew she wanted to accept Twila's request. I looked to Wren, who looked to me for direction. I glanced at Fira before I looked up to the canopy to see how much sunlight was left. They followed my eyes. "How long until we're out of the woods, by your mark?" I asked Wren.

Wren stepped in between Ela and I and blocked Twila from hearing as we spoke. "We might make it out before sunset if we leave now," her stress lines worsened as she continued to urge me.

I stepped around Wren and in front of Fira before I crouched down behind Twila. From behind, I untangled her surprisingly strong fists from Ela. Twila turned to me, and I saw fear and pain racing inside her eyes. I took a large, calming breath in before I spoke to her, careful to keep my tone even and calm. "We might not make it out even if we leave now. I know that your mom and dad would want you to come with us and survive." Twila's eyes bubbled up with tears as she struggled to breathe from her panic. "I don't know how you survived for so long in here on your own," I admitted.

Twila turned away from me and grabbed Ela's hand as I stood back up fully. "I'm ready," Twila sobbed. The coal inside my heart burned in spite of my calm exterior. I stepped out of their way as Ela guided Twila to the path. Twila cautiously stepped onto the trail. Fira and Wren followed as Ela led Twila down the path. I watched as the child turned to stare at the tree her father rested behind. At the last second, Twila's eyes glanced at me as I hung back in the foliage.

"Watch out for that odd traveler," Fira cautioned Ela as they walked.

When the child was out of sight, I was quick to take a few steps and crouch next to her father's deceased body. "I'm sorry," I murmured as I plucked feathers from his wings. "We've nothing else to trade for food." The stash of money Princess Wren had been given by Queen Aethra would last some time, but our journey had no end in sight.

Twilight swaddled us warmly as we stood some ways out of The Telling Woods. The four of us stared into its abyss as odd shapes danced this way and that, their arms outstretched as they tried to beg for us to return. The creatures danced serenely as I hissed lowly at them. Before us, Twila bowed to the woods, her tiny, fledgling wings outstretched awkwardly as she spoke. I averted my eyes as I gave her privacy.

"I wish I could have said goodbye to Mom," the child's final statement punctured my heart, and I turned away completely and instead pretended to size up the direction we were headed.

When her tiny footsteps stopped behind me, I turned to look down at Twila. I kneeled as I brought my small side pack around and rooted inside of it for a moment. "Here," I told her as I brought out two large white feathers.

Twila's face lit up in recognition as she took her father's largest primary feathers. "Thank you," she wheezed at me as she looked at them with awe, the tear stains on her face reigniting as twilight pinched at her face. Before I could stand, she had wrapped her strong little arms around me, and I felt something in me stall. *Is this how tiny I had been as a child?*

When I was released, I stood and rubbed at Twila's head only to quickly withdraw my hand and make a face as I rubbed the mud onto some nearby grass. Twila sniffled as Wren began to lead us to the general direction of the Swampy Marsh.

"Phaedra," Fira's voice stopped me, and I turned to see her looking towards The Telling Woods. I stepped close to her and followed her eyes to see the odd forms had changed. The creatures stared at us emptily, not moving. I shivered and brushed against Fira reassuringly as I turned to follow after the others.

The soft, gentle, lush grass stroked my feathers as we rested on the edge of the Teacup Hills. We sat in the shadow of one of the small hills. Large, lazy clouds drifted overhead. I stared at Twila and Ela, my wings stretched out as I soaked up the beautiful day. Twila had captured Ela's attention and avidly talked while they braided the long grass. My heavy eyes settled on Twila's wings.

I shook Wren off my wing as she tried to lean back onto it and her hand pressed in painfully. "Sorry," she murmured and adjusted herself to sit up fully, still on watch duty. She always volunteered to work when her smaller frame and limbs became swollen and needed rest. I flicked my wing towards her in acknowledgement while my eyes shifted to the clouds above. "It's difficult to travel with a child," Wren spoke to me quietly, and I slowly blinked. "Difficult."

Fira hummed in agreement from where she had sprawled out nearby on her stomach.

"We haven't come across any angels to hand her off to," I stated to Wren, thankful she hadn't voiced her opinion up until now. With the addition of Twila, we had been forced to rest half way through each day and to stop for camp sooner than we liked. Her child's wings were too small to carry her, and she easily fell behind as we walked. "If she would even be safe with other angels," I added as an afterthought as I allowed my eyes to drift closed.

I could feel Fira frowning at me as Wren spoke. "In The Telling Woods, why didn't you fly ahead and leave us behind?" She asked. Her vulnerability surprised me, and I peeked under my lashes to see her sitting facing steadfast away from me.

"I'd never force someone to endure something like that alone, if I can help it," I answered easily and watched as Wren's shoulders shifted slightly with curiosity. As my mind began to drift again, relaxation carried me away. I could almost feel Liraz's arms around me as I huddled in a corner of a training room, future bruises blossoming on my skin. *We had been so small.* I rolled onto my side to watch the child.

Clear skies stretched out beyond our heads to the edges of the world. Occasional clouds dusted high above where angel feathers couldn't reach. Before us, scattered lakes, lagoons, and ponds pooled on the northeastern peninsula. Lake Lakira stretched out in the distance to our side, and the shock of Egan's face briefly appearing in my mind made me flinch away.

"There's moss everywhere," Ela remarked as she crouched down to rip some up. Fira wrinkled her nose as Ela sniffed the plant before she squeezed it. Droplets fell from Ela's fist. I frowned as Ela tucked the moss inside the leather bag over her shoulder. The earth princess stood and seemed surprised at Wren's deadpan expression. "We can eat this," she stated confidently.

"It looks like it's spread to the whole peninsula," I remarked. The spongy green plant was thick under our feet and pulled at my feathers whenever I let my wings droop.

"It's going to grow over us," Twila fretted, her wellspring of energy replenished after our last break. Fira put a hand on the child's head but didn't say anything.

"What now?" My question caught Wren off guard, and she blinked at me.

"We look for the water fairies," Wren answered easily, her chest and wings puffed out in confidence. She began the trek through the streams, and I followed closely behind. The sunlight keenly jumped off the water into my eyes, and I covered my face somewhat as I tried to see beyond into the depths. So far, the wildlife had been much more plentiful than the northern peninsula which the Dragon's Den resided on. The shadows of fish played around us, interacting with each other and sometimes falling still as they examined us just out of reach.

Ela brought up the tail of our party quietly as she guided Twila to walk in front of her. "The water fairies, what do you know of them?" Her gentle voice was carried easily to Wren and I despite the breeze that fluttered over us.

"There's a rumor," Wren hesitated. "That when Queen Aethra was my age, she took a lover who was a water fairy," Wren glanced back at us to gauge our reactions before she continued on. "They say the water fairies live in a palace where water is always running," she trailed off.

Where the water is always running. I contemplated the legend as I spied seashells moving. Their spindly legs dragged them around inside the water and on the waters' edges. I purposefully stepped around one that had dragged itself up onto the moss and half pointed it out to Fira, who followed behind me. Fira let out a tight noise as she awkwardly maneuvered around it.

"Mom said the water fairies are all dead," Twila's blunt statement made me frown and half glance back at her calm face before I settled my eyes on the back of Wren's head. A tight sensation curled in my chest as I brought my wings tightly to my back.

As we walked, we started to examine each body of water closer. We'd take turns flying up over it and try to look in while the rest would peer over its edges. The wildlife would often stare back at us as if we were the odd ones. When the fish and other water dwelling creatures had their fill of us, they'd turn in a flash of brilliant color and flit deeper into the waters. We hadn't seen any other humans, angels, or fairies so we fell into a cautious relaxation. Our voices grew as we walked from hushed tones to loud, voracious laughter as we joked and discussed what the water fairies might be like.

"Maybe they ride sea serpents!"

"Can they do magic?"

"I bet they can talk to mermaids."

"Can they breathe underwater?"

"They must be wet constantly from living here."

Voracious laughter.

Despite our calm, we rested without campfires. I sat cross legged at the edge of the circle the others slept in, my eyes adjusted to the starlight and glow of the nocturnal water life as Twila snored easily in my lap. I turned my head to look far into the distance, thankful for the flat terrain that made my job easier.

My eyes fell to Fira's sleeping form, and I watched as she breathed evenly. In, out. In, out. *She hasn't complained at all since Egan passed.* His memory weighed heavily in my chest. *She's even enjoyed these fantastic ideas we've been spitballing,* I held in a chuckle.

I turned to look the other way as the tightness in my chest bore down on me, eating greedily from my desperation. *We need to find them soon.*

A delicate yet intense fog rested on us. The moisture gathered in between my feathers and inside my clothes and weighed me down. My flutter was quiet as they trudged on behind me. Wren fell to the back as she insisted upon examining the smaller pools that now surrounded us.

"What's that?" Fira gripped my shoulder to stop me and pointed to the deep fog. I narrowed my eyes as I focused on the dark shapes.

"It's not moving," I murmured to myself as I tried to decipher the spherical structure. My resolve fell into my feet as I placed the familiarity I was feeling. I shivered against an imagined cold breeze. "The Dragon's Den," I whispered to myself. Heavy shame pressed me down into the spongy earth, the moss eager to accept my still-warm corpse.

"The ocean!" Wren's voice startled me, and I spun on my heel as Fira let go of my stiff shoulder.

"We're at the end of the peninsula," Ela realized with wide eyes as she grabbed onto Twila as the child made to walk towards the presumed edge of the land.

I opened my mouth but no words came out. The others looked at me expectantly as my mind sputtered and turned over. *I failed.* Naturally, my eyes went to see Fira's reaction. I couldn't stop myself from seeking her approval and felt sick when I saw her dark expression.

My mouth closed and opened once more as I struggled to come up with a solution. "We'll head south and check the west side of the peninsula," I ordered, doing my best to keep my tone calm and unshaken. *We only checked the east side before. There's still a chance.*

"Good idea," Wren acknowledged and immediately began to walk as southerly as one could with the sun still hidden in the mist. The others followed her confident stride, but Fira remained stock still.

I stayed with her but didn't speak. My thoughts sped up and became even more frazzled. I felt as though I trailed behind Queen Mara once more after another session of being unable to keep Cynthia in my grip. Spindles grew into my heart and poked at me sharply as I averted my eyes from the former Princess of Fire.

There was a sharp tug on my cloak, and I made a gasping noise as Fira's hand tightened around my collar and clothes as she lifted me up. The tips of my feet sank into the moss unhelpfully as she snarled at me. Our eyes met. Her iron eyes blazed into my bruise-yellow ones. Then she thrust me away, and I fell hard and awkwardly onto the ground. My elbow dug into my wing painfully. I caught my breath as she walked off to follow the others without looking back.

We wouldn't be out here if not for me, I blamed myself. *She wouldn't have been reminded of Egan if not for me.*

Dear Sister,

Queen Mara has birthed a second girl heir. I'm not sure who the father is but a blessing nonetheless. Her Majesty favors this child over Phaedra. I have concerns that Max may be the root cause.

Hazel

Chapter Sixteen

The starlight calmed my nerves as it hugged the gently rolling lagoons around us. Ela was on watch, and I had been caring for Twila as she refused to settle down to rest. Her small feet carried us away from the others as she went on about the water life, the brilliant glowing fish that caught her eye. She held my hand tightly, and I bent down awkwardly to hold her hand back as she led me in a confusing pattern.

Please let this tire you out, I thought as I felt a sting in my back. Twila stopped at where two ponds met and crouched down. She forgot about me as she crouched down to stare at the fish. I frowned as they turned to state back at her. *Unnerving,* I decided and averted my gaze to enjoy the scenery.

I looked at a tree stump in the distance and enjoyed the way the starlight reflected off of it. It almost looked like the water had reached up into the air and stopped moving. The stump shifted, and my eyes dropped to its bottom to search for the animals that disturbed it. *I miss animal meat,* I longed.

My feathers ruffled as I saw something small shift. *No bigger than a foot. And Ela has the bow right now.* I sighed as the figure shifted. Something in me pulsed. A warm, tingly sensation raced through me from my fingertips to my wingtips, a gentle whisper in my ears. I swallowed.

A figure? I realized as they stood. What I had mistaken as a log was a volume of hair so great it reached almost all the way to the ground. The person then fell, and a loud, distant splash was heard. I jerked forward reflexively as if to catch them.

"Was someone there?" I jumped slightly as Twila startled me with the soft tone Wren had been teaching her. I looked down at her and purposefully relaxed before I smiled at her.

"Let's go back," I gently ordered.

We roused the others from their deep, comfortable slumber. Twila woke up Fira as I gently shook Wren. "What's happening?" Wren asked blearily. Fira echoed the question as she rushed to her feet.

"I saw someone," I said as I stood. I offered Wren a hand up as I looked to Ela, avoiding Fira's eyes. "Over there," I nodded into the dark, and they followed my eyes.

"Let's go," Wren stashed her meager belongings in a hurry.

"Right," Fira agreed and readied herself as well.

"A good night to be on watch," Ela remarked as she picked up Twila's pack we had just started to get her to carry on her own. I side-eyed the child as she pretended not to notice Ela carry her items. Ela's still packed pack was nestled over her free shoulder.

I slipped my belongings over my back as I led the group in between the bodies of water to where I had seen the person. The moss was extra spongy here, and Ela confirmed it had recently been soaked from interference. We all looked into the lake before us.

"This is the largest one so far," Wren commented as she stepped closer to the edge.

Fira agreed with a quiet hum.

A small fire burned inside me. Hope. "We'll stay until they return," I commanded confidently.

At this, Ela dropped her pack and made herself comfortable to continue her watch.

"Right," Fira agreed readily but anxiety still scratched at my insides. She hadn't addressed me since the incident. "Did you see wings?" She asked as she sat and made herself comfortable.

"I didn't," I admitted uneasily. "But they dove into the lake." I gave Wren a pointed look so that I could avoid looking at Fira.

"Humans don't swim well," she stated before settling down.

"Twila," Fira said sharply as the child started to yawn. "Lay down. You've been driving Phaedra mad." Fira laid back with her arms behind her head.

"I have?" Twila looked between us with large eyes.

I patted a spot between Wren and I as I slowly sat down, my back twinging. "Come here," I insisted. *You will sleep one way or another tonight,* I promised mentally as I saw her kick at nothing with her feet, a telltale sign she wanted to resist.

The figure haunted my thoughts to the point the others noticed my forgetfulness. *It was a her,* I affirmed myself silently. *She had been...* I hardly had seen her at all. Her swaying hair, her sudden falling forward

—

"Wash your hands," Fira checked me with a hard tap on the head as I went to grab the knife to descale the fish we'd shot. I frowned and dropped the knife, and my wings brushed against Fira as she walked away from where I crouched.

I sighed and rose and made my way to a pool of water somewhat far from the others to clear my head. My feet squished into the wet moss distinctly, and I crouched down with my hands outstretched.

She —

Wide, blue eyes met mine. A button nose, a slightly open mouth. The blue water swirled dramatically around the woman — *that's not the water swirling, that's hair!* I realized with a gasp and frightfully jerked back. Before my hands cleared the surface of the water, her slightly larger yet slight hands gripped both of mine. My tense form was pulled into the water, and I squeezed my eyes shut and flapped in protest. My heartbeat was a drum in my chest. Fear wrapped around me like water plants.

My legs kicked out uselessly as I broke my hands free. I squinted and struggled harder as I realized the light and see-through water that had been around us had started to give way to a deeper, more suspicious color. The woman before me observed my terror-stricken face and actions with calm.

I lost air involuntarily in bubbles as she reached out towards my face. I made to jerk away, but the deep water held me still as the soft pads of her fingers caressed my face. She seemed as though she was one with the water as she maneuvered herself closer to my face. I closed my eyes in fear as she overtook my vision.

Something soft pressed against my lips and all my actions ceased. My mouth twitched from the ticklish sensation as I tried to under-stand what was happening over the noisy clatter inside my mind. Her lips pressed against mine more firmly as her hand slipped around the back of my head.

My heart slowed. My body relaxed as I felt my mind slip. *Cynthia?* I wondered at the odd sensation. In my mind's eye, I was taken far away from this time and place. I was a long-forgotten royal meeting the princess of another Queendom. I was a human woman serving dinner to another with blue eyes. I was a library servant meeting a general. I was a dragon meeting a dentist. I was a woman traveling the stars meeting with the leader of a warring faction. I was, simultaneously, all of these lifetimes and none.

I was Phaedra, the Banished Princess of Death, being dragged underwater by a woman with impossibly long hair the color of waves and blue eyes. My heart was both more full than it had ever been and more empty than I had ever comprehended before.

I looked at this woman as we slowly parted. My hand came up to brush against the long bang that hung over her left eye and face. She looked away from me and up, distracted, and I felt a spasm of pain in my chest. The woman's eyes widened before she looked at me once more. She hesitated before she turned and the water carried her away like one of its creatures. I looked up to see what startled her and saw hands reaching out for me.

My lungs burned as reality returned, and I grabbed the hands and was pulled onto shore. I spluttered pathetically as I was dragged some distance from the water. "Ela —" I coughed pathetically as she helped me to sit up and thumped on my back hard.

Water spilled out of my mouth as I slowly recovered. My wings pathetically shifted as I tried to shake the water off of myself in a feeble attempt to straighten my thoughts.

"What happened?" Wren's face was distinctly close as she bent over, her light eyes a firm gust that went through me.

"She was dragged under by someone. I didn't get a good look," Ela looked between Wren and the water's edge. The hand on my back rubbed gentle and comforting circles between my wings.

I took a deep breath before I trained my eyes on the ground. "She kissed me," my voice was hoarse.

"What?" Ela balked next to me. Wren stood straight, arms over her large chest, and took several steps back. Fira echoed the confusion and knelt closer to give me an even look.

"How sharp were those rocks you hit your head on?" Wren nervously laughed. I frowned at her joke and squeezed the skin of my high chest. I felt as though I had lost something, as if I'd left a wing in the water accidentally.

LANA

I stared from under the water as the fairies and angels fell asleep on land with my fellows. While we patiently waited for an opening, I ruminated. *Why is Mother bringing these strangers down to us? Unheard of.* I leered at their feathered appendages. The smaller looked to have lost one wing and another ill-matching wing sewed on. The way their feathers moved with their faces and emotions unnerved me.

The act of going to the surface was forbidden. My soldiers oggled, all of us tense as we stayed alert for danger. *These beings are too different,* I decided as two of the fairies wandered off. *I'm scared of them.* I admitted to myself, and I balled my hands into fists.

Why would Mother want to learn from them? I shook lightly. I wanted to turn tail and head back to what I knew, what was comfortable.

PHAEDRA

I grumbled to myself and kept my head down. I knew what came next after Twila's innocuous question.

"You'll have to ask Phaedra. She knows best about taking a quick bath," I could hear the smile in Fira's words and kept sharpening Cynthia evenly. Cynthia didn't need it, she never needed it, but I hadn't been able to do much else around camp without being heckled by the others for falling in. I frowned out of frustration and assumed my expression was hidden.

"Phaedra —" Twila bumbled over to me as she jumped up and down as she tried to fly.

"Fira —" I started and began to turn around, exasperated at my friends' badgering.

Splash! Thud! Thud! Thud!

Out of the water, beings leapt up and around us. I dove to cover Twila with my body, unable to get Cynthia out of more than a low guard as they pointed their spears at us. Twila stared at Cynthia's blade with huge eyes.

"Wren!" Ela startled as the Princess of Wind was shoved to her knees from where she had stood guard. Ela was pushed down next to her.

"I'm fine," Wren grunted. Her eyes took in the soldiers slowly. They wore scale armor as if they were fish. No wings adorned their backs.

Fira met my eyes as she slowly knelt next to me and gave me a small nod, a spear at her throat. My wings bristled with anxiety as one of the strangers stepped out. She was young but not young enough to stand out as a leader. She was lanky, her short hair a dulcet blue. She too had a spear, but it remained aimed at the sky as she crouched down in front of me to meet my eyes. Twila grunted as I pressed her into the ground and hoped her wings weren't obvious.

I remained still. Twila's breaths pressed into me as a reminder for why I shouldn't lunge at the enemy. The woman looked into my eyes, unblinking. "Come with me," the woman ordered. Her spear tipped down as she stood. I grimaced at her weapon but relaxed slightly when she pointed it to the lake that they had come out of behind our group.

I risked a small look closer as the water swirled suspiciously. Something rose from the water, and I watched in confusion that slowly turned to horror as I took in what happened. A beast larger than any I had ever seen had risen before us. The skin of the serpent was old, scarred, and darkened in places, but we could all fit several times over comfortably inside of its gaping mouth.

My hands flew to cover my nose as I smelled the odor of rotting fish. The serpent was a deep green, its eyes faded and white. Large fangs were still as it waited patiently as we failed to hurry into its waiting maw to be the next meal. As my eyes watered, the brilliant lights that bounced off the jewels and adornments on the serpent caught my attention.

"Who are you?" I slowly rose to my knees to unveil Twila. *If they wanted us to be dead, we'd have died already.* The woman that had almost drowned me pulled at me like a siren from afar. *Can I see her again?*

The woman's eyes shifted to her companions as she made sure we were secured and unable to escape. "I am Lana, Prima Filia of Lakira's Oasis," her melodic voice was strong and confident despite her hesitance.

Dear Sister,

Princess Phaedra is healthy and well. Her Majesty has ordered that none talk to her as it will distract from her studies and training. The younger Princess Keres is growing like a weed, and she shows leaps and bounds every day. Max visits less often than she used to, so I have time to train the newest maid, Liraz. I hope she takes to the calling quickly. I've noticed Her Majesty pits her girls against each other. I think it's in hopes Phaedra will grow faster. Princess Keres is developing a sharp tongue.

Hazel

Chapter Seventeen

I stumbled off of the spongy tongue and gagged involuntarily as I wavered on the firm concrete. Twila clutched on to me as she cried. My hands tightened around her. Fira, Ela, and Wren rushed out after I exited. Each coughed as they suffered from the breath of the serpent. The people that accompanied us inside of the serpent's mouth followed slowly. They looked distinctly more green around the gills than their counterparts who now stood around the serpent.

I cleared my airway one last time before I shuddered and looked around. "Where are we?" My eyes narrowed as I looked behind the serpent. As it closed its mouth and shook its head, almost as if in distaste, I noticed that it seemed to be resting on a wall. Beyond the silver bricks beneath our feet, there was a sudden dropoff and a dark, dark blue. The wall of blue wavered as the serpent slipped farther back into it voluntarily before it slipped away with frightening speed.

"My ears hurt," Ela whimpered behind me.

"I'm dizzy," Wren warned us.

Fira gave a few spluttering hacks as I slowly turned to look at what was behind us. The military officers from earlier looked far more comfortable as they stood at attention behind Lana the Prima Filia. But what captured my attention instead was the expansive, glowing, castle behind them. My mouth parted as my grip on Twila loosened. I blinked as Twila took the opportunity to start to pull on me, and without thought I lifted her up and rubbed her back. She sniffled into my neck, her tears cold.

Stones of blue coloration formed the ancient architectural marvel. A myriad of shades, celeste, iris, periwinkle, powder blue, an unimaginable number, complemented each other to create a supreme pearl cloistered in the darkness that encased it. Odd plants grew around the castle, as if trained with purpose. Their gentle glows added an abyss one could easily be lost in.

"Welcome to Lakira's Oasis," the Prima Filia looked smug as she raised her hands to show off her grand home.

"Are you human?" My quiet question was on account of my stolen breath.

The Prima Filia frowned at me, displeased. "Come with me." She began to walk into the grand archway behind her and only stopped to exchange brief words with a guard.

Our weapons, I watched with longing as he carried Cynthia, Ela's shield and shortsword, Fira's dagger and sword, and Wren's bow and sword. I tried not to stare and briskly followed behind the Prima Filia as we were once again surrounded. The halls of this castle were large. The ceilings soared above. Despite their welcoming size, they were nerve-wrackingly empty. Occasion scuffles and small sounds could be heard, but other than the few guards we passed the farther we entered, no one greeted us.

I slyly examined a guard we passed from the corner of my eyes as I continued to comfort Twila. This guard was dressed differently than the ones we followed. His armor appeared to be some kind of dried leather hide, and he bore no weapons. I looked to the guards that flanked our leader. *Tailored,* I evaluated, *unlike a common guard's.* I looked between the Prima Filia and her warriors. *No difference in armor. Are they on equal standing?*

We slowed to a stop before two great doors. *White Wood?* I marveled at the rarity and felt a pang for Cynthia. The Prima Filia slowly pressed the two doors open until they opened on their own. I trailed behind her and fell back to walk closer to my fairies as I considered.

Before us, the grand hall sparkled. Every surface was illuminated and radiant, the grand colors of water both uplifting and threatening. I squinted up at the ceiling and covered my eyes as I frowned. A momentous plant had overtaken the ceiling, assuming there had ever been one and they had not simply built under the life. Light spilled from the being, and the room was illuminated in startling detail.

On the far wall, a large quilt hung floor to ceiling. It depicted the petals of the Goddess, united, as they fought against one of the lesser goddesses.

The throne of the room rose high above us. As we approached, I admired how sea plants had been interwoven with the stone in such a way to compliment the Queen who sat in it. Her blue hair cascaded down, down, down nearto the ground. Her long bangs covered the left of her face. She watched me warmly as I stopped before her, my eyes captured by her radiance. Her attire, a simple white dress, was doing more than I could ever hope to achieve. I swallowed nervously.

"I'm happy you were able to make it," her voice was deep, strong, and feminine. Her eyes, the same blue as the deep sky no one reasonable would ever dare fly near, blinked slowly. I tuned out of the simultaneous looks my group gave me as the Prima Filia stood next to the throne. *Ah, her daughter,* though no age would ever be able to diminish the woman before me.

Twila sniffled, and I slowly slipped her from my arms. *You don't know this woman — this Queen,* I tried to reason with myself over how I felt guilty hiding the child.

The Queen smiled gently at me, and the feathers on my wings slowly started to stand up in a strange excitement. "When I saw you at the surface in the distance some time ago, I had been shocked," she spoke evenly. "When you camped next to my Lake Lakira, I couldn't help my curiosity," she chuckled, a bell-like noise.

My lips tightened and stretched as I remembered almost drowning. At this, the Queen raised a hand to pretend to hide her laughter as she grew louder. "I didn't know what to do when you saw me!" She smiled large as she read my mind. Slowly, the Queen settled. Her eyes darkened as she looked down at me, and my heartbeat thrummed in my veins. "I'm sure you all understand what must happen now," her ominous voice echoed in the empty hall.

Wren grabbed my arm from behind, and I shifted back a step as we formed a protective circle around Twila. *Is she going to hurt us?* The possibility didn't seem real to me. *How do I know her so well? Do I even know her?* I forced my body to listen and started to purposefully lay my feathers back down.

"We're not barbarians," the Queen told us after the guards failed to react. "We're not going to kill you," she sounded exasperated as we didn't relax. "You will never be permitted to leave Lakira's Oasis. It has been over a century since a water fairy has revealed themselves, let alone the castle. We prefer to be forgotten by the dry world and its troubles," she explained.

The Queen of the water fairies. I looked her up and down before I began to examine the other water fairies. *Where are their wings?* I frowned. *Are they hiding them?* They appeared to be humans.

"Your Majesty," Wren spoke up next to me and dropped into a bow as the Queen looked to her. "I am Wren, Princess of the Wind Fairies," she paused, but the Queen remained silent. "I implore you to reconsider. Our people have had good relations in the past. My mother had a water fairy lover." Her ears slowly turned pink as she spoke.

"I know nothing of one of my people leaving," the Queen of Lakira's Oasis informed us. "But the late Matriarch did disappear from time to time," she traded a humorous glance with her daughter who smirked back. "Take them away," she ordered the guards without acknowledging them, our eyes engaged.

Matriarch? The guards advanced, and I held out my hand and slowly lowered it to signal to the others we shouldn't resist. *Where could we run?* Rather than grab us and escort us forcefully, one gestured for me to walk alongside him. I glanced back at the Matriarch before I obediently followed. My wings flicked as Ela followed too closely behind me and tickled my primary feathers.

No one spoke as we were guided through our supposed new home. Our feet clicked on the silver stone as we meandered in a generally a straight line. Our heads were on a swivel as we took in the new sights. Through the archways and carved out windows, I could see the darkness farther beyond. But the corridors were lit easily by the water plants the fairies had taken the time to train. Different hues overtook each other as we passed different corridors. *Is it color-coded?*

As we took a spiral staircase, the guards had us walk up the inner rail where there were no windows we could leap from. I frowned, and looked past my escort to see below. There were a few more people now, some handling bags and handiwork tools. *No wings,* I shivered.

We stopped before a corridor that was illuminated with gentle blue water plants. "You will reside here," my escort stopped to look over the others. I half glanced back and saw Fira's agitated face, Wren's blank expression, and Ela's concern as she held Twila and comforted her. My guard pushed open the nearest door, and I hesitated to enter. *Will I be locked in?*

"These are your chambers," the guard instructed me, and I picked up my leaden feet and entered. The door swung shut behind me as the others, presumably, were efficiently shuttled to their own areas. I sighed as I allowed myself the comfort of hugging myself. I shifted on my feet and waited, but I slipped my shoes off.

She's not going to kill us? The idea of her raising a hand to us seemed oddly far-fetched. *How do I know this woman? Why do I trust her?* Uncomfortable with my lack of knowledge, I busied myself with examining my new rooms. There was a small bathing area off to the side with a restroom, and on the other side, there was a small sleeping area. The largest of the rooms was a sitting area that had plush and leathery pillows on the floor. Two large floor cushions took up the spotlight. Beyond them, two large clear doors beckoned me. My hand rested on their ornate handles as I admired the artisanal glass, small water creatures subtly etched in the corners of each pane. I twisted the handles and stepped back as I let myself out.

The fresh air rushed in, a small breeze that surprised me. My bare feet cautiously padded out onto the balcony, and I gratefully stretched my wings in the free space. My fingers curled over the railing as I bent over to look. The castle seemed to be coming to life as the darkness beyond lightened. I could see the fairies as they walked about, stopping to talk or exchange items. I wondered idly where their social hub might be as I was drawn to stare up. The highest points of the castle cascaded above me, and above them, a small but growing sliver of a soft blue.

My eyes narrowed as I saw things shift above me, cleared to see in the light. I leaned my back against the rail for a better view before my breath caught in my throat. *Lake creatures?* I gaped in shock. I whirled, my hands digging into the railing as I peered into the softening darkness we had come from. *Are we underwater?!*

Newfound fear made me dash into the sitting room and onto a floor cushion as I stared out my open balcony doors. *I can't swim.* The helplessness tasted bitter. I took a deep breath and slowly let it out as I rested my elbows on my knees and stared at the cold stone floor. *What kind of magic does this?* My curious mind whispered to me. *Can water fairies do magic?* The tall tales we laughed over as we searched suddenly formed a hard knot deep in my stomach.

I settled into the negativity before I shook my head and scrubbed my hands over my face. *No. We've accomplished so much,* I reminded myself. *We need to get their help to traverse to Silver Top Island.* "We're on our way," I promised myself. The Matriarch's laughter was a poignant bell in my head, and my mind wandered and relaxed.

As I sat tightly on the settee, I eventually became restless. I slipped my shoes on and slowly crept from my room, surprised to see no guards in the hallway. I crept to the next door and softly knocked on it.

"Come in!" Ela opened the door after a beat and greeted me cheerfully. I gave her a relieved smile as I stepped in. Twila was farther back in the room, and she poked at the plants that gave light. Their rooms were the same as mine, but it seemed my balcony was unique.

"Have you seen the others?" I quietly asked Ela so as not to distract Twila and worry her.

"Fira is in Wren's room next door," Twila looked up at me, sharp as usual. I nodded and looked to Ela.

"Why don't we join them?" She suggested warmly as she saw my hesitation. I gave a tight nod as Twila wandered over.

Wren's rooms echoed Ela and Twila's. Wren had taken a small cushion while Fira and Ela shared a larger pillow across from Twila and I.

"The Queen wasn't effected by your story," Ela sounded regretful as she fretted with the sleeve of her traveling cloak.

"The late Matriarch must not have informed her daughter of what she was doing," Wren looked to be heavy with disappointment. I observed Fira next, cautious as my cheek remembered her punch. Fira seemed lightly agitated, not angry, and I subtly relaxed.

I tried to feed my optimism to the others as I spoke. "That leaves us with one less option, if the Matriarch won't honor her predecessor. But we've come so far," I put a hand on Twila's head and shook her lightly. She giggled at the roughhousing and Wren softened somewhat.

"What should we do now? Being under all this water makes me feel ill," Fira glanced out the window before looking down at her hands. I sympathized with her feelings as Wren nodded in agreement.

"We could appeal to the Matriarch's good side," Ela proposed, her words quiet as she faltered in confidence.

Fira scoffed at her and Ela flinched slightly.

"Fira," I warned my companion, and she looked up at me, grumpy, but settled. "The Matriarch didn't say or do anything to Twila," I pointed out in support of Ela.

"Did you really kiss that water fairy?" Wren's question caught me off guard.

"Uh. Yeah, but it was more the other way around," I admitted. The tips of my cheekbones burned as I recalled.

"Well, have you seen them since we've been here?" Fira crossed her arms as she leaned back to eye me.

I opened my mouth and hesitated. "It was the Matriarch who kissed me," I fell into a quiet mumble at the end.

"What?!" Wren balked. Fira and Ela echoed the notion.

I rolled over for the hundredth time on the plush futon before I finally gave up and sat up. I clenched my jaw and stared at the glowing plants that grew into the stone of the corner of my room. I had attempted to toss a blanket over them to darken them, but they had only grown brighter in response. So I had attempted to put the blanket over my head until I'd realized they'd still shine through. At that point, I'd abandoned the sleeping room for the settee in the sitting room, hoping this light wouldn't be so bright.

I glared out my still open balcony doors into the now dark lake water outside. I'd spent the entire day with the others. *Why is my room different?* The nighttime haze spun my thoughts on an axis while I sat. *The Matriarch — before I came here, I've only read sparing mentions of water fairies in the legends in the Royal Library.* My frown deepened to a grimace. *An entirely unknown, untouched queendom. What would that mean to Queen Mara? What would she do?*

My rooms were a faint reminder of what I'd had as Princess of Death. They had the same official feel, the fine quality of items, a similar grand view. It comforted me when I ignored what had become of me as a child. *What will happen if I can defeat Queen Mara?* I longed to feel Cynthia in my hold and the confidence she brought me. I tried to picture Keres on the throne, but my vision changed to the hateful eyes she had shown me when I defeated her at the edge of the Wind Territory.

Keres would do the same as Queen Mara, I concluded and brought my knees up to my chest. I wrapped my arms around them as I let my head drop. Instead of Keres, I tried to picture myself on the throne. My white hair would be longer, as long as the Matriarch's. I'd have Cynthia at the ready next to me. I shivered, chilly and uncomfortable at the thought.

The feeling of connecting with the Matriarch came to my mind unbidden as the shadows of the night stretched on inside of and around me. Even now, there was a restlessness that itched under my skin. I longed for her familiarity simultaneously with my deep curiosity to learn about her. I closed my eyes and recalled her soft hands on my face and the luxurious feel of her lips on mine. Unbidden, my feet carried me out of my chambers and farther into the castle, unseen and silent.

I arrived at a large fountain that widened well over my head. In and around the large pool around the sculpture, more of those awful glowing plants grew. The area bathed in their rainbow tones. I walked around them, eager to see what they hid. I slowly dipped my toes into the cool water of the fountain as I was drawn to admire the base.

A statue of a mermaid supported the fountain, her form large. From behind the naked statue, a giggle made my feathers floof out in alarm. The Matriarch swam out from behind the statue, the fountain much deeper than I had thought. She looked at me, a quiet smile on her lips while I felt my body heat up. I kept my eyes firmly on her face. They twitched as they tried to examine her unclothed form.

"I've never shared a bath with an angel of death before," her lips pursed and I purposefully stopped from leaning forward.

I looked away as my face burned. "Sorry," I murmured, unsure of these large feelings coursing through me. I stepped back out of the water to leave.

"It's okay," the Matriarch lurched towards me with her hands outstretched under the water as if to grab me to keep me still. "You're welcome in my personal bath any time," she assured me, her mischievousness falling away to warmness as she took in my hesitation.

"Surely Lakira's Matriarch can find more capable bathmates," my hands gripped my traveling cloak tightly as I doubted myself.

She laughed, a melodic noise my heart sang with, and I looked back at her. Her hand was outstretched, but a shifting over her shoulder caught my eyes. I gasped as her wings slowly stretched out, enraptured with their beauty. They were clear, as if someone had hand blown glass and connected it with the most delicate pieces of silver and black metal. They were thin, two on each side. *A water fairy.*

Her beauty was immense as she gazed upon me warmly, ready. My mouth opened and closed several times as my heart beat like a rabbit's.

I fled and tripped over myself.

Dear Sister,

They've caught a life angel in the village today as Princess Phaedra abdicated the throne, according to Her Majesty. I have my suspicions. I fear war is coming. Should I return home?

Hazel

CHAPTER EIGHTEEN

Breakfast the next morning had been a delightful affair. The Matriarch sat on the floor at the head of the low triangular table, the Prima Filia just to her left. I had been instructed to sit to her right, and I kept my eyes steadfast on the food before me. Wren sat to my right, and Ela sat next to the Prima Filia. Fira sat next to Ela, and Twila had been gifted the high honor of sitting across from the Matriarch.

"Mind yourself," Fira chided Twila as something small went flying in the corner of my eye.

"We're still working on manners," Wren assured the Matriarch as she attempted to gain her favor.

The Matriarch's hand slipped over mine as I held my knife upright, much to the chagrin of the guards stationed around us, and my feathers stood on end as fairies danced in my stomach. "Manners can be hard to learn," she said wisely. My large eyes slowly turned to her as I considered burying my nose into my plate. She gave me a small, warm smile, and my face turned beet red. "Little one," she addressed Twila, who had speared absolutely too much food onto her utensil,

"Did you find the child bed I had placed in Princess Wren's chambers comfortable?"

"It was!" Twila smiled toothily at the Matriarch. "But I still woke up when Phaedra ran down the hall and slipped and knocked over the fancy table." My horrified eyes turned to the child as she tattled. I suddenly regretted not handing her off to a random village.

My companions all turned to look at me simultaneously with varying expressions. I kept my eyes stuck on Twila as she innocently played with her food.

I pointedly started to gather my food up with my fork as I spoke without meeting anyone's eyes. "I had trouble finding a drink last night," I placed my agitation into my tone.

Twila's mouth opened, and I bristled before the Matriarch interrupted her. "My Toolkeeper tells me you wield a Weapon." I relaxed as we began to discuss business.

"Yes," I admitted.

"She is quite powerful. You must surely know how dangerous she is. Has she spoken to you?" The Matriarch took a long drink as I shook my head no. *Not personally.*

"She spoke to me as well as my late companion in The Nothing's castle," Fira confirmed my suspicions.

The Matriarch's eyebrows jumped up briefly in surprise. "My condolences," she frowned before she turned to me. "A Weapon can only speak to your soul. If you can't hear her, you're either not listening, or she hasn't reached out," she informed me. I could only nod dumbly in agreement. This short conversation had taught me more than I'd ever been taught about Weapons.

"Could there be two souls in one body?" Twila asked as she cleared the last of her plate. Ela and I frowned at her question as Fira discreetly looked away.

"No, you are one individual," the Matriarch comforted the child through her insecurity, and I felt my heart wobble. "The closest would be a Weapon. But one soul cannot be sealed into another," she continued.

A well-dressed water fairy announced himself as he stopped just short of the doorway to the hall. The Matriarch bid him to enter, and he approached to whisper quietly in her ear. She nodded and told him she would join shortly. "Please enjoy your day without my company," she finished her drink.

"Your Majesty," Ela said, and the Matriarch paused.

"Mmm?" The Matriarch hummed.

"It would be my honor to learn your name," Ela, ever polite and kind, made Wren tense as she brought our shortcoming to the Matriarch's attention.

Blue hair bounced as she covered her loud laugh, and the sound soothed my feathers back down as I relaxed. "Forgive me!" Her bluntness surprised me. "We don't have outsiders here. I didn't even think of it," her hand squeezed mine before she rose, finished. "You may call me Sumiko." She affirmed us with a welcomingly. She leaned down, and I shivered as she breathed into my hair near my ear. "Or Miko," she promised me before she quickly left.

"I need to prepare for the ambassador," Lana told us as she stood. I politely bid her goodbye. When she had left, followed by the majority of the guards, the others turned on me, and I began to sweat.

"What happened last night?" Wren looked at me with mischievousness as she leaned her elbows onto the table, her shoulders now fallen. Fira evaluated me, and Ela played off her awkwardness by cleaning Twila up.

I tried to hide my embarrassment with a cough. "It's nothing important. Just a misunderstanding," I lied.

"With Sumiko?" Wren pressed, and I could feel myself turn red once more. Wren laughed at me openly.

After I had evaded the others, I had been able to 'sneak' away and take some time for myself. My skin cooled slowly as I allowed a guard to discreetly follow me from a distance. *He knows I'm looking for a way out.* It was tempting to laugh over how obvious I was. *But what else can a flying creature do when underwater?* I walked about leisurely. My black travel cloak did not stand out as much as I thought it might in the small groups of water fairies I passed. Most had their wings tucked in. Some wore dark colors like me, and others prioritized soft pastels.

The market was small and inside a courtyard. More plants sprung up from nothing, 'corals' according to one merchant's sign. I stopped to examine the small seedlings he sold and admired their unique hues while he ogled me.

"Where might you be from, stranger?" He asked, arms stretched as he leaned welcomingly on his table. A knowing, crafty glint in his eyes made me smile subtly. Rather than give an answer, I waved him off as I wandered to another stand. His eyes, among many others, followed me with discreet intensity as I gathered an understanding of this new place.

The leather comes from fish, I recognized the shapes easier as they were splayed out in bulk. *And seaweed is in,* I glanced at a stall that sold snacks, makeup herbal remedies, *just about everything.* The bitter taste of breakfast haunted my palate.

I stepped out of the market and around a corner and jumped a few steps ahead. I laughed quietly as the guard rushed to catch up to where I had suddenly disappeared behind the stones. The small corridor I found myself in had plants in large vases on one side. I stepped closer, curious, and examined the spines protruding from them. When the guard caught up to me, his loud footsteps coming to a halt, I turned to give him a warm look before I continued my wander.

As I trailed around Lakira's Oasis, I stopped just behind some coral as I found Twila handling a bow. Her arrows were fair in their flight for her age and size, but many were just around the target.

"Breath into your stomach," Wren coached behind her, arms on her hips, while Ela rested a hand on Wren's arm nervously. I watched with interest as Wren reached out to lay her hand on Ela's to comfort. As Twila let another arrow loose, Ela flinched as it bounced off the corner of the target. *They're growing closer,* I noted adeptly.

"She crawled into my bed last night," Wren complained as she stepped away with Ela. I tensed from the other side of the coral as I listened in.

"Twila?" Ela asked.

"She refused to leave, and we had to hunt someone down for a second bed. She's not sleeping in mine," Wren finished gruffly.

"Why not share?" Ela slowly asked, and my frown revealed itself.

"I can tolerate her unnaturalness," Wren admitted in a hushed tone. "To a point."

Ela was quiet for a moment before she hummed. "You might have to get used to unnaturalness if we can't leave and stop the Queen of Death," Ela gasped and fear jumped into my toes at being found out. "Twila, stop!" She yelled. I heard the sound of her flying away and landing heavily. "Don't touch this plant. Spotted parsley is deadly!"

I took advantage of the moment and slowly slipped back the way I came. As I approached my personal follower, I nodded to him. *Unnaturalness.* Suddenly, seaweed didn't seem so bad.

WREN

The child couldn't string the bow for the life of her. Tired of waiting, I stepped away from Ela and bent the bow so she could notch the line. Twila smiled up at me, and I harrumphed as I retreated to a safe distance.

She's likable. I admitted to myself grudgingly. *But should we really be mixing?* I looked at her wings. *I suppose she's healthy enough.* I watched her utterly miss the target and sighed. I recalled how I had felt when I'd discovered how the life angels, our newest ally, looked.

They look so similar to me, I massaged the concept in my mind as I took Ela's hand in my own. I automatically smoothed my thumb over the back of her hand as I considered her words, and she gripped me back eagerly.

PHAEDRA

I stood farther back and off to the side as I watched what happened before me. Outside of the barrier that kept back the water, several fish people floated gracefully. Their colors were evocative, and their chests bare as they passed information with their hands. I scowled as their hand signs and gestures flew over my head and tried to mentally repeat what I saw.

What language is this? I could already see its effectiveness during flight. Before the mermaids, Lana the Prima Filia floated, her wings flexing every now and then to keep her in place. *Why can't she keep still like the mermaids?* My brain tugged this way and that as I came to terms with how out of depth my knowledge was.

"I was shocked too," I jolted into the air as Fira took shape next to me. She smirked at my reaction and seemed proud of herself. She looked back as the main mermaids' and Lana's exchanged gifts. "Mermaids. The stuff of fantasy," she scoffed softly. "At the water fairies' oasis, the place of fantasy," Fira stepped closer to me and brushed my shoulders as she dipped her head to look me in my eyes. "We're in fantasy land," she flashed and shook her palms uncharacteristically.

I chuckled at her high spirits.

"I'm starting to miss even the most tedious parts of being a princess," she remarked and looked up towards the top of the clear dome that protected us. My cheerful face faltered as my heart stung for her.

"I've never greeted an ambassador before," I admitted. Lana looked at ease as she performed her duties in front of us, her hand-talk fast and efficient as any knife. She looked proud, her shoulders set back, and her expression was open as the mermaids seemed to take the time to discuss something amongst themselves before one explained it to her with wide gestures. *Not afraid to learn. Mark of a good leader.*

My thoughts drifted towards Keres. *After Mother beat her for burning that one book when we were children, she never touched any of them.* My face softened. *Was it fear? Shame?*

Why am I assuming Keres is to be the next Queen of Death? I crossed my arms and rubbed my chest, ignorant of Fira's lolling head and curious look. *Do I desire to greet ambassadors?* My legs itched, and I turned to Fira. "Walk with me?"

"You'd be good at it," Fira's words confused me.

"What?" I asked for clarification, lost in my thoughts.

"At greeting ambassadors," she answered. I opened my mouth but couldn't find my words. Her hand landed heavily on my shoulder, and the air wooshed out of me at her exaggerated actions.

"You're too harsh on yourself. Let's walk," Fira offered with a shrug and slung her arm over me as we left. *Fira thinks I'd be good at that?* I looked over my shoulder at the ambassadors before Fira gripped the back of my head and made me look forward.

We should be able to see most of the Oasis before nightfall. I tried to distract myself from the warm wood-stove fire my companion had started in me.

It seemed as though not dining with the resident royals was not an option. And so we all found ourselves at the unique table again when the sun set. I admired the woodwork of the table and pressed my finger into it as I debated whether or not to take a stab at the purple goop on my plate the others found so sweet. While I slowly came around to the idea, I idly listened to Lana discuss the political visit of the other nation's officials with Wren.

"They told me that Phaedra is a banished princess from the Queen-dom of Death," Lana's fast words slowed as her tone turned. My eyes widened as my hand found my fork. My friends tensed but didn't overtly react as they glanced at me and between each other. Even the slow guard that had been tailing me was able to comprehend the sudden shift in the atmosphere. His eyes went wide.

"Lana," Miko's stern voice made me flinch slightly. "Do not gossip over our honored guests." She admonished her daughter.

"It's true," I spoke over Lana. I slowly raised my head to look at the Matriarch. *I have to be forthright now that they know. Maybe she'll let us go if she knows I'm a time bomb.* Cautiously, I began to explain. "I am the first daughter of Queen Mara of the Queendom of Death. Queen Mara is currently waging a war against the world," my eyes faltered as I hesitated, "and winning." I swallowed and found Miko's unhappy face. "I was exiled for my weakness. I'm not fit for the throne." I squeezed my fist over the table as if to show her and the others my strength.

The Matriarch made a gesture that surprised the guards. I started to retract my hand as they quickly filed out of the room obediently. When the final guard shut the door with a long look, Miko placed her napkin from her lap onto the table. She leaned forward, and her sharp elbows dug into the wood as her normally pleasant looking face fell into a solemn resolve. An alarm bell started to quickly ring inside of me. *This is the Matriarch.*

"I thought it was very odd so many dissidents came together," she eyed my fairies. It felt odd to not be the center of her attention. "I was worried an attack would be imminent," Miko spoke slowly, an invitation for any of us to interrupt. "I've been to the surface many times. The only thing I've found is a life angel scout and a white feather they left behind,"

Wren audibly gasped as the group tensed. Ela pulled Twila into her lap as the child sought comfort from the change of mood. *A life angel? All the way up here?* The information jarred me.

"Then they weren't with you. That's news, at least," in this light, her eyes looked almost turquoise when they fell to the table. "Our Oasis has been hidden for a long time. We're all but absent from recorded history since the fall of the final dragon." She traced her goblet with a finger, and something darted inside me. "Good riddance," she scoffed to herself as if she remembered the beast.

Egan's unmoving face, his crippled body before Min flashed in my mind. My eyes flung up to look at Fira. She glanced at me but then looked back to Miko.

"But I've started to wonder," Miko folded her hands before her plate, "if we are falling behind the outside world," her voice hushed as she relaxed. Her eyes were clouded like a summer day that promised too much rain. I couldn't bear to see it and not act.

Lana beat me to it. "Why don't we take this conversation elsewhere?" She suggested. The Matriarch blinked before she agreed. She looked to me for a long breath before the two departed.

Lana shut the door quietly after her mother. I surreptitiously looked over my shoulder before I shrugged.

Fira broke the silence. "Sumiko should be afraid of falling behind the rest of the world," she scoffed and shook her head.

"I agree," Wren confidently spoke as she sat straight and proper. "We can use this to our advantage, trade for information." *The first moment we've been out of surveillance and she talks like this.* I deliberately held a deadpan expression. *At least Fira and Wren are getting along,* I tried to stay positive.

"We still need help to get to the island," Ela leaned forward and whispered loudly. She squeezed Twila to settle her nerves.

Fira leaned back and threw an arm over the back of her chair while Wren opened her mouth to impose her opinion on Ela. Before Wren spoke, I interrupted. "Their lifestyle is different from ours. We should learn from them as we try to achieve both our goals," I proposed.

My fairies paused at my suggestion.

The soft black dress I wore was soft as it brushed against my legs. In an attempt to free myself of the dinner drowsies, I wandered to the section of the Oasis where I had encountered Miko's private bath. When I didn't find her there, I found myself next investigating a coral garden. Different coral sprung up around me. Some twisted high as others dived to grow down. Phenomenal colors and pulsating glows waltzed around me, but I only had eyes for sea-maiden before me.

"Phaedra," her lips curved around my name in a way that made my thoughts meander. She nodded to the guard that followed me at a polite distance, and I listened to him retreat.

"At dinner —" We both spoke simultaneously and abruptly stopped. We smiled, and I gestured for her to continue. I wrapped my hand around my elbow, unintentionally relaxed.

"I found myself so comforted by your presence that I lost myself," Miko apologized. *We should have definitely been thrown into your jail the second you brought us down,* I silently agreed. *Your people are so shielded.*

I breathed deep and held my breath as Miko stepped close to me, and I had to look up to see her eyes. I blushed, flustered. "This soul-deep longing I feel for you," I could almost feel her hands in my feathers I imagined as she pulled me under, "do you feel it as well?" she breathed on me softly. I wavered as I became lightheaded, and Miko's tender hands held me firm.

"I do," I admitted hoarsely. I looked down at our feet as my heart and brain trembled. "I feel as though I've flown too close to the sun."

I looked up at her suddenly with wide eyes. "And you are the cold dew on my burnt skin and feathers," I felt my tiptoes press into the stone floor. "I've never," my lips almost stung with want as they just touched hers, "felt this way about anyone."

I felt her soft smile tickle me before the sensation faded. I opened my eyes to see she had backed away to a respectful distance. "It is odd," she released me and held her hands together tightly as I watched her fight with her longing. "I feared you had bewitched me. But I see now that isn't the case."

I wanted to profess how I felt about her, how when she was near I felt as though the torrents of my life had soothed to a calm pond. *I'd scare her,* I thought sadly.

"Why don't you tell me about yourself, one who has stolen my heart?" Miko sat daintily in a nearby stone alcove. I felt drawn to her like a magnetized compass. I sat next to her. Our hands were close, our pinky fingers a hair's breadth away from one another. I began to explain myself, who I was, where I came from, my past. As I continued on, the words came easier and we relaxed. Miko listened intently to my ambitions, my fears, anything under the sun that I could think of.

When I finally finished, she began to share the same with me. A true nakedness that I had not experienced save for my lost friend Liraz. My eyes settled on Miko, fulfilled by her beauty, as I fondly thought she was much more approachable when I knew her and she wasn't a naked stranger beckoning me into a bath.

Miko slowly quieted as she ran out of things to talk about, her voice strained from losing track of time. "I'll have to apologize to Lana," she admitted as she poked at my foot with hers. "Do you long for that high life you used to live?"

Her question distracted me from prodding her back playfully. "I didn't have as much exposure as a regular princess should," I admitted. I recalled Lana meeting with the mermaid delegation. "I always assumed my sister, Keres, would take the throne," I sighed.

"You are firstborn?" Miko asked. I nodded. "You will join me tomorrow so that you can decide if you want to return to that life," Miko decided unilaterally.

"What?" I asked as if I didn't hear her.

"Go to bed and rest," she purposefully didn't hear my objection.

Chapter Nineteen

I stood in another unique black dress next to Miko's throne. She sat well above me, her throne the only one I'd seen that had stairs and was deliberately placed so she could stare at people's hairlines — *ehm,* so they know who to follow. In the Great Hall, her subjects lined up as they waited patiently to address her personally. The line soon grew out the door as they took their time voicing their complaints, ideas, opinions, and requests.

I watched as Miko took a genuine interest in what each individual had to say. Several of them informed her that they had an issue with my presence as well as my group's, and she took it in stride. She explained herself easily to the citizens, being transparent where she could be.

We broke for lunch when we finally reached the noon hour. The guards sent those who Miko hadn't had time to address away with a ticket number and a guaranteed spot at the start of tomorrow's line.

"This would be difficult with a large population," I worried.

She nodded as she poked at her fish. Just the two of us ate in her private garden. "The system would have to change," she agreed fluidly. "But a ruler can only know they're adequate by what the citizens say.

We have to listen to their opinions. What if they have a better idea?"
She proposed, and I eagerly took in the information.

"They have experience politicians don't have," I spoke to my empty
plate. Miko hummed in approval.

"Do you see that plant there?" I followed Miko's finger to the
generic looking seaweed.

"Yes," I kept an open mind. I watched as a few bubbles drifted off
and up from it.

"It produces air you can breathe," she told me as we approached the
bubble barrier that protected her castle. "You just have to chew it,"

I accidentally made a face. I glanced back to see the guards she
selected this morning looking lazy. "You want me to do that, why?"
I asked, skeptical.

She laughed at my distaste. "I can breathe underwater but you
can't," she reached out to stroke my cheek, and I leaned into the touch.

I closed my eyes as I enjoyed the attention. "Fine. I'll try it," I gave
in. *My feathers are never going to dry,* I resigned myself.

Miko smiled at me as she half stepped and half jumped through
the barrier. I admired her as her hair started to float up and around
her. Her wings slowly slid out of her back and flapped as she gave me
space to join her. One of the two guards yawned as they waited for me
to enter. Miko extended her hand, and I reached out for her without
thinking.

The water was pleasantly warm as my fingers dipped through the
invisible shield. My fingertips touched Miko's as I slowly dipped my
whole arm in. I stole one last large breath before I squeezed my eyes
shut and plunged in. I felt Miko's hands push and pull at me until
the familiar taste of seaweed was pushed into my mouth. I awkwardly
released my air in bubbles and then chewed. I cracked my eyes open as
I struggled to breath around the seaweed in my mouth.

"Take out the seaweed and then breathe it in," Miko's laugh sounded like a siren under the weighty water. I did as she said and made a face. I shrugged as she and the guards looked at me expectantly.

Miko hand-spoke to the guards, and they began to retrieve copious amounts of the plant from the natural garden. "You can't talk to me underwater," she pulled at my hand as she began to swim away from the castle, "but you can learn to sign. Or just listen," she smiled back at me, cheeky, as she pulled me along.

I flapped to try and help but found that we went faster when I drew my wings in and kicked my legs like the water fairies. I glanced back at the slowly shrinking castle and felt a foreboding feeling. *Has an angel ever come here before?*

Miko guided me through her Oasis's agricultural fields. Organized neatly, they grew plants in communal clusters. "They benefit each other," she told me in between hand-talking to the farmer. "Some make the soil stronger. Some stop pests. Together, they form a family," she told me as we moved to another field.

We stopped briefly to detour to a small cave. *Such a dropoff,* I looked up at the shore high, high above where we had been taken. The light faded as I was pulled into the cave, my body tired but my mind excited. I was pulled up and gasped when my head broke to air.

"These pools gather naturally from the seaweed below," Miko gracefully surfaced next to me and pointed down. I made an ugly face as I tried to see past the ripples in the water and Miko laughed. "Come on!"

She dragged me away to the next farmer's field. This farmer had prepared for our visit and thoughtfully provided us a bag of already-picked fruit from his field. I examined one as I accepted the bag with a polite face. Miko, momentarily distracted, grabbed at the leaves of the tall plants he cared for. She pointed at the yellow tinge to the leaves, and the farmer quickly signed back.

After Miko exhausted every agricultural novelty she prided, she dragged my dead tired body through several natural, carved villages. "They carve their homes from the stone or find a cave," she told me as she waved at those we passed. They eagerly waved back. Some laughed at my predicament.

I was allowed to rest inside one of the local taverns. They had carved a ceiling into the cave and cultivated more of the special seaweed below as well as glowing coral that climbed out of the water.

I eagerly dove into my fish as Miko talked. "The crop blight has effected that field because the land is tired," she explained.

"Tired?" I asked as I gulped down my drink.

"We had to order farmers to grow certain crops several seasons in a row. We needed the medicine for a plague that grew here," she looked down and I stalled, concerned. "We will revitalize the land in time," she soothed me as she stole a bit of fin off my plate. "If we grow the right crop on it. We can benefit along with the land," she taught me.

Hairs stood up on the back of my neck as I stared out into the unending blue. A guard stayed with me to make sure I didn't drown while the other accompanied Miko to the end of the tunnel. Corals grew and illuminated the eerie space. My sharp eyes searched the ocean for danger from my poor vantage point. *If this seaweed grew farther, I could join her.* I kept a firm hold of the guard so I wouldn't accidentally drift away again.

I eagerly waited for Miko to return as I realized how hopeless our situation could be. *You'd have to learn how to summon and control that serpent.* I'd not seen hide nor scale of it since we arrived. My wings fluttered as Miko approached us. She looked satisfied over the contraption her soldiers were building at the tunnel's end.

I somewhat fell as Miko helpfully dragged me through the bubble barrier. She grunted and buckled as my wings weighed us down. "Take her to the bath," the guards helped me stand. "Take her to my bath" Miko cleared her throat. Light link dusted her cheeks. "Thank you for coming with me." She looked a touch sad that our adventure had ended.

I smiled at her, ready to faint from exertion.

"I have to meet with my advisors. Please rest," she suggested, and I laughed weakly.

My bones felt heavy as I closed my eyes. The tub water coated the room in steam, and I had begun to turn pink. Despite the fact I was prepared to fall asleep in the tub, I smiled to myself. I began to lather the soap on heavily.

I could repeat today forever and be happy. The warm sunshine inside of me threatened to burn away the steam in my bath. I washed off, eager to dry, and stepped out of the tub. *I enjoyed those duties, meeting with the citizens.* Miko's heart for her people was undeniable.

I walked to the side of the room and crouched to look into the mirror that rested on the floor and leaned against the wall. I then examined the different perfumes, mists, and products the water fairies had prepared for me. My eyes lowered to Cynthia as she rested against the doorframe. Guilt tickled my palms as I considered not moving her. *They gave her back quickly. For a moment there, I...* I sighed. *I forgot about my purpose.*

I slowly put my palms on her. Her wood greeted me with a thrum, and as I lifted her to dry off her blade, emotions ran into me from where we were connected. Bloodlust, flashes of my memories of Keres, Queen Mara, what happened at the Earth Realm. *I have to defeat her,* the voice in my head had a sharp edge, a growly undertone. *I have to defeat Mother.*

My eyes narrowed as I dried her blade obediently and pushed the thoughts away. I swallowed the bloodlust down. I pictured myself sitting on the throne as the Queen of Death, Sumiko as Lakira's Matriarch by my side after we had completed our union.

She would never leave. I leaned Cynthia on the wall just outside the bath. *She has so much love for this place. It's so peaceful.* I could only hope it remained that way.

Miko, Twila, and Ela were gone when I reached breakfast. I eyed the leftovers on Twila's plate and settled on a suspiciously soggy steamed fish in case my stomach decided to disagree after what it went through yesterday. I listened to Fira as she animatedly told Wren about the Fire Sphere's waterships. Her wide gestures and happiness were infectious.

"Phaedra," Wren paused Fira. I raised my eyebrows at her. "Sumiko is waiting for you at the observation deck,"

I nodded and happily left with a skip in my step.

I found Miko high up in the castle. The observation deck had a curved body, and it stretched around the center mass of coral that illuminated the castle. I stood behind Miko as she stood at the edge of the deck and held the railing.

My heart thumped as I took in the sorrow she tried to hide. Without a look, Miko reached back and gripped my hand tightly. I held her back. I looked at where we joined as I understood what she felt. Miko felt lost, confused, conflicted, sad. I winced, and she turned around and embraced me.

Her arms wrapped around my shoulders, and she tucked her head into my neck. She spoke into my neck, muffled. "They're pressuring me into letting you and the others leave. First, they wanted me to kill you," her arms tightened as her voice wavered. "But I talked them down."

"Your advisors?" I guessed as my tears started to fight me.

"Yes," she whispered sadly.

The idea of being apart from Miko made my gut twist. *I know she'd be happy here. I know she's safe here.* I felt guilty for wanting to be next to her.

"You and your friends speak of such fantastical things," she continued. My neck grew damp despite the chill. "Wooden creatures that fly over water. Surely, if you could teach us such things, I could convince them to let you all stay," Miko finally looked at me. Her red rimmed eyes searched mine in desperation.

I gripped her face and wiped away her tears. *This is all I can do,* I thought hopelessly. *This is all I can do.* I spoke slowly. "As much as my heart yearns to nest deep in the stones of your castle, never to see the light again but for your beckoning eyes, I cannot stay," my voice broke and I squeezed my eyes shut as my tears fell.

Miko pressed our foreheads together as I continued. "There are people depending on me. And for their sake, I must continue on," I forced my lungs to steady as we rubbed each other's tears away. "I cannot stop," I whispered. *Make me stop,* I begged her silently. *Lock me away so that I might have hope of not feeling this guilt of giving up.* I hiccuped as I cried.

Miko kissed me on the forehead, and I was momentarily soothed. "At least take my daughter with you." She touched our foreheads again. "Let her learn the ways of as many people as she can before she returns to us." She pleaded.

The revelation made me open my eyes. I leaned back as Miko looked at me. Her clear, deep, beautiful, magical eyes had red veins gathering in the white as she struggled not to openly sob. All I could do was nod. I didn't trust my own voice.

LANA

"You want me to what?!" I raised my voice as Mom sat on her futon in front of me. She looked tired.

"Please, I've been with the Board all day," she gripped the side of her head, and I knew she had a headache from their incessant chatter.

"Sorry," I lowered my voice before I started to pace in front of her. "I just don't think I need to go with them," I told her firmly, my hands animated.

"Lana —"

"They know the dry world better than I. Why would I go and hold them back?" I reasoned mostly to myself. "I can't even fly that well," I dropped my hands and reminded her.

"Lana —"

"Oh, and they're a different species!" *If I start in on how Mom and that angel are being — I'd like not to plow the fields again.* I told myself I was being wise by not continuing on that thread. "And they have a child!" I started down a different argument.

"Lana!" Mom raised her voice as she gave me a look, and my mouth snapped shut, and I stopped pacing. "I'm sending you because you're terrified," she explained, and I gave her a confused and angry face. "We're going to fall behind the rest of the world. And what then? Hope they don't discover us and take advantage?" She pressured me.

I shrugged and looked away.

Mom breathed as if to ready herself. "You need a chance to go out and meet new people," I looked at her with startled eyes. "You're different from the others here just like me," she told me knowingly, and I felt my confidence crumble. "We have to stand apart and can't truly have the friends and loved ones we desire," she whispered the last part. *Is that why you chose her, Phaedra?* I wondered as I sympathized with her pain.

Mom was silent as she gave me a moment to speak. But if I admitted how badly I wanted a close confidant, someone to talk and chatter away the days with, I might start to cry.

"I trust Phaedra," she told me. *I know.* I wanted to say. *We all see what's going on.* "You'll be in her care. It's going to be fine," she promised me.

PHAEDRA

My eyes were large as I held down my grief. I stared at Miko's face as she was flanked by her daughter and advisors. I paid none of them any mind, consumed by my Love. Miko stared back at me despite us not being able to meet the other's eyes. She introduced her daughter once more and informed the group Lana would be traveling with us to learn

about the outside world and to fight alongside us. I ignored my fairies'
responses as I tried to memorize Miko's luscious mane one last time.

Miko had one of her soldiers present my friends' weapons back
to them. Then she addressed me as she gave Cynthia a hard look. "I
tried to draw out the spirit of yours for you," she told me, her voice
faltering to a more emotional whisper. "If not to simply talk to her
myself, but she would not appear," Miko sounded frustrated, and I
squeezed Cynthia in anger for what she did. Cynthia's wood groaned
in my hands as if upset.

"I wonder if we both have done something that's agitated her?"
Miko guessed. *That can't be the last thing she says.* I dropped Cynthia and rushed forward to wrap my arms around her middle tightly.
Her advisors exclaimed while Lana took the opportunity to join my
friends. Miko coughed from the sudden rough treatment.

"I'll return," I whispered to her. She stilled as the world outside us
fell away. "Once I've taken the throne and become the Queen of Death,
I'll return," I promised. I squeezed her before I quietly added, "and I
have a boat."

Miko laughed, and the mood lifted considerably as we parted. I
gave her a sad smile as she wiped a tear from her eye. I had taken the
opportunity to scrunch my tears into her fine white dress. I turned to
see my fairies had already clamored into the mouth of the serpent that
brought us here. They watched me, unusually quiet, as I followed.

As the serpent closed its mouth, my eyes met Miko's. In the dark,
we shifted and were thrown around as the beast swam through the
tunnel to the ocean and then to the surface. I struggled to keep my
composure and was thankful for the wild ride to distract me. *It's
irrational to cry when I'm going to see her again.*

"It's okay to cry," Twila's small voice was hard to hear over the
complaining of the fairies as we were tossed around ruthlessly. "But

only sometimes. Not all the time," Twila quoted what Fira had told her during The Splinter Moment.

I reached out blindly and dragged the child toward me. I held in my loud noises as I tried to drown myself in her lovely hair.

I managed to scrub my face clean when we broke to the surface. The serpent's maw opened, and we clumsily tried to fly out. I allowed the others to go first so I could use the new space to unfurl my wings. Lana jumped into the ocean to the delight of Twila.

We hovered in flight above the serpent. Fira and Ela looked at me warmly, Wren expectantly. "Let's go to Silver Top Island," I delicately landed on the large serpent, careful to not let my feet slip on its scales. Lana expertly climbed up. Her practice showed. She sat at the head of the beast, near its eyes, and she bent down as she talked to it. The serpent began to flex underneath us as the coast trailed away.

"Open water is best to avoid being seen," I remarked, and Lana nodded.

Chapter Twenty

I LAID BACK ON my elbows while the others entertained themselves. I watched Ela pick through and organize Twila's tiny wings as she groomed her. *For someone without feathers, Ela has become an expert.* I watched as she took care to clean around Twila's back. Behind me, Wren and Fira had joined forces and started to spear at fish with the driftwood they had found. They used the rope already tied around it to bring it back to the serpent after each failed attempt. I cracked a smile as they failed again and exclaimed loudly.

"Are there even any fish out here?" I asked Lana as she joined me. She copied me and laid down. She crossed her ankles, and I suppressed a smile.

"Yup," she agreed with Wren and Fira. We fell quiet as we enjoyed the scenery. "I played up what the others told me so that my mother could use it to keep you by her side," Lana suddenly said, and my neck cracked as I looked at her in alarm. "You're a bad liar," she judged me.

"I'm not a liar," I automatically denied, used to the words coming from Queen Mara.

Fira and Wren started shouting in alarm as they got something. I made a face and grunted when Wren almost stepped on Lana and I.

"We got one!" Wren grabbed the poor fish and shoved it into our faces. It was tiny and still moved.

I gave Wren an impressed look as she showed her catch to Ela and Twila.

"Can we start a fire on this creature?" I murmured to Lana. She chuckled.

Wren and Fira reached the conclusion that they would cook the fish by holding it above their now-on-fire driftwood. I watched them, suspicious, as it cooked unevenly. When they deemed it to be as cooked as it could be, they split the meager portions among us. I kept my expression neutral as Wren gave her portion to Twila when the child finished her own in record time.

LANA

The small child plopped into my lap as I sat on the helm of Sally. I tensed immediately, surprised she would approach me at all.

"What's her name?" She babbled as she traced Sally's hide.

"Sally," I answered curtly. I suppressed my shudder as her feathers pressed into me sharply. *How unpleasant.* I frowned down at her small head before I glanced back. The others were relaxed as they talked amongst themselves. *They're not protective of their young?* I wondered. The child looked up at me expectantly. "What?" I asked.

"I said," she huffed dramatically, "could you take the stick out of my feathers?" She pointed towards her back and turned around. "Please," she leaned forward.

I made a face as I saw her issue. I cautiously plucked the twig out of her feathers and shuddered at the thought of what else she might be hiding in there.

"Thanks!" She chirped, jumped up, and left happily. I watched her go with a blank expression. *I suppose that wasn't the worst thing in the world.* I examined my hand. *No blood. Didn't get cut either.* I looked back at Phaedra and wondered if angels really were killing machines.

PHAEDRA

At night, we slept side by side. Fira would hold me tightly in her sleep, and I would take whichever side was closest to the water. As we traveled, Wren or Ela or Twila would sometimes take my other side as we huddled for warmth in the open ocean. Without any semblance of privacy, we were forced to grow closer.

Lana attempted to teach Fira to swim, but Fira panicked and remained tense. Lana ended up dragging her through the water next to the serpent as Fira did her best impression of a drowned rat.

At sunset, we would tell stories to try and ease Twila to sleep. Wren talked about the glory of the mountains, their hidden treasures. Ela explained the forest and her people lovingly. Fira missed the heat of her sphere as well as the steady ground beneath her feet. I told Twila of what I had learned of the world through the books in the faraway library, of myths and legends, of history between our queendoms. I believed I was the best storyteller, as Twila would always quickly fall asleep when it was my turn.

I recognized in my heart when we passed by the distant speck on the shore that could barely be identified as the Queendom of Death. The others intermingled busily and pretended not to notice my sudden silence as I watched it go by. *If I want the crown,* I gulped, *will I have to fight Keres?*

We, eventually, came to an odd place. When we passed by, we all grew quiet and stared. A simple island, large in size. It had a small beach, but impossibly gargantuan white trees cramped in. I reached back to hold Cynthia. *Is this where White Wood comes from?* There were no animals here, and no one suggested we stop for any reason. The island had a presence. It felt heavy, as if it saw us watching and stared back at us, unblinking.

The sensation reminded me of when Cynthia took control in the presence of Fira and Egan, and I felt an unseasonable coolness in my toes. Lana patted the serpent in a complex pattern and we sped away. We breathed easily when it was out of sight.

Something was wrong. Silver Top Island was a ghost town. We didn't see anyone as we approached, only a smooth bone white surface. As we landed, I furrowed my brow as I looked at what remained. The structures looked like they used to be houses, shanties, but they seemed to have been destroyed. Some spilled across the island, carried by the wind. Others barely stood as they were.

"Driftwood?" Wren questioned the mix of White Wood and regular wood.

"Something's wrong," Fira gathered.

"Look at this," Ela pointed at an odd glass ornament on the ground. Twila hastily picked it up and held it up proudly for us to examine. We gathered around as the child started to turn in circles to show us every side.

"An apple?" I took it from Twila as she started to get dizzy. I scrunched my nose as I pressed my thumb into the glass stem and glass leaf. "Ah!" It sliced me, and I dropped it as I bled.

Shatter!

The object shattered at our feet messily, the fine shards catching the sun.

"There's no one here," Wren frowned as she looked over her shoulder at the dilapidated village. *What happened here?*

"We should talk to the mermaids that swim here," Lana suggested. The others looked to her for guidance, and I nodded.

The Turbulent Sea lived up to its name. We steered clear of its vivid boundary as we aimed for Mermaid's Bite and hoped our map, given to us by the ambassadors who visited Lakira's Oasis, was accurate this far out. The mood was dampened with this new revelation. Fira and I steered clear of each other.

Ela had asked Fira if she wanted to fish with the rope Ela had gathered at Silver Top Island, but Fira had made a scene of rejecting her, and now the two sat quietly in opposite directions on each side of the serpent as far away from the other as possible.

Ela wouldn't understand Fira because Ela got to fight against the death angels, huh? I mulled over what Fira had shouted. *Ela is a worthy princess,* the bite of the admission wounded me. *I would be proud to be Ela, Princess of Earth.* I ignored the twitch of jealousy in my gut.

We landed at Mermaid's Bite some ways away. From a distance, we could see different forms and colors as they commingled on the shore. Some were tiny, and others threatened to rise above the treeline.

"I didn't realize mermaids could get so big," I remarked to Lana as she stretched and got ready to swim to shore.

She laughed. "The biggest ones don't come to the surface,"

"We're going to stay," Fira volunteered from where she was working on Twila's hair. Twila cheered and threw her little fists up. I nodded towards Fira.

I shook myself from Lana's ominous statement as we took flight. As we approached, we were spotted, and some mermaids turned away and headed back to the depths. Our landing disturbed the open and friendly atmosphere. I looked up at the largest mermaid, her orange and pink tail twitching as she looked down at us blankly.

"Hello, I'm Phaedra," I began.

"And I'm Lana," the expert took over. "We come from Lakira's Oasis," Lana began to explain how she was close with the clan of mermaids there, and the deep eyes of this mermaid lit up as she asked about someone in particular. Lana happily answered, and the mermaid laughed and flapped her tail loudly. Smaller mermaids that I hadn't seen before scattered from under her, no bigger than minnows despite their angel-like features.

"If you would honor me," I looked back up at the large woman as she smiled down at us while Lana continued. The pink and blue mermaid next to her of equal stature picked at her nails as we spoke. "I was hoping you'd know what happened to the people that lived on Silver Top Island."

The companion of our mermaid tensed and glanced at ours. The other mermaids that were closer to our stature whispered. Some peeled away at the prompt, their faces worried. Our mermaid quieted, the happy shine in her eyes gone. She glanced at the other. Her companion put a hand on her orange tail and uttered something in a different language.

Our mermaid turned back to us while her friend frowned. "They fled suddenly into the night some time ago. The next day, a figure appeared with an ominous aura and searched for them," she stated. Her companion made a shushing noise and grabbed her, but she shook her off. "You can find the people that lived there, on the skull, on Star Isle," she told us as her friend shuffled back into the water with a loud splash.

"On the skull?" I looked at Wren in confusion as our mermaid followed her companion. "Let's go back," I decided as more mermaids left, unnerved.

We gathered back on the serpent, far from the now almost empty Mermaids Bite. Fira tied off Twila's new braid as I told her what happened. I clasped hands with Twila as she showed her new look off.

"Do you think the figure could be Queen Mara?" She asked.

I paused as I thought. "I don't know," I admitted.

Star Isle had a dock. As we approached, I stood at the front of the serpent with Lana. My feathers started to stand on end as I saw that the island inhabitants stood on the shore and around said dock. All of them stared at us with pleasant faces.

I glanced back and saw the others were just as worried. I leaned down to Lana, who directed the serpent to stop at the edge of the dock. "Stay sharp," I whispered.

I walked off the serpent and to the dock and tried to hide my sea legs. The others followed me slowly, likely not eager. One woman stepped out of the group. Her soft silver hair matched the others, but her wings caught my eye. It seemed as though tree branches grew from her back. White Wood sprung forth behind her like butterfly wings, branches curled and poked out. Some held glass fruit. *That's what I dropped,* I shivered. *What kind of magic is this? They grow glass fruit?*

"Hello," she greeted us pleasantly after a beat. She bowed to us. "We have long awaited you.My name is Danica," she explained as my companions stepped close behind me. " She turned and the crowd parted for her immediately. She walked a few paces before she looked back at where we stood.

"She wants us to follow," Twila stated from the center of the casual circle the others formed.

I sighed and followed. Danica seemed pleased and slowly continued on the stone path. We passed houses as she guided us. Most stood empty. The inhabitants of the island still stared at us from the dock.

"Is it okay to leave her there alone?" Lana feared for her pet.

"She'll be fine," I felt confident in my hope. I spied into a few shanties we passed, each used as storage. Something moved in the shadows of one, and my wings beat in alarm before I forced them to quiet. The path came to an end as we reached a forest. The trees were quiet as we walked through, and I began to sweat from the overhead sun. *Where's that sea wind?* I longed for a reprieve as I tugged on my cloak collar.

"I'm getting warm," Lana remarked as she swiped at her neck.

"The wind will come," the woman remarked from well up ahead. *Sharp ears!* As if summoned, a small breeze curled around us suspiciously. *Thinking the wind is off. Have I lost it?* We slowed to a halt as the woman brought us to a shack. This one was built entirely from White Wood. It seemed structurally sound. Blankets had been hung around it, and they toyed in the imagined breeze. She stood just to the side of the entryway, her hands pleasantly folded in front of her.

I frowned and let out a tight breath as I slowly walked in. I paused just in the doorway as the others filtered in and brushed my wings.

Someone rested in the corner of the small space. They sat upright but were weighed down by the different blankets bundled around them. The dark purple materials had strange patterns and unknown writing embroidered in. I squinted into the tiny opening I should have been able to at least see their eyes through, but I saw nothing but shadow.

I froze as their eyes slowly opened. From within the darkness, twin lights shone out. They looked like glass as they reflected the light. *Like the fruits.* The blankets subtly shifted as the figure breathed, and I had the sinking sensation this individual was far older than I could guess. Cynthia pulsated on my back.

Have I met them before? I idly wondered.

"I am the caretaker of the Prophet of Stars," we all jumped as the woman materialized over my shoulder. *How did she get behind me?!* I controlled my breathing. She stared at the bundle. "The role has been passed down in my family for a long time, until the green light reunites their souls." She cut herself off as the prophet shifted. "The Prophet will speak to you now." The woman left, and I carefully avoided my feathers from touching her.

A ghostly noise slowly began and grew louder. It sounded like wind flowing through a chasm of a newly opened ancient cave, a suction of air into long forgotten depths. The Prophet spoke.

Within the realm where shadows dwell,
A prophecy unfolds, a tale to tell.
A queen of death, her dominion vast,
Shall face a challenger, a destiny cast.
From the depths of darkness, a hero shall rise,
With purpose burning in their eyes.
To challenge the queen, her power supreme,
And bring an end to her eternal dream.
With earth's strength and fire's blazing might,

Through air's guidance and water's gentle light,
The hero's courage, a potent blend,
Confronts the queen of death, her reign to end.
In a final confrontation, the hero's blade gleams,
As they clash with the queen, breaking her scheme.
With each strike, her hold begins to wane,
And the queen of death feels her reign's bane.
In a moment of truth, the hero's strike finds its mark,
Piercing their hearts, piercing the dark.
Her immortal essence fades and departs,
As her reign of death crumbles and falls apart.

Fira's raised voice came as the Prophet quieted. "What the hell is this?" I could hear her teeth grinding. "We can't keep chasing possibilities!"

I ignored her and looked at the large quilt strung up behind the Prophet that stretched over most of the inside of the shack while Wren held Fira back.

This quilt showed the Goddess' petals united and reformed back into the Goddess herself. The Goddess of All was in battle with another goddess. The lesser goddess' form was pure white, and they were both portrayed with angels wings. *Why are these quilts everywhere I go?*

"You think your anger and violence is going to help your sphere?!" Wren's raised voice startled me back to reality. I turned to see Fira was ready to attack the Prophet. I went to grab Fira's shoulder, but she smacked my hand away and stormed out of the shack.

I emerged after her and stopped the woman from following her. "Let her go," I ordered the stranger. Danica turned to me patiently. "We were sent here to find a way to stop the Queen of Death," I was upfront.

"We have no great weapons here," Danica slowly shook her head.

Anger flashed in me. "Why are we here?" I asked her impatiently. "Why have we come all this way?" *How much time have I wasted?*

"I am not wise like the Prophet," Danica raised her hands to try and calm me. "But I believe you should put down the Weapon and take a rest here on our island."

My hand tightened around Cynthia at the mention of her, and I looked down. *When did I grab you?* The confusion set in and I breathed evenly. "Come on," I ordered the others to follow as I hunted down Fira and replaced Cynthia onto my back.

Fira had stalled in her walk at the coast. The others took the opportunity to rest on the firm sand while they listened to Fira yell at me. I stood there and took it. *I've wasted so much time.* Fira finished her speech with a, "I don't have time to rest!" directed at the others. She began to throw stones into the ocean to let out her anger.

"Fira," Twila approached the angry fairy as she pulverized the water, "my hair fell out. Can you please tie it off with some grass?" She asked innocently, her eyes large and round as she pleaded. I watched Fira soften at the request, and they retreated to the edge of the beach.

I stared off into the waves in defeat with Ela and Wren. Eventually, Ela spoke. "This is not a place of war and conflict," she concurred. She sounded regretful despite her soft and kind nature.

"She'll be rested and ready to head out at first light," Lana rested her chin on her knees while she drew in the sand.

"I'm going to go see what we can learn," Wren stood and shook off the sand as Fira's comment got to her. Her awkward tone and uncoordinated actions betrayed her lack of usual confidence.

"Leave them alone," I sighed. *They make me uncomfortable, and I don't want you to bring them here.*

Wren ignored me and walked off, and I sighed as I followed out of obligation. I found her at the edge of the village and jogged to keep up. We found Danica and another villager. Baskets of glass fruits filled their hands.

"We're harvesting fallen fruit to make wine," she explained as we stopped before her. I eyed the baskets. *Are they devouring themselves?* At my curiosity, she continued. "If you pick them before they fall, they'll cause horrible dreams and illness," she warned.

I was about to offer to help when a terrible sound ripped through the air. We all gasped, and Danica and her villager dropped their baskets in surprise.

"That way!" Wren pointed towards the dock, and we took flight to avoid the glass shards. We easily avoided the small crowd of villagers below as we landed on the dock. My yellow eyes turned to the sky as I watched lightning race across. It cascaded over the clouds and illuminated the already bright day before it slowly receded back to where it came.

"I thought the green light was upon us," Danica sighed as she approached and looked towards the mainland where the lightning had originated.

"You said that once before," Ela pointed out as she landed with Fira, Lana, and Twila. "What is it?" She steadied Twila from her poor landing.

"When the Prophet is unified through death with her other half, the final dragon, a green light will guide them to the White Wood to become one with the Goddess," Danica explained heavily. *Is she speaking from firsthand experience?* I wondered at her tone and noticed she glanced at Cynthia on my back. I couldn't help but glance at Fira at the mention of the last dragon, and she returned it with an alarmed look.

"How long have you been on this island?" I asked as I recalled the ancient books that spoke of the Campaign of the Dragons.

The woman smiled at me pleasantly. "I don't know. We don't measure time," she said simply.

I reeled back and glanced at the villagers who stood in the same positions they did when we arrived. *There's no children,* I realized as I went to point one out and question their age. The woman saw our confusion and said, "It would be unusual for descendants of the Great Seamstress to pay particular attention to the date," she confused us all further.

My fairies shifted as they picked up on my uneasiness. "The Great Seamstress?" Wren questioned.

"One of her works lies in your throne room, does it not?" Danica nodded to herself.

I took half a step back to get distance from the strange fairy. The others subtly made their way back to the serpent. *How does she know that? That room is such a long way away.*

The woman laughed as if she had enjoyed a private joke. "Now you see why we don't leave the island," she explained pleasantly while some of the villagers laughed. Apparently fulfilled by her torment of us, the woman turned and left. I followed the others onto the serpent as the crowd slowly dispersed.

"I'll take first watch," I told the others as I sat cross legged at the serpent's head closest to the dock. "We're leaving at first light," there was no argument.

At first light, Danica brought us large bags full of supplies: rope, non-glass food, bandages. We eagerly accepted them, ready to be on our way. *Anywhere but here,* I repeated to myself as I exchanged good-bye pleasantries with Danica. We all flinched when another large lightning bolt exploded and spilled through the sky.

"We'll have to avoid that storm," Lana worried as she patted the serpent.

"It's not a storm. It's just the life angels trying to cross the Field of Lightning with their newest invention. Again," the eternally pleasant woman almost sounded annoyed as she bit the inside of her cheek.

Life angels? I kept one eye on Danica and one eye towards where the lightning had emerged. "Promise me that you will tell no one we're here," Danica suddenly requested.

"I promise," I agreed too quickly, unwilling to curse another poor soul with the mistake of coming to this island. We were quick to shove off, and the serpent seemed pleased as it headed in the direction we had arrived.

I took a deep breath as I evaluated free of worry. *I've visited all the fairies. I've been to the farthest reaches of Ouranios. Save one.*

Chapter Twenty-One

"We are going to the Life Domain," I turned and announced to the others. They dropped what they were doing to watch me. "For years, Queen Mara has worried they have superior technology, information, and strength," I informed them. "Life angels are opposite to death angels. They have to be able to stop Queen Mara." *Our last hope.*

"Is that it?" Fira questioned, surprised. "We're leaving without a weapon?" She was annoyed.

"No. We're leaving to go to the weapon," I redirected her agitation. "Her dominion vast, her power supreme." I quoted the prophecy.

The Wind Territory has an alliance with them. I looked to Wren and she nodded. *Wren will be vital.*

As we encroached on the far side of the Wind Territory, the cold began to set in. We were still on the serpent to travel faster and avoid any unfortunate run-in's. Twila huddled under my wings for warmth, Ela on her other side. Fira conveniently toiled away at something on my other side.

"We won't be able to swim through the ice," Lana warned me from up ahead after she dipped a hand into the water. *I thought we might be cutting it close with the snake.*

"Wren," Ela asked as she rewrapped Twila in her arms, "how far is it to their island from the tip of your territory?"

"Half a day," Wren answered from where she sat up ahead with Lana. "For a strong-flighted fairy,"

"Stop," Fira pulled her work away from Twila as she made a grab for it over my lap. I caught her small hands in mine when they shot out a second time.

The goodbye left Lana in tears. As the last living remnant of her home swam away with the letters full of ink she had created for Miko, Lana was truly left alone and in my hands. I put a hand on her shoulder and used my wings to block the continuous breeze that promised to tack on to her misery.

"I could still call her back if you want to send a message," Lana looked up at me as her nose ran.

I shook my head again. "I have nothing to show her," I said heavily.

We stood at the edge of the peninsula, and we stared across Heartbreak Fjord to the closest tip of the continent the Life Domain controlled. *Are they even out there?* If not for them being spotted repeatedly, one could believe they didn't exist. "It's too far for me to fly," I deemed. *I'm not going to risk falling into the ocean.*

"We should aim for Heartpeak Fjord," Wren suggested. "Instead of going directly to their island."

Between their continent and the rest of Ouranios, the terrible momentous Passage of the Dead stood. I stared into it as the rapids swirled, impassable by boat, and threatened to drown any who tried and failed to fly across.

I turned to our smallest member. "Twila," I caught her attention as I kneeled down. "We're going to have to fly across," I told her. Her eyes went big as her face went a tad pale. *Oh, you're bigger than when we first got you,* I saw as I threaded a hand over her head and into her hair. *Even on a diet of fish.* "But I think you can do it." I glanced at her stubby wings which she flapped proudly. "You're the strongest of any of us," I gave her a strong smile as she laughed. I rubbed her head and straightened.

"As long as you're there to follow, we'll all be fine," she told me, and I messed her hair.

I turned to Ela, who stood next to her, and spoke quietly. "We're going to need a system," I told her, my face drawn tight. "She's not going to make it."

I brought Ela to Fira, Lana, and Wren, who stood a small distance away. "I need ideas. What do we have?" I asked as Ela started going through what remained.

"We're going to have to ditch most of this," Wren frowned at the heavy bags.

Ela pulled a tangle of rope out of one of the larger sacks.

"Okay. Good," I affirmed as I took it.

"We could put her in the bag," Fira proposed.

"In the bag?" Wren echoed and dumped the largest one out completely. She held it up and we leered inside.

"She might fit," I proposed as my hand traced the reinforced rope closure on each side. "But can one person carry her?" I looked at my comrades.

"We could all hold the rope if we cut it up and use sections," Lana proposed.

I sighed. "I think this is our best option," I looked back at Twila. "Hey, come here."

The rope pulled at my wings awkwardly. I had tangled my hands in it to try and pull it up so the weight wouldn't rest on my back, but I couldn't lessen it completely. I looked over to see my flutter doing the same. Wren looked determined as she flew directly behind me at some distance, her flight wings the strongest of the fairies. Ela flew to my back right, and Fira on my back left. Lana flew alone, unable to support any weight, between Fira and I so we could keep an eye on her while she captured my updraft.

The sheer winds buffeted us as we approached the sudden cliff that started the life angel's perceived territory. They pushed and pulled at us, upset at our transgression, as we prepared to land. As we cleared over the cliff, I yelled, "I'm going to land!" And I hoped the others heard me over the wail of the wind.

I beat my wings down as I slowly lost altitude, unable to stop myself from being pushed awkwardly into and then away from the others. I stumbled as we landed, Twila safe on the ground as she started to move inside her bag. I bent over and gasped as I wiped the sweat from my brow. "How — how are we?" I asked but didn't look.

"I made it," Lana reassured me as Fira grunted and Wren moaned.

"All good," Ela gasped back.

"We're going to need better clothes," I remarked as I eyed a few houses far away.

"I'm freezing," Twila reminded me as she came to cling against me again. I patted her back.

"We should only send one person in," I held my wings tight to my back as I spoke to Wren. "You're the only one of us who could reasonably be here," I informed her.

"How much money do we have?" Wren dug through the small pack she had been able to bring.

"Here, trade these," Fira produced a few small glass fruits from her bag.

"Will they care about that?" I asked as I stripped off my thin cloak.

Fira shrugged. "Do they care about your coins?" She asked Wren.

Wren faltered and accepted everything we gave. We sat in a miserable, cold silence until she returned. Our last large bag was overfilled with cloth on her shoulder. We eagerly put on the new clothes, and I held myself as feeling started to seep back into me.

"Let's go see if we can get a fire going in between those two hills," I pointed with my wing. "I'm exhausted." *I don't want to do anything like that ever again,* I decided.

We had the fire lit after we dug a hole for it in the earth. We crowded around it, and Twila shoved herself in between Wren and I. The others dozed lightly as I stared into the dark. I felt a gnawing guilt for my final meal at the Castle of Death. The long meat, seared to perfection with a brushing of herbs. *Life angel meat.* I shivered and looked down at Twila. I recalled the life angel who had looked at me as I left so long ago. *If I knew what I knew now, would I have helped him?* I wondered.

I absentmindedly tucked Twila's hair behind her ear, and she roused and yawned.

"Does this look familiar?" I asked her exhausted little face. "Have you been here with your father before?" I pressed gently.

"I don't remember Dad's face very well anymore," she whispered loudly as she at least tried to mind our sleeping companions. She rubbed at the feathers I knew she kept at her chest.

"Me either," I admitted to comfort her as her eyes began to close again. *I wonder why that is?*

I woke when the sun rose to see Wren had relinquished her watch to Ela. I smiled warmly at Ela as she pet the sleeping child on her lap, and she returned it. I walked off, eager to stretch my legs, and headed towards the village. Conscious of my feathers, I hung back behind the houses.

Singing? I couldn't place the words as they raised their voices. I listened and enjoyed the tune until I pieced the lyrics together.

In angels' care, we find our place,
Guided by love, with heavenly grace.
Working together, our spirits aligned,
Spreading their light, so divine.
Working for angels, with hearts that sing,
Lifting our souls on ethereal wings.
In service we find purpose anew,
Bringing their blessings to all we do.

They repeated the words as my heart sank. *They worship angels,* I realized. *This place might be more dangerous than I thought.* I quickly returned to the group and shook Fira awake while Wren and Ela shared breakfast. I explained my worry as Fira tamed her hair from sleep.

"They're leaving and carrying things," Fira yawned as she pointed to the village. I turned, hopefully we hadn't been seen.

"Stay with Twila," I ordered Wren as I brought Ela and Fira to sneak closer and observe. *What are they doing?* We peered around one of the smaller houses as the humans put their valuables and food in the center of their village. "Offerings?" I guessed.

"It looks like someone important is going to come get that, doesn't it?" Fira saw an opportunity.

"Yes. Should we leave?" Ela looked up at me as I stood over her crouched body.

The worn down path was barely visible at the best of times, but we still followed it obediently to where the next town hopefully was.

"It's so flat, anyone could see us coming," Wren commented as she kicked the dry grass. The frost that coated the ground and made our steps crinkle delightfully flew into the air.

"You're right," I tucked my wings in closer. "I'll go around the next village if you're comfortable gathering food and information about their castle alone," I proposed.

"The first merchant almost refused my coin," Wren mentioned.

Twila looked up at me with worried eyes as she held my hand with her gloved smaller one. I squeezed her reassuringly. *My presence is so disruptive here. What if I hold the group back?*

Twila spoke confidently, "If I ruled the world, everyone would have money." She misunderstood my worried face. But she did make us chuckle.

"Thanks, kiddo," I laughed.

Ela paused for us to catch up and she fell into step with Twila. She pinched Twila's cheeks. "When," she corrected the fledgling.

The old, stone church provided a windbreak for Twila and I to rest as we waited for the others to return. We had come across this town as we traveled farther into the unknown territory of the life angels, and we were eager to see what information and goods we could gather. *Leaving most of our things behind to transport you was worth it.* I looked down at Twila, who had curled up in the crux of my body and wing. I resisted the urge to reach down and start preening her feathers, not wanting to wake her.

My feathers shifted as I noticed a fall in the wind. The lack of large animal life, of birds, made me feel uneasy. With the fall of the wind, even the insects fell silent. My eyes narrowed, and I hesitated before I gently dislodged Twila to stand.

Someone's here, I decided on intuition. I stepped to look down the closer edge of the church and came face to face with another angel. I gasped and jumped back, my hand curling around Cynthia naturally. "A life angel!" I gasped.

The man's white wings flapped as he brought up the knife he had, his posture defensive. I shook my head to clear my thoughts as I recalled my final dinner under Queen Mara's direction, the sight of the life angel being put down when I was banished.

The cold air rejuvenated Cynthia as she unleashed against the life angel. We parried his blade with ease, our footwork natural. Twila stood behind us, ready to run as she peeked around the cracked stone of the church we had taken shelter at.

His white feathers were a distraction as I drew out the battle. He did not count on his smaller stature and smaller wings. Instead, his blows were hard and relentless. He did not take the attack and withdrawal tactic that many of the fairies I had seen fight used. It was overwhelmingly close to how I had been taught to fight when I resided at the Castle of Death. If I could take ink to his feathers, he would be no different than any other death angel or myself.

I left a purposeful opening for him to strike, but I did not expect to be smacked with his wing. *How dangerous! The most important part of our bodies. Reckless,* I judged. My eyes widened briefly as he flapped for a quick burst of speed to try and get me before I raised Cynthia to guard. *He's copying me!* I realized, startled.

Agitated, I took one of his accidental openings and deeply gashed his ankle. He collapsed and dropped his knife, and I raised Cynthia for the killing blow. I hesitated as I looked down into his scared eyes. He took the opening and scuttled away. I watched him go and awkwardly fly off.

After he was well enough away, I turned to examine Twila. "Are you okay?" I asked her as I began to rub her shoulders and look for wounds.

"I'm fine," she answered, still scared.

I looked up as I heard the others come barreling towards us. Fira grabbed Twila and got the child on her back.

"We have everything that we need," Wren told me as she secured her bag.

"But there are assassins in town," Ela finished as she caught her breath.

We ran.

We ran out of breath far from the village and gave up on running. We blindly followed the single path we'd discovered before. "I had some trouble at the church," I stated softly.

Wren interrupted me. "We weren't attacked until Fira dropped some coins and the life angels saw the money,"

"They were triggered by it?" I asked for clarification.

"They probably have their own currency," Wren assumed. "Because they don't contact the outside world."

"They contacted your territory," Ela pointed out.

Fira spoke over Ela thoughtlessly. "There's a wagon!" She pointed out. *Ah, I miss the snake doing the work too,* I sympathized. *Stay on guard,* I reminded myself. "Think we can manage one more transaction?" She held up the last of our money.

"We're far enough into the middle of nowhere to try," Wren placed her bet.

The two of them flew ahead while Ela, Twila, and I hung back at a distance. I pressed my wings as close to my back as I could manage as I watched. The two beasts that pulled the wagon looked strong, their powerful horns somehow not knocking against the other. The wagon itself looked fairly nice. *Must be a well-off merchant,* I decided.

I watched as they spoke to the driver. The driver gestured towards us, and they waved at us. "Are they waving us over?" Ela asked beside me.

I hummed. "Let's go." I decided they'd gesture if they didn't want me to approach. We stopped before them, and the driver stared at me. I gave him a mean look, uncomfortable.

"An odd group," he remarked and turned to Wren. "You sure you want to go to the castle?"

Wren nodded when I ascended. *I don't trust this driver. But we're in the middle of nowhere.*

"I can do that," he informed us. "Trading at that town is never good anyway." He frowned behind us.

The back of the wagon was full of supplies, but we were allowed to reorganize and get some legroom. It also smelled, but it was worth seeing Twila's happy face as she watched the animals pull us. The merchant was kind enough to spare us drink and food, but we were slow to accept. Even after a week together and not one misstep from him, I couldn't get my gut to agree with trusting him.

"The castle!" Twila excitedly pointed out on the fourth day.

The driver chuckled. "It's about three days away yet," he tampered our expectations. *It's huge!*

I examined the structure keenly. The Castle of Life did not rise out of a cliffside and bones. It rather reminded me of the Castle of Fire with its high walls and lack of windows. The stone used to build this fortress was white and reflected the sun powerfully.

"Reminds me of home," Fira wistfully commented to me.

We had drawn the flaps on the back of the wagon and moved the merchant's items to hide us before the large fortress doors creaked open and allowed us in unwittingly. I listened to the voices outside as Twila huddled into Wren across from me. I couldn't make out the words, and I grew more and more tense.

"He sold us out!" Fira exclaimed from where she peeked through the flaps, and we jumped up. Some boxes spilled as we knocked them over. The flaps to the wagon were swung open as the fortress doors closed with a resounding bang. We were overwhelmed as soldiers rushed the wagon, and I froze when they grabbed control of Twila.

"Stop!" I ordered my companions. "They have Twila!" Fira looked back in alarm before she was ushered out of the wagon. I followed, resigned.

Chapter Twenty-Two

OUR ARMS WERE BOUND behind our backs, mine on top of my wings painfully so I couldn't escape. They bound my fairies' wings separately. We were escorted through the main square. Life angels on all sides surrounded us, but the many guards mostly blocked the view. We passed around the central watering hole, and Twila's cries increased. Wren tried to calm her from a distance and called out desperately.

The doors of the castle were opened by the guards stationed on either side, and we were quickly zipped down staircase after staircase until the air became damp and moldy.

"More strange persons?" We stopped in front of a row of cells. Another guard stood at the far end of the hallway. "The Beyond must be more awful than the studies provide," he remarked.

"Shut up," the guard that held me remarked when we were individually locked up. The concrete walls between our cells made my ears sharper. *Where's Twila?* I realized that her wails had ceased and that she wasn't among us. *Where's Lana?!*

One by one, we were returned and taken for individual interrogation. We didn't speak in the cells, cautious of the stationed guard.

Eventually, it was my turn. I was the last. I obediently followed the guard's commands, and I was rewarded with my hands being restrained in front and my wings unbound.

I was guided back up the stairs. My knees wobbled when I reached the main level, and I was taken to a luxurious white room. The carved wooden furniture matched the white stone floor. The gray drapes behind the grand chair that sat in the middle of the room reminded me of the Castle of Death. I was sat down on the couch.

I stared at the obvious noble that sat with his legs crossed in the chair. His long blonde hair and blue eyes examined me keenly. "My name is Patrick," he introduced himself. "What is your name?"

I remained silent. *But if I'm silent, will it hurt the others?*

"Same as the rest then," he sighed. "You know we won't feed you until you can answer our questions." He gloated. "We even locked you up separately so you can't cannibalize each other. Can't have that again." He laughed, and the guard joined in when Patrick glanced at him.

The doors behind me bursted open, and I jumped and looked around to see Twila being dragged in too tightly by her arm. I stood to go to her, but my guard pulled me back to the couch. I hissed at the guard that stood her before Patrick.

"What's this?" Patrick asked, confused, before he saw her wings and gasped. "Get the Princess!" Patrick stood and shouted.

"It's okay, Twila," I leaned forward to try and touch her. She turned around, her eyes red, and cried out when she saw me. She tried to reach for me, but she was forcefully picked up by her guard like an item. "Put her down!" I struggled to get out from under my guard's firm grip and get to the child. Twila sobbed loudly as tendrils of fear clawed inside me. *I should have given her away,* the ruthless thought jarred me.

A side door built to blend in with the wall to my left opened swiftly, and I sniffed back my emotions as a woman came through. Her gray eyes surveyed the room and stopped on Twila's as she cried and struggled. Her fine hair was white as mine and also dropped down to her waist. *The Princess?* I gaped at her flawlessness. A pang of jealousy hit me as I compared us, my dirty and banished exterior to her clean professionalism. It was easy to replace her face with mine in my head with our matching features. Like the other life angels, her wings were shorter than mine. But they looked warmer, her white feathers thick as they enveloped her back.

Patrick bowed when he saw she had already arrived. "Your Highness," he began as she unfroze, "this group was found by a traveling tradesman and turned into the castle guard."

The Princess was silent as she bypassed him for Twila. I struggled to get in between them, to protect her. I growled as the Princess took Twila from the guard and cradled the crying child to her chest. I frowned, disturbed, as she began to gently rock and comfort Twila and pat her back.

Patrick tried to win her grace. "Your Highness, isn't she the spitting image of the late emissary?" He pleaded. The Princess grasped Twila's face and forced the sniffling child to lean back so she could get a clear view of her.

Blood dripped down as I continued to test my bonds. "She does," the Princess's voice was sweet and melodic. *Her coldness reminds me of Keres.*

"I bet the Outside soldiers kidnapped the emissary and tried to escape with the child," the noble baselessly drew his own conclusions. The Princess drew Twila in as her small figure shook with fear.

Her stormy eyes turned to me next. "Then why would she bring her back to us?" She questioned him.

Patrick became flustered. "To extort you, Your Highness. Surely they could have found out about your close friendship," the Princess squeezed Twila in a caring hug before she let the child down. Twila threw herself onto me, and I wrapped my bound hands over her.

"Even if you are right," the Princess humored him, "at this point, we are keeping someone who returned the precious child to us in chains. Release them and make sure they are fed and have accommodation," she ordered. The noble shrunk under her judgmental eye. She turned to me. "Thank you for returning her to us. I do not know how you discovered the fact she was missing, but you will be rewarded, Outsider," she promised me, any reluctance well hidden. I slowly nodded at the revelations.

She glanced at the guard who then released his grip on me and walked around to undo my bond. The Princess opted to use the side door to leave, and I stared after her.

ASHA

I couldn't deny the pleasure I felt when I saw the death angel in chains as Lord Patrick interrogated her. But I had to turn my attention to the Blessed Child that had been returned. My hands reached out to take her from Patrick as I soothed her, her cries unpleasant.

"It's going to be okay," I shushed her and patted her back. I ignored the Lord while I got a good look at her face. *Truly a copy of her father.* Annoyed as the man kept jabbering, I coldly questioned him as to why he was keeping the Blessed Child's savior in chains. *Even if she is a death angel, we have standards!* The Queen would be upset to learn this.

PHAEDRA

Patrick squeezed his eyes and took a deep breath. "Go free the others," he commanded the second guard in the room as the life angels that had gathered in the hallway dispersed. "And bring them to the guest wing." My hands unbound, I scooped Twila into my arms as she held me back. Her little nails dug in painfully.

Patrick extended his hand, and I looked down at it. He coughed when he realized I didn't understand the gesture. "Do forgive me for my earlier actions," he insincerely apologized, and I glared at him. "I am but a simple servant of Her Majesty." He bowed. "Now, please allow me to guide you to your new home." He spoke the last part to Twila, and she turned away to hide her face in my neck.

Patrick took my silence as acceptance and led us through the Castle of Life. My wings were pin pricked by the stares of the life angels we passed, some maids and others soldiers. We passed several that were well-dressed like Patrick. *No coincidence the nobles are here.* I glared at them so they might not enjoy the show, and they shriveled away.

The clean cuts of the castle and the spotless outfits and politeness of the life angels were to be admired. As we passed the maids' quarters, I noticed an instructional list handwritten posted on the inside of the door. *Big on rules then.* We passed several lifelike statues, but it wasn't until the third one I realized they were vestiges of their royal family. *The Princess!* I observed the carved mineral.

They think the royal family is of the Goddess. I recalled the tune the villagers had sung. *I bet those were the humans' offerings to them.* Our path took us outside, and I was able to observe life angels praying in many rooms. Each room had depictions of the royal family, but above those, rested a depiction of a woman with long curls. The figure reminded me of Max. *It's been so long,* I thought sadly. *I would have liked to see her again. I wonder how she's doing.*

In one of the rooms, an ancient quilt hung instead of any visages. It showed The Goddess at her classic flower podium, all seven points done in white thread, as she ruled over All.

"This is your room," Patrick told me with faux warmness as he gestured to the door. "Her room," he paused to make sure Twila watched him, "will be next door." He smiled down at her, and I shifted so I was between them. Patrick grimaced.

"She will be staying in my chambers at least for tonight," I warned him.

His mouth twitched. "So it shall be," he acquiesced. "We will move a second bed to your rooms." He paused. "Your associates are staying on a different floor. You will be able to see them tomorrow at mass," he instructed me before he abruptly left with a frown.

"Mass?" I questioned the foreign word as I entered our rooms. I put Twila down before I checked for enemies. I found none and put her to bed. The poor child fell asleep fast. *She must be exhausted.*

I continued to dig through the rooms as quietly as I could. *No windows,* I huffed and felt like I had been buried alive. *And nothing of interest.* I flopped into a plush chair.

I sat next to Fira on the pew. I had taken the end seat and saved the rest of the pew for them. We sat tightly as life angels squeezed in for worship. "Fira, what's going on?" I whispered, only to be shushed loudly by the head figure in front. He wore long robes, and the now-familiar shade of gray adorned him.

"Your Royal Family," the man announced loudly before he hurried off the stage. I watched, confused, as the Princess walked on. She was followed by two little people, a woman and a man. "Queen Abella, King Chai, and Princess Asha," the man announced proudly. The life angels around us clapped, and we slowly followed suit. *They all have white hair like me.* I was intrigued by what I saw. The father and daughter shared eyes while the Queen's sharp green flashed to me before she looked over the audience.

The man waited until they had taken their thrones before he walked onstage before them. He began to speak, his powerful voice moving the life angels around us. He spoke of the royal family's divinity, their godliness, and their grace. My attention dipped in and out as I wondered why these people would worship them. I wondered at where we were. The walls were white, but the ceiling formed a point like one of the singing theaters back home. Still, no windows.

"And thank the Goddess of Everything for their creation," the man made a show and bowed to the royals before he left the stage. The life angels around us clapped as he departed. *Is it over?* I hoped.

I faltered as Queen Abella stood. "A new hope is upon us." The others leaned forward eagerly as if they could capture her words before she said them. She held out her hand towards my companions and me, and I frowned. The life angel who sat behind me pushed me in the back rudely. I took the hint and held Twila's hand tight, conscientious not to hurt her, as I brought her to the stage.

Twila looked at me, and I nodded when the Queen guided her up the steps. The Queen spoke as she reached up and rested a hand on Twila's shoulder. "This child is a perfect unity of life and death," she exclaimed proudly, her voice powerful. "She will unify our lands as well as our hearts. This death angel," my eyes flew to the faces in the crowd as I froze, "brought her here to us. As you go about your daily lives today, remember to be thankful for those around you and for the unexpected."

The life angels stood as they clapped with fervor. The Queen guided Twila back to me and then went to speak with the earlier man. I stood and watched as the life angels slowly began to leave. Some stopped to speak to their friends or associates, and some came up to speak to the Queen or the man. My mouth twitched at Fira's obvious agitation as she avoided those who dawdled.

"It's time to relocate to the throne room," the Queen returned and looked up at me. "Follow," she glanced at the others as they finally reached us.

I followed her as the others naturally put Twila in their protected center. I spoke to Fira in a hushed voice. "Are you all okay?" I half glanced back as we walked.

"Yes. You?" She asked. I was flattered her concern showed.

"Yeah."

When the Queen, the King, and the Princess had taken their thrones, I bowed lowly to them, my wings outstretched properly as my primary feathers brushed the ground. I gestured for the others to follow my lead, and they copied me, their wings stretched as far as they would go. *These people rely on customs. I need to fit in if I want their help.*

When we straightened, Queen Abella spoke. "You brought the blessed child back to us. Tell me what you wish for a reward." Her order was phrased as a request. The quick draws of breath behind me showed my companions' shock.

"We are before Your Majesty to ask for your gracious kindness. However, we did not realize this child was of your domain," I clarified.

The Queen smiled gently as Twila tangled her hands in my lowered flight feathers. "She's not," the Queen explained. "Her father was one of my most experienced emissaries. Unfortunately, it seems one his last experiences was being bewitched by a death angel woman." She murmured this almost to herself. "But the child is better off with her own people, isn't she?" The Queen had not failed to notice our protectiveness.

I fell silent as I contemplated Queen Abella's comments. *She's been in danger over and over because of me,* I reasoned. The Queen interrupted my thoughts. "Now, tell me of this help you require."

A deep breath helped me clear my mind and focus on why I had brought us all here. "Your domain is the only one that can stand against the Queen of Death," I paused as her eyebrows shot up into her dainty golden crown. "Your technology," I recalled the lightning, "and strength," I recalled the warrior that ambushed Twila and I outside the church, "are the only ones that can stand against her. I fear that when she takes the Wind Territory," I gestured to Wren, who stepped forward with her hands behind her back as she flexed her wings to look bigger, "They will control our continent completely."

The Queen breathed slow and took her time to speak. "Your fears are unfounded. We have recently allied with the Territory of Wind to prevent this from happening," she revealed. Only Lana reacted with surprise. *So what Ela's nurse said was true.* "We are safe on our continent," Queen Abella assured.

Think, think! "It was quite easy for us to enter your domain, Your Majesty. Are you sure there are no agents of death here?" *Why else would there be a bounty?*

Her eyes narrowed at the threat, and she pursed her lips. I continued, "Now that Queen Mara controls the Queendoms of Fire and Earth, she outnumbers you," I warned. I struggled to keep my feet still as I argued my case. "She will continue to grow her queendom as much as she can. When there is no more room to grow, when the only land left is your domain, is it possible you will find yourself fighting against the world to keep your ancestral land?" I struggled to politely catch my breath.

The Queen was silent for a moment. "It is true we've had troubling news from our informants," she admitted and seemed to be lost in thought. "I will consider your words," she dismissed us with a wave.

I screamed as my door swung open, my top all the way across the room as I changed into the clothes they'd provided. "Close the door!" I tried to cover myself as Wren and Fira barged in.

"Why? Obviously, you're good enough for queens," Wren mocked me as she threw the door shut. It rattled on its hinges as I slowly dropped my arms and shook my head as I changed. "Any of these peasants should be grateful to look upon you," she scoffed. I blushed as I pulled my new outfit over my head.

"Come out," I grumbled and knocked on the bath door.

The door swung open to reveal a laughing Ela and Lana and a half-drowned Twila. Twila squealed and tried to jump onto Fira as the fire fairy scrambled to avoid her.

"Why are you wet?!" Fira stressed as she took advantage of the high ceiling and flew out of reach.

"My bed," I sighed at the child-shaped wet splotches.

"The other handle makes the water warm!" Twila answered as she grabbed Fira's toe. Fira panicked and flew higher, and I winced when I heard her toe crack.

"Popped your toe!" Twila cheered as Ela threw a fresh dry towel on her.

"Why were you using the tub to wash your hands?" I leered at Twila.

Wren, curious, disappeared into the restroom. I heard her amazement and the continual shutting off and opening of the water valves. Eventually, we settled to sit on my oversized bed.

"I haven't heard of the alliance being officially announced," Wren admitted to us immediately. "But it makes sense geologically. We're the last thing standing between here and there," I glanced at Ela as she soothed Twila. *Must have been a politics thing,* I guessed at why she knew life and wind had been in talks.

Fira agreed with Wren. "So the Queen wants to keep —" she glanced at Twila, who was still awake as Ela distracted her.

"Yes," I drew Lana, Fira, and Wren's eyes while Twila and Ela played. "It seems the father ran away to be with a death angel." *I wonder how they met.*

"Does this place seem odd to anyone else?" Ela asked as Twila did her hair.

"That's an understatement," Wren judged. "I know I suggested we leave her in someone else's capable hands, but..."

Fira interrupted. "Finally softened?" She mocked and poked at Wren's middle.

"No," Wren smacked her away sharply. Lana laughed at them.

"I'm also in agreement we stay together," Lana looked warmly at Twila. Twila's small face pinched with the effort of braiding. "But how do we get her away and secure the Queen's help?"

Ela sighed. "Assuming she gives it to us." She brought reality back.

"I don't have all the answers," I tried to appease. "But I think we should be extra polite and try not to overstay our welcome. An opening will come." I tried to comfort their varying emotions.

A knock at the door roused me from my private slumber. I thought it was Twila or Fira, eager to start the day, and I scrubbed my eyes and yawned as I opened the door. A note was thrust into me as the tall and imposing soldier stared down at me blankly. I accepted the message sloppily.

We have received reliable information that states Queen Mara has killed the Queen of the Water Fairies. We will go to war.

I slammed the door in the guard's face and rushed to the bathroom to vomit.

CHAPTER TWENTY-THREE

FIRA

I STOOD ON THE other side of Phaedra's door and silently listened. She wailed inside. Her haunting pain carried through the wood and down the hallway as a ghost might. It was cold, and I was worried for her. I wanted to go in and light her fire.

But I couldn't step forward. I couldn't rest my hand on her door for fear it might shudder and reveal me. Her pain resounded into me, and my chest ached. Egan's kind face came to me as I bathed in her sorrow just out of reach.

'She had the opportunity to stop Queen Mara long ago.' I had told Egan in private when we first began our journey. *'I'll never be able to trust her.'*

And yet here I was, faithful in my belief that she had no opportunity in the past. Phaedra howled for her lost love, a noise that broke off as her voice cracked, raw. *How am I supposed to hold you accountable now?* I longed for the past when things were simpler.

PHAEDRA

I had not emerged from my room in some time. Grief made my head spin. My heart sometimes seemed to stop, and other times it beat so fast I thought it might rip through my chest. My anger, and sorrow, and regret, and love surged through me without respite. All I could do was react as they came to the forefront. My rooms were demolished.

My thoughts had begun to circle. My anger would lead me to remember Miko to comfort myself. I would then feel sorrow over her loss as it struck me anew. And then I would regret as I found only myself to blame. *If I had never gone to Lakira's Oasis, she would still be alive,* I promised myself.

I held my face as my breathing shuddered. My sobs came out as wracked, incoherent noises as I suffered. *I killed her. I killed her!* My sorrow was a whale breaching in the ocean, the anger a hurricane. My regret was a knife sliding down my throat, threatening to undo me from the inside out. My love was a fleshy thread, a promise to untwine my very body if pulled too hard.

I could no longer eat. My stomach stabbed at me with a vengeance, but the act of eating, trying to live when Miko could not, felt a betrayal to her honor. *If you are too good for this world,* my hands collapsed as I prayed to her, *then surely I might see you in another,* I hoped.

Time had no meaning in the face of my awesome grief. Memories of my lover circled in my waking mind as well as my dreams. I could scarcely comprehend her absence. *I had her back, and now she's gone.*

I need revenge.

A pulsating in the floors breached through as I replayed the memory of Miko as she begged me to lie.

"Come...find....me..."

My wings beat as I threw open my doors and found the nearest staircase. Down, down, down, I half fell, half glided to where she called. I entered the armory easily after I overwhelmed its doors. My hand gripped Cynthia firmly as I felt her surety rush into me. "I'll kill Mara myself," I vowed to the blade, Cynthia's shifting eyes in the blackness watching me as she smiled.

I turned and came face to face with Princess Asha. She spoke, "I ordered this armory cleared when your blade began pulsating. Its bloodlust rocked the entire castle."

"I don't have time for this," I tried to push past her. Her hand on my shoulder stopped me. *Keres?* I slashed with Cynthia out of fear for what Keres had planned next.

Cynthia cried as she was met with a shield. I blinked as Princess Asha jumped away. *I attacked the Princess.* I shook my head. "I — I didn't know —" *I've messed everything up. My whole life, I've been a failure.* Mara's voice confirmed as it danced around my mind. I let Cynthia drop as I grabbed my chest.

I fell as everything became too much. The air pressed against me was *too much.* Princess Asha rushed to me. "What's wrong?!" She faltered and her hands waved over me.

"Miko was my," I couldn't finish.

My eyes popped open as my breath returned. I gripped the bed sheets as I turned to see my companions around me. Lana gripped my hand as Wren had dipped her head to hide her face. Fira noticed me first. "Come on, everyone." She ushered everyone, save Lana, away.

I squeezed Lana's hand after the door shut. I opened my mouth and found I couldn't stop apologizing as we both let our tears free. Lana nodded over and over as we shared our grief.

"I promise. I'll stop the Death Queen and anything like this from happening again," my words felt paltry in the face of all-encompassing loss.

"I would like to go home now," she whispered, and I embraced her.

This anger, I decided as she shook in my arms, *I can use this to move forward. This promise, it's mine to keep.*

I stood before Queen Abella in the throne room, the others behind me. My insides were cold, my mind empty. *I'm going to hold on to Twila.* I couldn't bear to lose another. I could only force down so much. *Luckily, Mara trained me in this, even inadvertently.*

Queen Abella spoke when the doors to the throne room closed. "We are now readying ourselves for war," she promised. "Perhaps it is fate that brought you here to my doorstep," she mused. My face showed no emotion as I remained silent. "I see the news has also darkened you. Forgive me," a rare apology from a monarch, and she nodded to Lana. "Had I been informed you were one of the water fairies spoken of in legend, I would have delivered the news more carefully."

I held the sneer off my face while Cynthia pulsated as she begged me to take her out. Since my conversation with Lana, the scythe hadn't left my side.

The Queen saw through my mask. "Let's not mince words," she spoke faster. "I can see we all feel the same here. In 30 days, we will meet the Queendom of Death in the first, and, hopefully, last great battle of our generation." *She's not counting the fairies' wars with Mara?*

My eyebrow twitched. "You may fight with us or leave. You have my permission to come and go as you wish." She gifted us that small freedom. I thanked her and bowed as she and the King left the throne room.

Princess Asha subtly relaxed into her throne when her parents departed. She had a sinister glint to her lips, and a dark look in hurricane eyes. "What'll it be?" She crossed her leg as she waited.

"We'll fight." I replied, no trace of fear in my voice.

I walked with Princess Asha in her private courtyard as we avoided prying eyes.

"Training in front of people would show them we're fallible," Asha explained.

"What's wrong with that?" I challenged abrasively.

"Queen Abella is keen to control her subjects through worship," she slowly worded.

"And you not so?" I inquired.

Princess Asha laughed, good natured, at my question, and I felt my feathers flatten as I calmed. "Who needs prayer when there's money?" she asked playfully.

Queen Abella had promised to walk with me today as I continued to tour the castle. She had invited me to her private garden and extended the usual pleasantries about the weather, if the accommodations were okay, if the food was prepared well enough. I was agreeable as I waited for her to get to the topic at hand.

"I would like the child to go to the frontlines and see the war." My feet stopped and forced Her Majesty to turn back to address me. The small group of guards that followed a polite distance away also paused. The Queen read my shocked face accurately. "The child has the potential to unite the world. She needs to see its realities," she reasoned.

The anger that simmered in my chest burned into a bright star as I wanted to yell. I swallowed it down as I let my rational side take over. "You may be right," I continued to walk and passed her. She had to discreetly hurry a few steps to catch up to me. *And this may be the best opportunity to take Twila away.*

"I'm surprised," Queen Abella quickly fanned herself. "You seem fairly protective of the child."

Ahead on the path, Ela and Twila enjoyed the flowers. *Ah, she planned this,* I disapproved.

"I can't let my feelings hold her back," I pictured Miko saying her goodbye to Lana.

The Queen placed her hand on my elbow, and I looked down. "Good girl," she judged. I didn't respond as she returned the way we came. I resisted the urge to glare at her as she retreated. The Queen stopped and turned as she gave me one last morsel of information. "Oh, and I'll have my daughter protect her personally. I know you two are well-acquainted."

Ah, so that's why Asha wanted to learn my fighting style.

The night before we left, my companions having returned to their rooms, I stood in the Queen's private garden alone. I stared over the walls of her castle at the flat landscape, unable to see the continent in the distance. *Tomorrow, Miko.* I squeezed my arm and dug my nails in as I held back my emotions. *Tomorrow.*

The ground shook suddenly beneath my feet, and I gripped the rail in confusion. The ground quieted before it shook once more. Then, in the far distance, a green light shot into the sky. I watched with wide, shocked eyes as it lit up the sky like a world-encompassing storm, green light illuminating the clouds above my head. *The last dragon egg has passed.*

The Queen and King emerged from their private entryway and were startled when they saw the sky. "What is that?" Queen Abella asked, fearful.

"War," I turned around as the night sky grew dark once more.

When I returned to my rooms, I found the others had already gathered there. It was refreshing to see them all daily, excluding my mourning period. A squeal from the bath let me know where Wren and Twila played. Not sure how much longer Wren could preoccupy her, I sat on my bed with the others and explained my plan to them. They were appalled.

"You want to let Twila see war," Ela stated.

"It would force Queen Abella to give her a smaller detail. Less people are less likely to be noticed," Fira weighed. "But if we can get Twila to the edge of Abella's forces, we can sneak away that way," she proposed.

"If we do it your way, we might have to deal with the rear troops trying to stop us," Lana pointed out. "Why don't you just grab her and fly away?" Lana asked me, confused.

"Everyone but you can fly well, Lana," Fira sighed.

"You're a fairy too," Lana leered at Fira, more playful than offended.

"I don't see any other options," I crossed my arms.

Twila laughed as she scurried into the main room, and Wren looked exhausted as she hovered in the bathroom door. I smirked at her and held in my laughter at how wet she was. She joined us but stood off to the side, not eager to soak the bed. "We could hear," she remarked as she took a deep breath. "What if we involved the death angels?"

We jerked back at her proposal. "Just think about it," Wren continued. "They might have just as strong an interest as Abella," she suggested.

The group looked to me. "The death angels..." I started and then crossed my arms. *The death angels might eat her,* I looked at the young girl as she bounced around the room, chattering excitedly. "Won't have as strong an interest," I fell short in my explanation.

"Why?" Ela asked innocently. Her big eyes looked up to me, curious.

"Mixing is, supposedly, impossible," I began slowly, trying to find an adequate explanation. "She would be deemed an enemy of the state." I settled on. *One way or another, they wouldn't let her live.*

"It's dangerous, what you suggested first," Wren circled back to the first idea.

"It's stupidly dangerous," I agreed before the others could interject. "But it's the opening we need."

"What do you mean?" Lana asked, confused.

"I'm going to fight Queen Mara," I affirmed to her. Lana tensed at the reminder of her mother's murderer. "While I'm doing that, the eyes of Queen Abella will be on us," I surmised. "She'll want to confirm I'm not going to turn against the life angels," I rationalized.

"You know about their castle," Ela stated. "And their forces just from being here,"

I nodded along.

Fira nodded. "So you want us to take care of the small guard detail for Twila while you take care of the Queen?" She crossed her arms.

Cynthia dug into my back as we shared a quiet bloodlust. Anxiety jittered inside my heart. "If you want to help me defeat her," I offered, and Fira closed her eyes. *I was so young when I trained with Queen Mara last.* Lana, Ela, Wren and I watched Fira decide. *Has her style of scytheplay changed?*

"We'll have to play it by ear," Fira decided and opened her eyes. "The battlefield is chaotic." Ela and I nodded along.

We had taken our breakfast in Ela's rooms when Ela answered a knock at the door. Princess Asha stood somewhat awkwardly on the other side. "May I come in?" She inquired.

Ela echoed the question back to us, and she was either ignored or given shrugs. Ela held the door open as Princess Asha entered. Her servants followed her and placed a chair at the table for her as we made space. We all stared as they set her breakfast, nice and tidy, before she sat. Fira poked at the single flower they had set out in a vase in front of her with her fork.

"So," she grabbed her fork and held it properly. "I'm happy you're all enjoying the food." She beamed at us.

I softened as I saw what had happened. "Yes, it's delicious. I'm glad you joined us," I welcomed her.

"I've wanted to for some time," Asha had a light blush on top of her cheeks while her maids lined up in front of the door. "I wasn't sure if Outsiders viewed it the same as the Inside," she admitted.

"Things are much less rigid there," Ela put her hand on Asha's and gave her a warm look.

"Is that so?" Asha inquired.

ASHA

I held my breath before I knocked on the door. Just off to the side, my maids held a chair and my breakfast. We had noticed the Outsiders gathered together frequently. The way they looked out for each other and shared their responsibilities —

The door opened and the earth fairy looked surprised. I began to explain myself hurriedly. *I want that.* The urge began as soon as I saw their camaraderie. *I've not had that before.*

I relaxed as the earth princess allowed me to enter, and I eagerly waited for my maids to set my place at their table. Not sure how to take their sudden silence, I began to ask about their accommodations. *What is it that they enjoy talking about?* I wondered helplessly.

I was relieved when Phaedra took the lead and welcomed me into their midst.

The life angel armor fit me much better than the fire fairy armor I had beaten over our adventure. My wings could flex as they liked without the metal plates shifting, and it was much more suited for flexible movement. There had been an ongoing commotion around the castle the past week as they readied themselves to depart. We seemed to be on the last legs of becoming ready.

"We don't use metal armor where I'm from," Lana pointed out to me.

Princess Asha clamped Lana's naked back with her metal glove on, and Lana jumped into the air. "This is special metal," Asha assured the fairy who rubbed at the spot. "It's built for flexibility and to be lightweight. But I'll watch your back," Asha looked to me as Lana softly smiled at her. I nodded in agreement.

I turned so I could watch Twila be specially fitted. Her small body matched the royals in stature, and so she was graciously allowed to wear the King's previous armor. My heart cracked as I watched them push a helmet onto her head. *I'm so sorry you'll have to witness this. But this is not a place to raise a child.*

Twila looked up at me, and I fixed my face. "Am I going to have to fight?" She whispered, her voice still overly loud because of her youth.

"Of course not," I knelt in front of her and adjusted her cloth collar so the armor wouldn't bite her neck. "We just want you to be safe," I promised her.\

I stood off to the side with Princess Asha, my fairies, and Twila as Queen Abella addressed her army. "I have called you all here for a higher purpose," she roared. "To protect our future."

Twila shifted next to me, and I was distracted by how tiny she looked in her new armor. She carried a small shield on her back. To distract myself, I looked over the soldiers that stood at attention, proud, before their Queen. *I'm going to kill Queen Mara.* Cynthia pulsated on my back as my legs felt like I had stepped onto the serpent again.

Ela whispered next to me, and I was glad for the distraction. "Asha told me they still haven't responded. Do you think she'll march all the way to Death Castle?" She fretted. Her soft face looked unnatural in the sharp geometrics of her helmet.

"No response?" I asked, confused.

We broke apart as the soldiers began to march to battle, their foot-falls heavy. *What is Mara playing at?*

Tomorrow, we will reach the battlefield. I had snuck away from the group to take a moment away from the madness of camp. *I need to collect myself if I'm going to do this.* I stared down at the small pond at my own reflection. Tired, yellow eyes with sleep marks stared back at me. My skin looked dull.

"I'm going to kill my mother tomorrow," the words tasted foreign in my mouth. "Liraz," I closed my eyes as I pictured my best friend.

Her boundless smile and — *ah, I've forgotten her face?* A tear slipped down my cheek. *How long has it been now since I left?*

I let out a shaky sigh. "For Liraz," I told my reflection. "For Miko," pause. "For all the others who she's hurt," pause. "For Keres," *If I can salvage her, I can save her.* I squeezed my eyes shut as I threw water into my face. My hands shook as I pictured what our fight might look like.

A small hand on my shoulder made me leap sky high. I exclaimed and looked back to see Twila. I took a deep breath and calmed my heart as she spoke. "It's okay to be scared," she reassured me. "Do you want a hug?" She held out her arms expectantly.

I smiled at her and grasped her tightly. *How could Mother have hated something so small, so fragile?*

Chapter Twenty-Four

WE AWOKE TO SENTRY horns. I and many others had slept in our armor, suspicious by Mara's lack of response, and it was a relief to be ready. I shook Fira awake as she slowly opened her eyes next to me. I pulled her onto her feet as I kept up. Lana was my next victim as I forced her to rise and abandon our small personal camp. I made sure Lana properly put on her armor while my hands shook from the emotional strain. *I need you to live, Lana. For Miko.*

Princess Asha entered our tent without fanfare. "They're here." Two soldiers flanked her. "Give me the child so we can keep her safe," she demanded. Blood rushed in my ears as we positioned ourselves between Twila and Asha.

"We can't trust she'll be safe with you," I hissed, emotions high. "The Death Queen is too dangerous. We'll come with you,"

Asha blinked in surprise, but we all turned when another sentry ran past us. His horn bleated unevenly in alarm as he sprinted.

"Fine," she agreed in a snap. "But you listen to me. I scouted the land last night. I know where to go." I raised my hands to show I didn't want to argue.

Princess Asha led us through the chaos in the camp with skill. We avoided the worst of it and followed her to where a high hill broke off into a cliff. The tallgrass of the plains reached up the hillside, and on our other side, the trees of The Telling Wood sprung up. Behind us, The Nothing's forest began.

"Make yourselves comfortable," Asha instructed us as we stopped. "We'll be able to see everything from here. And if trouble comes our way, we can just pick a side and fly."

I shook my head, upset. "The Telling Woods and The Nothing are not options. They're too dangerous."

My sudden aggression made Princess Asha go quiet. "Then you'll take the high grass, it seems." She sat down as she stared over the battlefield. I frowned and sat next to her as the others took the cue. Far afield, we could see the camp for the life angels. *Bide your time. Bide your time.*

"The death angel camp," I stuck my chin out at the black tents even farther away across from them.

"They camped in the long grass," Wren observed. "Wait, is that my army?"

My head turned back to the camp full of white tents. Next to them, a slow moving mass had slowly stopped. I hummed as Princess Asha confirmed it.

"Only half," Asha continued. "They didn't want to leave their territory completely unprotected."

We grew quiet as we watched the death angels amass and slowly march to the chosen battlefield. At the head, I could see Queen Mara. She hadn't changed since I last saw her. Her black hair was still kept long but now rested back in a braid. Before her dark eyes, the earth seemed to shrivel and decay. Keres marched just behind her shoulder. I squinted. *Is Keres afraid?* I tried to make out her face as I watched her wings beat, uncharacteristically nervous. Cynthia hummed in excitement on my back.

I had spent all of last night awake as I imagined the different ways Mara could die: impaled, struck, bludgeoned. I hadn't been able to imagine my face as the attacker. *I'm scared of her. Like a child.* Cold hate settled in my gut. I started to shake as I imagined how she had annihilated Miko, the possibilities endless.

Fira shook me lightly. "Are you okay?" she leaned in and whispered.

"Yeah. Just excited," I half-lied.

"Her reign of terror ends here," Fira agreed louder.

The two armies paused from across one another. Queen Abella and Queen Mara flew to meet in the middle. Keres, for some reason, followed Mara to the center.

"What are they doing?" Ela asked, confused.

"Letting each other know they won't back down," Princess Asha kept her eyes glued to her mother. We watched as the royalty returned to their own side.

I took a closer look at the army of death and frowned when I noticed bits of red and green mixed in. "They're forcing the fairies to fight."

"Some of my people might just be bloodthirsty," Ela admitted quietly, and I sighed. My eyes narrowed as the horns blared on each side. I began to nervously chew my lip as the armies clashed.

Angels and fairies collided midair, on foot. Some that flew were struck down by arrows and spears. Some that walked were lifted up and dropped. My stomach flip flopped at all the blood as the killing began.

"Why do they have to fight?" Twila walked on her knees to hug me around my neck from behind. I gently stroked her arm. *I'm sorry.* Ela gathered her from me, and they began to quietly talk.

I turned my attention back to the battlefield. The life angel armor did give an edge to their fighting. They could not fly as fast or high as death angels, but the death angels were hindered by their inability to move freely by their inflexible and heavy armor.

Bang!

We all jumped as a life angel collapsed suddenly from the air. "There!" One of Princess Asha's two soldiers pointed out an odd contraption behind the enemy line. Fire fairies tinkered with the device.

"They're using a rock crusher to kill?" Fira questioned.

A large mass landed on the cannon, and I sharply looked away when innocent lives were squashed. "They have a catapult," Wren pointed to her own army's weapon.

Howls echoed through the battlefield. "They're releasing the dogs," I told my companions. The bred beasts used scent to identify the enemy. They easily shouldered their way through the ranks to snap at the legs and wings of the life angels and wind fairies. I cocked my head when the dogs bypassed the 'friendly' earth and fire fairies.

We watched with restless sorrow as our comrades fought for peace and dominance. I hollowly stared at the death. It felt as though someone had taken a shovel to my insides and carved them out, then tipped my head back and forced me to devour all the pain and suffering I could until I became bloated and slow.

I shivered occasionally as a storm rolled in. The first drops of rain made the scent of blood, death, and the stone crushers significantly stronger. *It's the sky trying to clear itself,* I reasoned, *of all this needless pain.* We sat in the rain together and shivered, unwilling to light a fire and be seen. I closed my eyes to feel the grass beneath me when Wren startled us.

"I think I see the Queens fighting!" She shouted over the downpour.

"What?!" Princess Asha and I gasped. We moved to try and see where she pointed.

"Mother!" Queen Asha cried as she ran that way.

Wren stood and yelled at the guards, "Go to your Queen! We'll protect the child." They dumbly looked at each other before they followed Princess Asha. I stood and looked at each of my companions' faces. I pretended the rain obscured my red eyes and tears as they stared back. *We all know it's time.* I stepped through them as I headed down the hill. It was as if an endless chasm had opened between us at this crux just to separate me from them.

Fira stopped me with a warm hand on my shoulder. "You know what you need to do," she squeezed me firmly, and I stroked her hand with mine before I walked her away. Her hand fell as I flapped and flew off alone.

When was the last time I flew alone? I tried to think back.

WREN

When Phaedra departed, I looked at the others who still watched where her form had disappeared into the sheets of rain. "I need to go to my army," I stated with resolve. They looked at me in surprise and confusion. Ela frowned. "It only makes sense I'd fight with the other wind fairies," I gestured for her to understand.

She shook her head and simply adjusted Twila's hood so the child might not become soaked. I slowly made my way down the hill as their eyes followed me. *It just makes things easier to be with the others.* I brusquely argued with no one.

As I flew high and alone over the battlefield, no one else idiotic enough to fly in a thunderstorm, I saw the dead and the living. Both sides were exhausted, but more death queendom troops remained. *How many of them are fairies?*

I saw the small clearing Mara stood in. My hand twitched before I took Cynthia off my back. I ignored all the rules of proper engagement, my surroundings, and my wellbeing as I brought my scythe blade up. Still in flight, I brought it down to cut into her skull.

Mother twisted and her dark eyes calmly met my terrified yellow eyes as she blocked me easily. I bounced off her and landed. I readied Cynthia as I stared at her. Mother was covered in blood, none of it likely her own. Her empty eyes gave me the chills.

"I thought you might be here," Mother flicked the blood off her own scythe nonchalantly. "We lost track of you after you proved yourself against your sister." The idea of Mother's looming shadow following me all along, watching my every move, my every Love — I was perturbed.

Cynthia rumbled in my hands to steady me. "No more words," I ordered.

Mother obeyed. She dashed towards me with a beat of her wings to boost her speed. She aimed a slash to cut me through knee to shoulder, and I rolled my back to dodge as I copied her move in the opposite way.

She hissed as Cynthia was faster and knicked her wing. She paused and looked down at the injury. *She bleeds,* I realized. I brought Cynthia up as I glared. Mara looked at me and her cool exterior cracked as she smiled smugly. She dashed towards me again and swung down the same as I had before, and I brought up Cynthia with both hands to block her blow.

She pressed me into the mud underfoot. I took advantage of my shorter height and flexibility as I leaned towards Mother. I snapped at her neck with my teeth and she jerked back.

I flapped my wings to get closer to her. She butted me to the side with her staff as her blade cut into my head. I hissed and jumped to the opposite side. Blood erupted down my head, but I didn't dare touch it and slicken my hands. Mara and I circled as we tried to gain an opening. I spun my scythe, and she copied me.

She's been fighting for hours. I observed her heavy breathing. *It'll come down to stamina or speed,* I realized. I pressed my feet into the grounding form Max had carved into my soul and stopped circling.

Mara grinned at me, showing off her top and bottom teeth. She bent forward as she readied herself for me. I strode across to her and spun Cynthia. She blocked as I tried to swipe at her wings. I parried as she tried to take out my ankles. Our blades sung as they danced, her tempered steel no match for my White Wood Weapon.

As we fought, I felt something blossom in me. It brought me confidence against my Mother's deranged, twisted, pleased face. I felt my limbs become more sure and stronger. My wings beat stronger, and I felt a high as my lungs expanded. My heart slowed as I observed her movements. I felt my mind expand as I calculated what would happen next. I felt like a black rose that had bloomed under a midnight sun.

Cynthia roared in my hands as I felt my transformation end. *She's slow,* I realized suddenly despite nothing having changed. Mother dashed towards me as I brought my scythe back. *I can out speed her.*

Splash!

Blood flew into my vision from behind me while Mara lunged at me. I half glanced back and gasped. At the end of my scythe, the point had dug into Twila's face. Someone gasped. Twila's left eye had been severed clean in half, its remains smashed farther into her skull. The end of Cynthia could be seen over the top of Twila's head. The Weapon drank in the child's blood as it seeped in. Twila's remaining eye was already absent of her soul. Twila went limp as the momentum slowed.

"No!!" I swung my blade forward as Mother readied hers. Cynthia slid through Mother's neck like warm butter. I struck Mother's scythe to stop it from flying towards me wildly, and I dropped Cynthia.

I twirled on my heel and pushed Mother's twitching corpse off of my child. *"Twila, Twila!!"* I screeched as I unearthed her. I wailed as I shook her small body. My hands fit completely around her shoulders. She was still warm in my hands. I held her to me, strange noises I didn't recognize around us. *Is that me?* I realized dimly as I made to wipe Twila's hair to the side so she could see. I started to hyperventilate when I saw how her face had been partially destroyed.

I held the child to my shoulder. My body shook. "What were you doing out here?" I asked her. My voice trembled. "Why are you on the battlefield?" I looked around and saw no one. "Why is a child on the battlefield?!" I raised my voice, desperate for an answer.

"Help!" I tried. "We need a doctor!" Twila slid in my grasp, her blood making it hard to keep hold of her. I tried to bundle her up into my body. My wings curled around us to try and keep my child warm. "Help!!" I screamed desperately.

Wails met my ears, and I looked up to see my companions, the family I had chosen, land next to me. "It was me!" I screamed as they began to blame Mother. "It's my fault!!" I cradled her to my chest like a broken toy. "I'm a failure!" I wailed into the sky. I was dimly aware of the fact Princess Asha had joined us with a sentry and troops, but

I couldn't bring myself to care. I screeched into the clearing storm clouds and begged them to return her.

Ela dropped to her knees next to me. "It was the final blow," I tried to tell her, my ears shot from my own actions. "I didn't look," I babbled as snot ran down my chin, and I shook my head. Fira dropped to my other side and wrapped her arms around Twila and I. I wailed again into her shoulder.

FIRA

Phaedra had wrapped herself around Twila. I couldn't see what happened through Phaedra's hair that had been dyed red. But I easily recognized her death wail. I hung back as Ela approached. I was rooted to the spot, frozen as I stared at our dead child and the deceased Queen that had been forgotten next to her.

She decapitated the Queen. Phaedra looked up at us and her mouth moved. I looked upon the crushed corpse of Twila, and my stomach twisted in on itself.

How am I supposed to be happy like this? My feet moved on their own as I dropped next to Phaedra, careful not to disturb Twila, and embraced her. She pressed her face into me as her pain overwhelmed my senses.

"Twila!" I whispered as my hands knotted in Phaedra's familiar white hair. I held her tightly as I pushed my eyes shut. "It's not your fault," I whispered to our leader and my best friend. "It's not your fault," she did not respond to my whispered chant.

PHAEDRA

"How could you let this happen?!" Princess Asha yelled.

Wren stepped in between her and I. "I left to fight with the other wind fairies," she begrudgingly admitted. "With my kind," Ela patted what remained of Twila's skull before she stood. *There's blood on her feet.* I dimly looked up at her brave form. *Has she ever killed before? She's so calm, too kind.*

"You didn't do your job!" Ela screamed at Princess Asha as she strode up to her. "We were ambushed by death troops. Where were you?!" She dug her pointer finger into Asha's high chest.

"I told her to run," Lana stared at Twila's corpse from a distance. "To run to camp since they had come from the high grass, and the woods aren't safe," her voice wavered, and I slowly looked up to see her tears. *Ah. She's crying again.* "What's done is done, then."

ELA

I cradled Twila's broken head in my hands as if I could stop the blood from flowing out. Her blood mixed with my blood which had already been tarnished by the death angels I had had to kill when they ambushed us.

"You ran like a good girl, didn't you?" I stared into her remaining eye. It was empty as she stared at something over my shoulder. *I can't take it.* I decided as I looked up at the screaming princesses. *This needs to stop. All of it needs to stop!*

I rose and unleashed the torrents of emotion onto Asha. *It wasn't enough. Why wasn't my faith enough?!*

We sat silently in our tent. Twila rested on a cot we had procured with a blanket over her. Her blood loudly dripped onto the ground from where it had bled through. I didn't turn as I heard the Queen enter.

"I see the news is true," I stared down at Twila as the Queen spoke. "A shame." I surged up, ready to behead her, but Princess Asha stepped between us. The Queen, unaffected, spoke to Princess Asha while she left. "Make sure she is buried soon, separate from the others. I intend to create a monument for her," the tent flaps swung shut unceremoniously behind her.

My family and Asha flinched as I took the nearest object, a book on fairy tales, and flung it into the wall of the tent as hard as I could. I screamed at the sky above the dirty white tent.

LANA

Alone, I sat by Twila's bedside as I said my final goodbyes. My hand curled around her cold wrist as a reminder she was truly gone. My eyes ran painfully as I spoke in a hushed voice.

"Thank you, Twila," I rested my head lightly on her stomach. I needed the touch, but I didn't want to disturb her and hovered. "You were my best friend." I smiled at her sadly. *So much loss.* The dry world seemed rife with misfortune.

"But if you and I can be friends," I reassured her quietly for whatever it was worth, "I'd overcome my fears again and again."

WREN

Twila's body looked tiny on the adult sized cot. I hovered near her head as I judged the poor blanket she had been covered in. "I'm sorry I left," I stared at her feet, ashamed, as I confessed my sins. "If I had stayed, you wouldn't have died." I slowly lowered myself as I held my head in my hands. My insides ached in a way I had never felt before. My heart felt as though it had been shredded by a wild animal.

"For someone as full of love as you to be born into the world," I whispered as I looked up at her hidden face. "It's truly a blessing." I swallowed. "I'm going to see your wings in my dreams forever, aren't I?" I hollowly questioned, alone. *Please, someone,* I looked at the ground. *Judge me. Scream at me. Punish me.*

We each said our goodbyes privately. When the guards came, we each kissed her on the forehead one last time. As the guards carried her through the camp on her cot, the surrounding life angels and wind fairies bowed to us.

Princess Asha selected to have the grave dug cleanly before a gathering of boulders to mark it. Strangers gathered around for Twila's funeral, and the Queen was long-winded as she used the dead child for political gain. I watched as they finally lowered her in.

We stayed until the grave had been filled and tamped, all the others long gone. My family pressed in around me, and I was thankful for their warmth as I cried without tears. After what felt like centuries had passed, Wren spoke. "I — I should return to my territory. See how our warriors have fared," she justified.

I looked up into the clear blue sky, not a cloud in sight. "It's finally over, isn't it?" I asked no one in particular.

"For us, anyway," Fira answered as I turned to look back at those who had lived.

Lana looked concerned. "What will you do now?" She questioned. *Now?* The question echoed inside me before I remembered my promise to her mother.

"Home," I gave a weak and hopeful smile. "I'll return home."

Wren nodded at me. The four seemed pleased by my choice, and I felt my cheeks heat up in an odd embarrassment. "Should we raid the armory before they pack it up?" Lana suggested innocently.

I blanched as I started to walk towards camp. "We need to fix this mischievousness before you go home."

Ela laughed. "I don't see anything wrong with it!"

We left our armor at the edge of camp. We didn't want to steal too much to carry, after all.

"You'll stay in touch, right?" I put a hand on Wren's shoulder as she stood nearby.

"I intend to," she assured me. "The letters will be slow to arrive such a long distance, but I'm sure Fira's waterships will speed it up a fair bit." She winked and Fira laughed her off with a small blush.

"I think I'll be going home too," Lana surprised us all. "I want to head straight there. I'm not afraid anymore."

I nodded knowingly. "I understand," I put a hand on her shoulder. "Will you be coming back on land anytime soon after you arrive?" The thought of losing the last connection I had with Miko — *let the girl live her own life,* I fought with the guilt.

She embraced me suddenly, and I returned it. "I'll come see you," she promised. "I think we need to join the world." She stepped back and wiped her eyes as she announced her decision. I smiled sadly. *Miko's legacy is going to be just fine, I think.*

"I'll be traveling with Wren," Ela hooked their arms together, and I smiled. "I'll write the second I arrive at Agee," she assured us. Lana sniffled and Ela bearhugged her. "It'll be okay!" Ela sniffled into her hair.

"I know!" Lana started to cry. Then Ela started to cry.

"I'll write to you all individually once I'm stable," I said as they separated. Ela rubbed her hands together in worry while Wren gave me a knowing look.

"Same with me," Fira assured our loved ones. With a bit more chatter, our feet grew fatigued, and we said our final goodbyes. Fira and I stood close together as we watched everyone go their separate ways, together now or not.

This reminds me of when I first left Max's, I identified the sad nostalgia inside me. Whatever fairies were present that belong to their individual homes followed them into the distance. *We're all probably eager to get back to normal.* I watched them go. I felt a pang inside my heart at all the hurt that the world had gone through.

Fira and I located and rounded up the last of the fire fairies on the battlefield. They had elected to stay behind when they had heard their princess was here, somehow, miraculously alive. She guided them confidently home, and I watched proudly from a distance as she instructed them on things she had learned through experience. *She's going to be a good Queen.* I didn't want to interfere as they rebuilt their trust and relations, and so I stuck to the fringes of the group. Being able to observe the fairies as they let go of their fear and strife made it worth it.

KERES

Mother had passed by Phaedra's hand in the war. My heart beat steadily as I awaited for her to come home. *She has to.* I stared down at the crown. *I can't. It's too evil.* The cursed object stared at me tauntingly. I sighed as I placed it upon my head. *Save me, Phaedra.*

Chapter Twenty-Five

ELA

Upon my return, I was crowned. Then I decided the courses of action for myself and for my realm. *I can't let war happen again,* I promised myself as I dipped my quill in ink. *Peace is the only option.* I began my letter to the other lands. *Faith isn't enough. We need to build those bonds today.*

PHAEDRA

We paused at the edge of the Sphere of Fire. "I don't want to experience that heat again," I laughed as Fira smiled.

"You won't have to," she promised. "But are you going to be okay on your own?" Concern painted her face.

I smiled softly at her. "Yeah," I decided, "I think I will be."

She gave me a sad, hopeful look that morphed into love as she embraced me warmly. I held her back and relaxed. "I'll miss you," we whispered to each other.

"I'll do anything and everything to help you rebuild," I left Fira with a promise.

"Let's not become strangers," she warned.

As I traveled alone, it felt odd not to hear the constant chatter of my companions. Instead, the wilds opened up to me, and I appreciated the birds' songs. I did not appreciate how immediately upon entering the proper Queendom of Death how afraid the humans became when they saw my wings, however. I gasped as I saw the beautiful forest I had once collapsed and fainted in so long ago had been stripped bare, an ugly bald patch that revealed my home.

The crops were weak, and I took note of how we didn't use the way Miko had shown me. Rather, it seemed we industrialized the replanting of the same crop over and over. *Was there a food shortage? Is that why Mother met us in all-out war?*

I walked into town and paused. There were no gasps, no screams, nothing being thrown my way. I walked through the cobblestone streets as a regular citizen. I was pushed this way and that through the shopping district and then hassled by the guards when a bright and shiny carriage came through.

Fairies still lived here. Fire and earth fairies seemed to have made a number of businesses. A bakery here, a wood carver there, a tailor, and diner. *This place is booming in growth!* I stopped before the main castle door, but it did not open.

"State your business!" The guard on the right stomped as he shouted.

Never had to do that before, I mused. "I am the rightful heir. Princess Keres is expecting me." The guards fumbled as they bowed and opened the doors.

Keres sat on the throne, Mother's golden crown atop her head. The jewel-less crown caught the light elegantly and instead showed the pinnacle of our home's craftsmanship through its unique shape and high quality.

Keres looked stressed. She pinched the bridge of her nose while she stared down at a stack of reports. Commander Bruno seemed to have made himself comfortable hovering around her, and the poor messenger was on his knee before her as he waited.

Keres looked up at me and gasped. The others looked up to see what was wrong. "I thought you might come," Keres greeted me solemnly. She stood, and my hand wrapped around Cynthia. I deadpanned when Keres laughed and waved me off. She removed the crown, placed it on the throne, and took her rightful chair next to the throne.

KERES

My sister stared at me, dirty and tired looking, as she waited for me to give her the crown. *What if it changes you?* I couldn't voice my concerns and risk sounding like a madwoman in front of her. When I hesitated, she drew her Weapon, and I began to tremble subtly. I stood and removed the crown. "I'm not going to fight you for it," I waved her off. I was happy to return to my proper seat.

PHAEDRA

She noticed how I had frozen. "I'm not going to fight you," she insisted. "It's yours." I slowly approached while the others gaped openly at her abdication. *Is it a trap?* I picked up the crown and found it surprisingly light. "You will need an advisor, will you not?" Keres questioned as she watched me try it on. *Bit tight.* Keres' fingers tapped and gave away her anxiety.

I turned to face the still open doors of the great hall. I tried to imagine myself, a young, small little girl, fleeing for her life with but a scythe. I rested Cynthia on the ground by my feet and sat on the throne. I looked at Keres. "Sure," I agreed, and she visibly relaxed.

Bruno, apparently having scurried away per his old self, came into the room through the regular entrance. Behind him, an entourage followed. *Where did he get these angels?* I idly wondered as they began to bow, introduce themselves, and pledge their undying fealty. The idea of having to fight Keres until one of us was bloody and beyond recognition was happy to depart my mind as they chattered before me. Soon, my eyes drooped, and I realized I was much too tired after my long travel for this.

"Princess Phaedra?" One of those who'd come to see me questioned as I began to nod off.

"How dare you disrespect your Queen!" Keres' shout as she stood startled me awake. "Out of here, all of you!" She ordered, and the nobles made quick work of themselves as they rushed out the door.

Keres walked around to approach me and bowed. "Your Majesty, my humblest apologies for our nobles," she remained lowered as she waited for an answer. *I never imagined her like this,* I frowned, uncomfortable.

"It's likely a difficult change considering you were acting as queen earlier today," I reasoned.

Keres' bow dipped lower. "No, no, no, I would never presume. I was merely readying the throne for you. Ask anyone. Since we returned —"

"Drop the act," my tone went frigid, and she turned to stone. "I know you despise me. I know you want the throne," I stared through her.

At this, Keres raised her head. She sneered at me. *Ah, that's the Keres I know.* "I want our people to have a strong leader. Are you not that?" she challenged.

I recalled her face when she lost the duel and sneered back at her. "Your cruelty during our younger years went beyond that," I didn't fall for her lie. *She's likely backed by the army and the nobles. Am I safe here? I'll need her support to rule.*

"I hated your powerlessness," she looked me in the eye, unforgiving. "I hated that you got the special training, special education. You squandered it." She accused me.

I stood above her, acid on my tongue. "Well. At least it's out in the open then," I turned and fled into the recesses of the castle with Cynthia. *I need her support!*

My feet had been captured by memories, and I found myself at my old quarters. I put my hand on the doorknob and wondered how many times Liraz must have done that herself. I twisted the knob and entered.

The room was barren and empty. There was no evidence I had grown up here. Not a hair, not a book, not a feather. I had been erased. The sound of guards marching on their security rounds startled me as I reflected. I slipped into my room and silently closed the door. A sweat broke out on me as the guards stopped at the other side of the door.

"Your Majesty," they spoke through the thin wood, "We have been sent by the Princess to protect and guard you."

I glanced around the empty room before I swung open the door. They jumped back in surprise. "Thank you," I gave them a brisk smile.

I next went to the Queen's rooms and found they had been redone. Most of the items and pieces of furniture had been removed but not everything. The dresser was familiar.

"Forgive us, Your Majesty," my second guard paused at the entrance and pleaded. "I will find someone to clear this out at once." He ran off before I could tell him that it was fine and I was exhausted.

"Wait outside," I dismissed my first guard, who had awkwardly followed me into the room to perhaps move out the things I didn't like.

I've spent so long revisiting that memory from the door, I looked at the open doorway. *That looking at where Liraz died from where Mother must have seen her doesn't phase me.* I wondered if I was hardening my heart as Mother had done.

I shook my head when I saw how plush and comfortable the bed looked. Instead of sleep, I decided to get ahead on things, and I began to drag the too-familiar extra large dresser across the bare stone floor noisily.

"Your Majesty, allow me!" My first guard appeared next to me as he offered his hands.

I grunted at him. "Things are different from today forward." The middle drawer opened on its own and my hand punched through accidentally. "Now, please, fetch the closest bed." *I will not be sleeping on my deceased Mother's bed no matter how squishy it looks.*

I awoke before sunrise and dressed myself. A bit complicated, but I ignored the extra layers that didn't suit me. The maids gasped when they entered, and I looked down at myself. *Did I make a mistake?* The maids apologized for their slip up, and I let my shoulders relax as one of them finished tying my dress in the back. I stopped them from ordering breakfast and instead asked for a simple fruit plate as I headed out the door. They hid their perplexed faces by bowing and thanking me for my patience.

I laughed and left, my two guards hot on my heels as I practically skipped downstairs. The throne room was mostly empty save a few well-dressed nobles that loitered around in hopes I'd make an early appearance. *I need to show them I'm a strong leader.* I touched the crown on my head and reminded myself to ask the jeweler to put some weight in it so I wouldn't have to look in a mirror to know it was there. *And I need to be a strong leader before I attend to personal matters. Just like Miko.*

I strode into the throne room slowly, elegant as I took my throne. The nobles gathered before me and eagerly bowed. I bid them to raise their heads, and the one in front took the lead. "Please, Your Majesty, would you hear us out despite the early hour?" the man asked.

I gestured for one of the maids stationed against the far wall to attend to me. The nobles averted their eyes as she approached and leaned down to hear me. "Where is the scrivener?" I wonder at her absence.

"She does not usually attend unless requested," she answered. "Shall I retrieve her?"

"Yes, and see to it that we have 10 more of her," I sent her away. She bowed and departed. I addressed the nobles. "We will have to wait for the reporter, I'm afraid," I smiled at them pleasantly and they returned the look. "A very popular profession these days," I hoped.

When the scrivener arrived and was ready and not a second sooner, the nobleman began to explain his plight. He complained of his crops not growing and growing weak from overplanting. "Your advice, Your Majesty?"

"Well, I'll have to visit the field myself and see to it," I answered. "It could be a few issues." I motioned for the scrivener to mark that down for the scheduler, and the elderly woman nodded.

Keres emerged from the depths of the castle and took her throne, her princess tiara noticeably present.

"Visit the fields, Your Majesty?" the nobleman echoed.

"Yes," I affirmed. "It's important I see the problem for myself," the nobleman bowed to hide his open mouth. *Miko.* The quiet thud of pain inside me.

More and more people filtered in to watch as I addressed the worries. But we weren't able to open the doors to the citizens before we broke for lunch in the private garden. I ate alone. My two guards stood watch as my selected three maids patiently waited to refill my cup and plate.

"May I join you?" Keres approached. I nodded, and the maids set her a spot.

We ate in silence as I enjoyed the new spices I'd not had the opportunity to try. Keres broke the quiet first. "I apologize for not having your rooms cleared out fast enough."

I shrugged. "How fast were my princess quarters cleared out?" I inquired instead.

Keres paused before she answered quietly. "Mother did it herself the same night you left."

"Banished," I quickly reminded her.

"Banished," Keres agreed.

I wiped my hands and enjoyed the flavored water. *The nobles were shocked by my hands-on method. Did Mother not ever leave the castle?* I stared into my drink before I looked at Keres, who ate politely. "I would like to go through her things. Where are they?"

She scrunched her brow as she thought. "I'll have them brought up from the crypt and placed in your drawing room," she poked at her plate. *This is not the Keres I know. This is a whole different Keres.*

"Perhaps I was too rash yesterday," It hurt to admit. Keres looked up at me in surprise. "Only time will tell," I answered her look. *I don't trust her.* Keres slowed down and put her fork down before she agreed.

I swirled my drink thoughtfully and took another drink. "Tell me what happened to the Water Fairy Queen," I kept the emotion off my face.

"One of our regular patrols found their caravan on the edge of Witch's Pass approaching the castle," Keres stared at my goblet. "They were brought before Mother and she decided to —"

My eyes narrowed as Keres stuttered. "Was it painful?" I settled on a question. Keres shook her head no. "Where is she buried?"

"In the back of the old garden with the rest of the family," she looked up at me, and I saw my own red rimmed eyes reflected. *What did Mother do to you, Keres?*

"I see," I stood and began to leave for my Love. *You were under my nose, Miko!*

A clatter from behind me made me look back. Keres stood and supported herself on the table. Her chair has fallen to the ground in her rush. "Your name was the last sound from her lips. Why is that?!" Her wild, lost eyes reminded me of a rabbit being hunted for sport.

I turned, my heart beating faster than a hare's as I pictured Miko's last moments stained by red petals.

I flipped through one of Mother's journals, the rest stacked almost to the ceiling in the corner of my drawing room. *She wrote so much,* I marveled at the large writing. It was a good distraction.

I sank into my chair as my mind was once again haunted by Miko. So far, I had made it to the entrance of the old garden. From memory, I knew a small, forgotten path had been laid in cobblestone through the graves. Beyond that, I saw it. At the end of the path, a new statue likeness had been placed. I hadn't been able to step forth into Miko's unblinking gaze.

The pain of loss pumped through my veins, and I flipped another page loudly and began to read to distract myself. *You were engaged?* I questioned the first entry.

I stood just inside the entrance of the old garden. I stared at the end of the path where she rested. The entrance was simple, a stone arch that had seen better days. Dirt and grime had caked onto it over time. The rose bushes that had always guarded the perimeter here had overgrown into brambles.

The crops are failing from lack of foresight and plant sickness. What would you have done? My face crumbled as I couldn't bring myself to approach closer. I retreated to read Mother's journals for hints. *Why did she kill you?*

This passage spoke of Mara's fears for her queendom. She felt that we had already fallen behind the rest of the world. *It would have been hard to tell, what with every race thinking they're too good to socialize with the rest!* The root of her fear was that they had uncovered a life angel spy. Her solution was to propose marriage to her mother. *Marriage to a fire prince?!*

"We have fixed the disease of the crops, Your Majesty," the two citizens remained on their knees before me. "We seek a reward for our troubles."

"Explain," I readjusted how I sat.

"Human farmers often allow spiders to live in their fields to cure the pests that cause the sickness," they explained.

"When I observed the crop, I saw no pest," I pointed out.

"The pests are too small for any living thing to see, Your Majesty," they replied and kept their heads low. From within their person, they produced a vial. I bid a guard to hand it to me. I held it up to the light and frowned at the spider within.

"I'm skeptical," I handed the vial back to the guard. "But we will test the idea. If it works, you'll be compensated," I promised.

The humans smiled up at me and stood. They bowed repeatedly as they spoke. "We will stay at the local inn and wait for the good news," they assured me.

I smiled at them and they returned the look. *Didn't I read a book that said spiders are bad luck to crops?* I pondered as the next in line dropped to one knee to address me. *Perhaps our old traditions need to be reworked more than I thought.*

Under the starlight, I stood just past the overgrown brambles and stared into the abyss of bones my ancestors had been chucked into. I could almost imagine her as she stood behind me, her hands on my shoulders in support.

"Miko..."

Another day, I stood just past the first few graves near the tree that marked the halfway point in the path. Miko stood, immortalized in minerals, some paces away. I unfolded another letter from her daughter and read it for her.

Lana thinks she found what you were searching for, that you couldn't have found it without worldly experience. My heart missed Lana just as dearly as she'd written she missed me. *I don't know if I want her calling me Mom. I'm not going to replace you.* I looked up at Miko.

"So she asked me to go with her," I quoted the letter. I looked down. "So I'll be gone for a while. I need to know what you were looking for." My eyes watered as I looked up at her still visage. *What could have possibly pulled you from your lake?*

When I left the cemetery, I paused in the archway. I leaned around the corner, thankful to be free of my guards, as I saw Keres hand a large basket of fruit to two humans. I watched their mouths move before the two departed.

Chapter Twenty-Six

Lana and I greeted each other exuberantly while our parties held back awkwardly, unsure of each other. I held her tightly, and she jumped up and down. The best place to meet had been the edge of the woods right before the Witch's Pass. After I had arranged Keres to babysit the throne after she refused to even temporarily wear the crown, I had set off.

As we released each other, that familiar dull ache of leaving the others behind was poignant like a single rain cloud. We chatted excitedly as our parties meshed and divided up the duties. It felt odd to walk with one of my old companions on a path and not fear whoever came toward us, but I soon put that feeling aside as we discussed our homes.

"When I returned, I found Mother's notes for me," Lana admitted as the Key Stone Mountains came into view. *Always so worried, Miko.* "She wrote about someone coming to see her, but she didn't write down the woman's name," Lana shook her head. *It's unlike her to forget something like that.*

"Is that what troubled her?" I wondered aloud. "You know, her grave is always ready for you to visit," I reminded her once again.

"Thank you," Lana glanced down and I pretended not to see her emotions overtake her. "She's exactly where she wants to be, by your side," she reassured me, and my heart swelled.

We camped at the base of the mountains for the night just inside the trees to avoid the dastardly wind that rolled off of them.

"Okay," Lana stood in front of us all with crossed arms. "We only have until sundown. And then we absolutely have to be back here," she pointed down.

The mountains were a challenge to fly over. The winds were odd and uncoordinated, but we popped over the peaks after we learned their patterns. Lana followed me expertly in the sky, and I felt a bit sad my eye on her wasn't needed anymore.

Instead, we hovered as we took in the civilization nestled in the center of the circle the Key Stones formed. Our group split up as planned, and I followed Lana deeper in. We flew in the air, not wanting to take the time to walk, as we searched for clues.

SUMIKO

The Matriarch of Lakira's Oasis toiled away in the library. While not unusual, her strained face was worrisome to those who passed. *That person who appeared before me... I've heard that name before. Where?*

She thought, grateful to accept the challenge to distract her heart from her recent loss of both lover and child.

The Matriarch selected another book from the nearby shelf she had sequestered at. The book opened to a hand drawn picture of large mountains that formed a circle. 'KEY STONE VALLEY' it read boldly.

PHAEDRA

"There's no one here," I told Lana.

"Look," she approached the house window I peered into. I hummed in question. "Do you see the reflection?" She pointed out, and I backed up and realized I couldn't see my own face. I moved about so the window might catch the sun but couldn't manage it.

I dropped down to peer into a storefront. "This reflection has people!" I startled back with a few flaps before I landed. Lana followed suit.

"What magic could freeze reflections?" She asked, and I shook my head, ruffled by the idea. "Let's head to the city center," she proposed, and I followed behind her. As we approached, we began to see different technologies that littered the streets and rooftops.

"Do you know what any of this is?" I asked Lana, alarmed.

"I don't," she admitted readily. "How long do you think this has all been here?"

SUMIKO

"This is an ancient village that worshiped a lesser goddess and was destroyed for its hubris by a different goddess," the Matriarch's soft whispers were the only noise in the library.

PHAEDRA

"I don't know," the feeling was eerie. We approached the central circular building and let ourselves in. "I'm freezing!" My breath showed in the wintery air.

"People," Lana breathed and I turned to see statues.

"Statues?" I guessed as I approached one. "So lifelike," I resisted the urge to touch as I looked towards the large machine in the center of the room.

"This reminds me of one of Fira's rock crusher devices," Lana remarked as we approached its shiny exterior.

"It does," I puzzled over what it might have used to do. Lana followed me as I approached the two women that stood in front of the machine. The long, blue hair of one and the low fire yellow eyes of the other made me feel warm and sad at once. The yellow-eyed one was being dipped by the blue haired one as if she had been surprised by the passionate kiss.

I grew woozy from the sudden deeper cold as I stood there. My vision darkened briefly as I observed the sculptures.

My finger trailed my lips as I saw how close theirs were to each other. Lana stopped beside me, and my hand dropped as I looked away to distract myself. My eyes locked onto the reflection on the base of the machine.

SUMIKO

The Matriarch spoke to herself. "I'll have to go in person to see the truth. Which goddess were you, Max?"

IN THE PAST

PHAEDRA

My hand curled around the clear glass Max had set before me on the table. *If she knows who I am and what happened to me, she'll throw me out*, I decided. *I can't tell her.*

"So how does the Princess of Death end up in the Dead Forest?" She poured herself a glass of clear tea. A sudden strong fruity smell enveloped us.

I tensed slightly. Pricks of pain reminded me of what had happened last night. *That's what I get for trying to fly nonstop.* I enjoyed my drink to drown out the memory of the forest floor. Max's crystalline eyes flicked up to me.

"Is something wrong?" She cradled her drink.

"No," I said too quickly, too sharply. "No," I calmed myself as my hands rubbed the glass.

"I need you to do something for me," Max proposed, and I looked up eagerly. *I need to pay her back for saving me.*

"Yes, anything," my aching muscles hoped it wasn't physical labor.

"I need you to kill Queen Mara," Max looked into my eyes unabashedly. "She refuses to worship me even through combat,"

I gasped as though I had been struck in the face. "Excuse me?" My hand trembled as I nursed my tea.

"And then I'm going to need you to go to the Sphere of Fire. She'll try and conquer them next," Max almost spoke to herself. Her eyes were latched onto mine, and I found myself unable to look away. She looked as though she was viewing something far away, something not of this world. She placed her tea on the table.

I tried to say something, anything, before she lunged over the table to me. Her surprisingly strong hand pushed me into the couch as her other hand tipped my drink to my mouth. "Drink," she ordered, and I tried to push her back helplessly. Her body felt stony and unmoveable above me while I spluttered and coughed over the liquid. The more I drank, the more the odd, warm, and wiry sensation took over my body. My mind felt slow as I took in the magical potion.

"You need to gather the petals," her large eyes didn't blink as she brought the empty glass away from me and placed it on the table as she leaned back. I coughed and dumbly looked down at the empty glass, not sure what just happened. My memories trailed each other down into a whirlpool of forgetfulness as they dispersed into nothingness.

PHAEDRA

"Max?"

"Who?"

"Your Majesties!" We turned to see one of my guards and one of Lana's. "It is time to depart!" We rushed back to camp. I followed Lana closely as she flew as fast as she could as the sun raced us. As we cleared the peaks and crossed their boundary, I turned to see the entire city abruptly freeze in a cold burst. *It doesn't extend beyond the peaks?*

I admired the magic before I followed the others down. When I landed, Lana asked, "What happened?"

My explanation started slowly as I told her how the sculptures reminded me of Miko and I and how I had seen Max's reflection. When she looked confused at the name, I explained Max was my mentor and had helped out Fira, Egan, and me long ago.

"Mother was right to be wary then," Lana frowned at the ground as she thought.

My mentor is the reason Miko is dead. The frigid ice inside my heart was insurmountable to the frozen city above. "Max never," I reviewed my memories, "told me anything substantive about herself," I realized. I looked down at my hand. *I broke the cup.* I realized. *Did I drink what was in that cup? Did it get into my blood?* My head began to pound from the pressure of the revelations, and I abruptly sat and laid down.

Who are you, Maximum? And what happened during that missing period of time when we first met?

I hovered out of earshot while I supported Lana from a distance. *I still haven't been able to approach Miko,* the shame ran through me. *What would you have thought, sweetheart, of all this?*

"We should reach out to the others about Max," Lana began as she emerged, and I straightened from where I leaned on the wall. "See if she's visited them as well," she proposed.

"I agree," I started. "But what did Max get from training me?" I questioned aloud. "Why has this ancient figure resurfaced?"

"I don't know," Lana nodded. "But we will figure it out," she promised. *Ah, she's grown just as confident as you, Miko.* "I'll send word to Fira as that's the way we're returning."

My stance shifted as I recalled the letters I had read Mother had tucked away in her journals. "That's best," I agreed.

"Did something happen?" Lana questioned, like worried because Fira and I had been so close. I disagreed, and she didn't press.

"It's an honor they came here. Do you intend to open trade negotiations with them?" Keres asked as the doors closed behind Lana's entourage. She stood just to my side.

"I already have," I answered her as I realized I had been too absent-minded to inform her.

Keres gave me a nod of approval. I looked up at her and recalled her laughing when she held me down when we were much too young to be playing with scissors and forcefully cut my hair.

"Why did you hate me so when we were children?" I asked her again.

I watched Keres pale and put my eyes forward to the main doors as our citizens bustled about. Keres' slow words were deliberate. "There will never be enough apologies in the world to pay the debt I owe you," she whispered before she left.

After dinner, I summoned Keres to my rooms. She stood politely, hands clasped behind her back, as she waited for me to speak.

"Were you aware that Mother despised me for the actions of my father, her first husband, and my crossed lineage?" I interrogated her on my findings from Mother's journal. I had compartmentalized the information and slowly sorted it out when I had the time.

"No," Keres whispered, her eyes on my feet.

"You hated me because, as her child, you copied Mother." I recalled Twila as she attempted to hold a book the same way I did. Keres looked up at me in alarm. *Is that why I feel so wrong when people call me intelligent and compliment me?* I questioned internally.

"But the night you were banished, Mother commanded your prior maid be disposed of without funeral." She was forthright with her memory. My lip curled in displeasure at our birther. "She said — called her a crossbred mongrel. Up until then, I had never witnessed her make a face like that." Keres shivered, and I felt pity. She looked up at me. "I wanted to tell you but —"

"You thought I'd treat you the same way you treated me," I interrupted her with my distaste. *I've not been kind to you since my return, Keres. I intend to change that.* I couldn't quite bring the words of 'I want to be sisters' to my mouth just yet.

"I'm sorry," she whispered as she backed away and fled.

I sighed and leaned on my chair before I once again took my seat. I flipped through Mother's journals as I searched for my final day here.

That cursed abomination created by the loose-legged maid and Cyrus, the Prince of Fire of all people, revealed herself to me today by name after I caught her poisoning my evening tea with water hemlock. She stole my weakest daughter from me. A sad day for a mother, a bullish day for the Queendom of Death.

Her proud signoff made my stomach roil. I snapped the diary shut and threw it against my wall as hard as I could. I tried to remember Liraz's face as my head spun. *I'm half fire fairy. I'm Fira's cousin. Liraz was my half sister. Max intimately knew Mother.* I resisted the urge to scream as I sat alone.

My feet ached as I missed the days I traveled with my companions. I missed their company, and I missed being able to sneak away and feel my emotions.

Lana's letter arrived by the waterships that now traded at our closest shore. I watched them absently from the viewing deck, careful not to let her words drop down the sheer cliff. Her letter described what we had found out about Max, the village, and Miko.

Fira's letter arrived shortly after. She informed us that Max hadn't visited her yet, likely as her father still controlled the throne, but she had visited her father in the past and he had rejected her. She informed us Max had sought out worshippers and 'requested the whole of Fire worship her daily for her grace.'

Wren and Ela sent one letter together. Max hadn't made contact yet, but they were firm believers that something that hurts one land hurts them all. I sent out a memo to my comrades in support of that statement.

Asha, as she requested we call her now, responded and said that they had begun dismantling the part of their religion that focused on her and that Queen Abella was hesitant to let go of her control. She inquired if Max still resided where she did previously.

I sent out a letter that expressed my acceptance of Queen Abella's decision and that a power vacuum in her domain would cause great issues and should be avoided. I questioned if we should travel to Star Isle and speak with the prophet as to Max's location as my spies had returned empty handed.

The others sent out at least one memo each that expressed a resounding no. Ela followed up her memo with, 'Didn't that odd woman say something about a goddess in the White Wood?'

My memo was simple. "Let's go to the White Woods. Let's meet at the Agee Tree."

KERES

I found the present after Phaedra left. It sat on my desk, unannounced and suspicious. I ripped it open out of curiosity and paused when I unveiled my prize. A rare portrait of us, tiny and painted in watercolor. We smiled at the artist who captured us, too young to have been set up against each other. I held it to the sunfall and turned to examine the shadow cast by the other side.

To my precious little sister. I love you.

Ela's realm revived steadily. We discussed it as we waited for the others.

"We don't want to grow too fast. Get growing scars," she nodded.

I laughed and agreed. "Those can be troublesome to lose,"

"You didn't travel with Fira?" Ela questioned while we waited in the drawing room with Asha.

I was saved from answering when the doors opened and Lana, Fira, and Wren entered together.

"Fira, Wren!" I hugged them both together, my arms curled around Wren's neck and Fira's waist as I bent down. "I'm so glad to see you both," I smiled at them and pinched their cheeks.

They slapped my hands away in tandem.

"Not enough to travel with me," Fira remarked and I blanched. Wren laughed as she went to snag the remaining treat from Ela's plate. Ela huffed in annoyance.

"I'm ready to go," Lana suggested.

"Hey, Fira," I rolled over to face her. The snake undulated underneath us just like old times.

"Hm?" She rolled over to face me.

"What do you know about your uncle?" I asked out of the blue.

"He was swept under the rug. Don't know much," she admitted. "Dad says he'll give me the crown when I get back," my eyes went wide as I pictured it. "Probably something to protect Dad's image," she imagined.

"It was probably to stop a war," I guessed.

"The war happened anyway," Fira half shrugged the shoulder she didn't lie on. "How do you know about him? Mom forbade anyone to speak of him." She tucked her loose hair behind her ear.

"My Mother did too," I answered.

Fira's eyes went wide. "Are you my cousin?" She gasped. I nodded, and we smiled and tucked our heads together under the stars.

Chapter Twenty-Seven

In the morning, we reached the White Wood. Its uncomfortable presence smeared across our skin and minds as we dropped onto shore. The ground thrummed beneath our feet as we headed in. We grew quiet as we noticed the woods were silent. The trees caused a heady feeling, and when I looked up, it felt like I was a flightless human.

"Ow!" Ela exclaimed as she flapped her arms and tried not to fall. My toe began to throb. *Sympathy pain,* I wrote it off.

"Don't fall," Fira remarked from behind me.

"I was looking for a place to sit," Ela snapped back, and I laughed. I felt a small yank on my hair and reached around to slap Fira's hand away from me.

When turning back around, my wings and feathers fluffed up and held wide, I smacked my right wing into a tree. I hissed as the bark dislodged a few of my feathers.

"Tsk!" Wren, who walked ahead of me, paused to rub a hand delicately along her wing.

I looked up, curious to feel like a human again, and a sudden pressure on my back pushed me forward.

"What?" I asked, confused as I helped Fira catch herself from where she had fallen into me.

"Just disoriented," she claimed, a hand on her forehead. I raised an eyebrow and hummed. We walked on and quieted down until my burgeoning curiosity got the best of me. I broke a small branch off of the surprisingly spry white trees and dug the sharp end of the stick into my palm.

"Ah!" Lana looked down. I stopped to look at what had happened and Fira walked around me.

"You're bleeding," I remarked, brow furrowed.

"What?" Wren asked, ahead.

"She's bleeding?" Ela echoed.

The others looked to me with expectant eyes. "We're connected," I realized. *They turned to me before I spoke as if they had read my mind!*

What is this place? "What is this place?" Lana's delayed question overshadowed her voice in my head.

"We need to move on," Asha pressed forward. *This place is not for us,* her words danced around my mind.

The animals slowly appeared to us. Their forms gathered similarly to the shadow creatures in The Telling Woods, but as we lost track of time and the sunbeams remained unchanged, their forms became more solid.

"It's white," Ela pointed out a faraway deer.

"The falcon too," Lana pointed the bird high above that stared down at us.

A strange feeling began to make itself known inside of me. Not an emotion, per say, but a sensation. *What is this?* Our thoughts echoed, all of us taking part in the experience.

"All of their eye sockets are empty," I felt Wren's unseasonable shiver as we were haunted by these ghosts.

We came out into a clearing that boasted a thick coat of star flowers. In the center, with crystalline eyes and dark, tight curls, she stood. *Max.* I didn't know whose voice it was that echoed in my head. She smiled as she saw us. The lush grass in the clearing flattened beneath her feet as she turned and stood on a stone structure.

It's a star flower pattern, Ela recognized silently.

A strange sensation that had grown inside each of us began to peak. I drew breath, conscious of the fact that I was still awake and not about to faint. *We're in danger,* we all realized simultaneously. *That's what this sensation inside us is, a warning.*

"I've been desperate for recognition for so long. I thought I finally had the tools to get it," Max sighed and her voice echoed across the clearing. "Since I can't get it," her voice lowered, "I'll have to destroy everything and try again,"

The stone flower beneath her began to glow, and simultaneously, all six of us reached out to stop her. *"No!"* I drew Cynthia, and the flowers around us exploded.

I drew my first breath in a millenia. To the side, the six keepers of my being, my petals that united to reform me, laid face down in the flowers. *Six petals to reform the Goddess,* I counted them slowly to confirm I had been reformed correctly. *They still draw breath,* I noticed, curious. *It seems they had souls that overlaid the bits of me they contained.*

I looked down at my hands and found a Weapon in one of them. "Who are you?" My bell-like voice rang clear. Her White Wood staff and long, curved blade were both illuminated and darkened as the sun, moon, and stars circled high above us. The sun and moon took turns dipping beyond the horizon to rest while the other darted overhead.

My name is Cynthia. Who are you?

I laughed. "Cheeky thing," I looked up at my child, Maximum. "I'm The Goddess,"

Maximum stared at me as the light of my podium faded away. "Mother?" Her voice cracked. Her powers were weak. Her form flickered, her sister not being there to support her like I had wanted. I closed my eyes to find Minimum.

"She's destroyed her sister," I spoke aloud for the Weapon, Cynthia's, benefit. The Weapon curiously listened, confused about what was happening. "Maximum cannot survive without Minimum," I elaborated. "Just like she tried to destroy me when I wouldn't worship her,"

Without warning, I attacked. "I can't forgive you for damaging me or destroying your sister." As I swung Cynthia, the White Wood breathed around me. The stars shone along with the moon as they twirled around our world only to be replaced by the sun. With every flash of light and turn of our ever-changing sky, I pushed Maximum to her brink.

Cynthia sang in bloodlust as Max summoned weapon after weapon. I swung down and cut through a simple spear easily. Cynthia lapped at the lesser goddess's blood. I brought Cynthia around and stepped forward as I slashed at Max's side. My daughter summoned a simple sword and parried me. Cynthia bounced off, and I simply let go of the scythe and instead kicked Max's feet out from under her.

Max fell with a pained shout, and I reached my hand out and summoned Cynthia back to me. The Weapon chattered with excitement as I brought her up and swung her down. Max threw herself to the side to avoid Cynthia and was quick to roll up.

"Stop!" Max cried, her eyes red-rimmed as she drew a bow from the air, a simple creation. She drew it back and loosed an arrow towards me. I reached up and grasped the arrow by the shaft. I stepped forward,

Cynthia's blade close to the ground and angled up. "I just wanted you to recognize me!" my daughter cried out. Her features glowed in the moonlight as it pranced above us.

I surged towards her with an upstroke of Cynthia, and Max created a simple wooden shield in between breaths. The wood splintered under Cynthia, and Max threw herself to the side once more as it broke. "I just wanted your love!" she pleaded to me as the moon fell.

Pain twisted my face as I stepped up to where Max laid on her back on the ground. Tears and dirt streaked down her face. She looked at me with large, wobbly eyes, eons of pain and desperation in their unknown crystalline depths. The sun began to arch over us, its unforgiving brilliance digging into our features like nails on a chalkboard.

"I'm sorry. I love you," I raised Cynthia, brought the scythe down, and shattered Maximum. It was a small consolation. Max drank from my daughter eagerly, her simple mind thoughtless and she quenched her thirst. *Maximum brought me back to praise her,* I surmised. *Maximum destroyed Minimum over the course of eons to eliminate her competition.* I closed my eyes and tasted the air as the sun forgave its peak and began to set.

So much life in this world. I stepped onto my podium and looked down at Cynthia.

Where is my master?

"How loyal," I remarked, not in the mood to laugh. "I placed her on the shore of her land," Cynthia's agitation flowed through me. "Now, now," I soothed her with my thumb. "There will be no war anytime soon. You're going to stay with me for a long time," I promised her.

The Goddess turned to you, the reader. "And you," she remarked, her crystalline eyes swelling with potential and power, "this is a family affair. Leave," she flicked her finger, and Wren, Ela, Lana, Fira, Asha, and Phaedra disappeared, transported. You, the reader, disappeared a second later.

PHAEDRA

I groaned as my body ached intensely. "Hello?" I called out blindly as I struggled with sand in my mouth.

"Yeah," Wren grunted some ways away. I looked up and stared as I saw my companions in various states of disarray.

Fira rolled over next to me and coughed. I lifted myself up and found my body oddly heavy. I stood, struggled to balance, and tried to pull Fira up as she motioned for me to lend her a hand. I easily lifted her up, thankful for my strength.

"What happened?" Asha wandered over to us as Fira brushed the sand off.

My mouth opened and closed while we stared at each other. "We got there and confronted Max," I recalled.

"And then we beat her," Ela nodded confidently.

I frowned and tipped my head. "I don't remember," I disagreed.

"We must have been hit by a whirlpool," Lana rubbed her head as she looked out to the ocean.

"What's that?" Wren plucked a paper from my breast pocket.

I snatched it back. "It's mine."

"Then what's it say?" Fira plucked it from my hands. She paused. "You wrote a list?" She mocked.

I huffed, flustered. "Queens are very busy!" I defended myself as I ripped it from her hand.

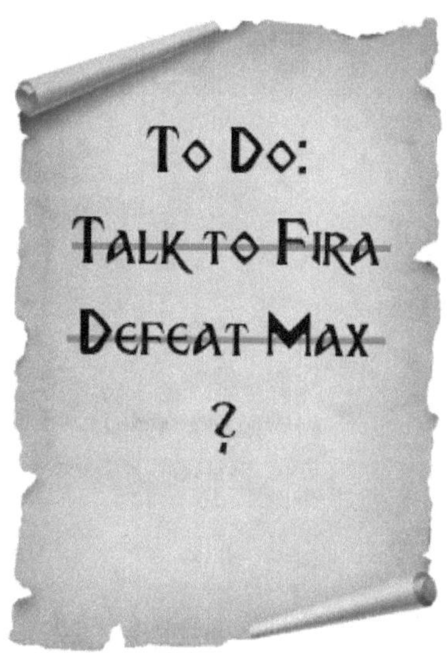

The first two items were crossed off. The others laughed as they started to walk towards where the Agee Tree rose in the distance. I hesitated and looked back out over the ocean. *Where's Cynthia?*

I sighed. *I suppose it's for the best. There'll be no wars for her to enjoy here anytime soon.*

My hands graced along her immortal face. Her minerals were soft under my touch. "Miko," I sighed, and pressed my warm lips to her eternally cold.

THE END

Dedication

I dedicate this book to the oldest daughters. I also dedicate this book to Kubo, author of Bleach. These two things shaped myself and this novel into their most successful and engaging versions.

About the Author

Tricah (pronounced try-kuh) is a private author who resides in a small village. She enjoys cats, femme fatale, and art.
"It is only by standing on the shoulders of our foremothers that we will reach the stars."-Tricah